Lost and Found in the Andes

By Lancer Gareth

Illustrated By Kenneth W Harvey

Copyright © 2024 Lancer G. Bailey

All rights reserved.

ISBN-979-8-3485-2529-3

Cover design Copyright © 2024

Kenneth W. Harvey

Printed in the United States of America

To my amazingly talented and infinitely supportive husband, thank you for blessing me with your patience and understanding during the writing of this book, and for the beautiful cover design and illustrations! You know this means I'm going to ask you to design all of my book covers from here on! You are my treasure! I love you.

Chapter One

"I told you not to get in my way," Dr. Malachi sneered, each phrase punctuated by a brutal blow to Edward's face. "You chose to meddle in affairs that didn't concern you—my affairs."

Bloodied and battered, Edward tried to gasp out a response, but Malachi continued, "There's nothing you can do now. All I have to do is press this button, and we reset the clock on humanity! Once the molecule is released into the atmosphere, there will be no stopping it. You failed, and now you and millions of others are going to die horribly!"

Dr. Malachi's underground laboratory was a sinister and foreboding place, hidden away from prying eyes in the depths of a remote mountain hideout. The walls were lined with cold, metallic panels, illuminated by flickering fluorescent lights that cast eerie shadows across the floor. The air was thick with the acrid scent of chemicals, mingling with the metallic tang of machinery and the faint hint of ozone.

The laboratory was a sprawling complex of interconnected rooms and chambers, each with rows of gleaming stainless steel equipment and high-tech consoles. Strange, otherworldly devices hummed and whirred ominously, their purpose hidden behind layers of intricate wiring and blinking lights.

In the center of the main chamber stood a massive containment unit, its reinforced glass walls housing the deadly molecule Dr. Malachi intended to release upon the world. Thick metal chains secured the unit in place, a grim reminder of the power it held over humanity's fate.

As Edward surveyed the scene, he couldn't shake the feeling of dread that hung heavily in the air. This was the heart of Dr. Malachi's operation, the epicenter of his mad quest for power and domination. As the countdown to humanity's demise ticked ever closer, Edward knew that he must act swiftly to stop the evil scientist before it was too late. He struggled fiercely against his restraints.

Suddenly, the room's atmosphere shifted as the door burst open. In stepped Agent Harrison.   An air of confidence surrounded him. "Looks like I'm fashionably late to the apocalypse party," he quipped, eyeing Malachi with disdain.

Dr. Malachi regarded Harrison with a sinister grin as the agent burst into the room, disrupting the doctor's meticulously laid plans. "Ah, Agent Harrison," Malachi began, his voice dripping with disdain. "I must say, you're more of a nuisance than I anticipated."

Harrison's steely gaze met Malachi's, his expression hardened with resolve. "Cut the theatrics, Malachi," he retorted, his voice a low growl. "I know about your little plan with the molecule. You won't get away with it."

Malachi's smile widened, a glint of madness flickering in his eyes. "Ah, the molecule," he mused as he waved around the trigger switch, his tone laced with arrogance. "My masterpiece, the culmination of years of research. Once released, it will usher in a new era, one where the weak are culled, and the strong thrive!"

Harrison's jaw clenched in anger, his fists tightening at his sides. "You call wiping out millions of innocent people a masterpiece?" Harrison fired back, his voice tinged with disbelief. "You're insane!"

Dr. Malachi shook his head, his expression one of self-assured superiority. "Insane? No, Agent Harrison. No, no…" He countered smoothly. "I'm a visionary! The molecule is the key to cleansing this world of its impurities, paving the way for a new order!"

Harrison's gaze hardened, his resolve unwavering. "You're playing God, Malachi," he accused, his voice filled with conviction. "And innocent lives will pay the price. I won't let that happen!"

Dr. Malachi merely chuckled darkly, a chilling sound that echoed through the room. "You can try to stop me, Agent Harrison," he sneered. "But you're too late! With one click of this button, the molecule will be dispersed into the atmosphere. Soon, humanity will face its reckoning!"

Harrison's fists clenched at his sides, his mind racing with thoughts of the devastation that awaited if Malachi's plan succeeded. "Not if I can help it," he vowed, his voice firm and resolute. "You're coming with me, Malachi, and we're going to undo the damage you've done."

Dr. Malachi laughed, a cold, hollow sound that sent shivers down Harrison's spine. "Ha! Agent Harrison," he taunted. "You're such a fool! You're pathetic! You couldn't even save your colleague here, or should I say your lover?"

Dr. Malachi turned to look at Edward, momentarily distracted, and the agent seized the opportunity. In a swift move, Harrison disarmed the button-wielding scientist, setting the stage for their final showdown. "Guards!" Malachi screeched.

Three armed mercenaries rushed in from an adjoining hallway to protect the embattled scientist.

Harrison rushed the men, delivering a flying kick to the first man's groin while simultaneously disarming him. He quickly pivoted to his left and drove the butt of the newly acquired rifle into the mouth of the second assailant, crushing his mandible.

With another pivot, he threw a sidekick into the sternum of the third gunman, spun the rifle around into firing position, and fired a round deeply into the man's chest. He then fired another two shots finishing off the first two attackers. The battle was so swift and decisive that it all seemed to happen in a flash.

Harrison turned again to give Dr. Malachi a malevolent glare. "Looks like the plot thickened, and so did your demise."

Dr. Malachi lunged in a final desperate attempt to reach the detonator switch, but before he could reach it, Harrison shot him twice in the chest. The doctor collapsed to the ground, dead.

With the villain defeated, the agent sauntered over to Edward, bound tightly to a chair. His eyelid was beginning to swell shut and blood dripped from his chin. A mischievous smirk graced the agent's face as he began to loosen the restraints. "I didn't know you were into this kind of thing," he teased, blending levity with the gravity of the moment.

Once freed, Edward tried to stand up but his battered and bruised body lacked the strength. "Here, let me help you," said Harrison tenderly as he leaned in close to pick Edward up onto his feet. Edward threw his arms around the agent, squeezing him as tightly as he could bear, his breath warm on the agent's cheek.

As the smoke of the gunfire slowly dispersed around them, Harrison and Edward stood together, their hearts pounding in their chests. In that moment of shared vulnerability, their bond felt stronger than ever before.

"I told you I would come back for you," Harrison whispered, his voice barely above a breath.

Edward's eyes brimmed with tears as he reached out to grasp Harrison's hand. "Yes, you did," he choked out, his voice thick with emotion.

Their gaze locked, conveying more than words ever could. In that silent exchange, they found solace and strength, drawing courage from each other's presence.

Their lips met in a tender kiss, a silent affirmation of their love and commitment. It was a fleeting moment of intimacy amidst the chaos of the world around them, a reminder of the enduring bond that held them together.

"Come on, let's get you out of here," Edward said softly, a smile tugging at the corners of his lips.

Harrison chuckled, a sense of relief flooding through him. "We need to hurry. There are two C130's inbound to bury this whole facility under the mountain."

"Cutting it kind of close aren't you?" Edward replied playfully.

"You know me. I don't like to spend too much time on foreplay," Harrison said with a devilish smile.

As they stepped forward, out into the uncertain future, their hands intertwined, Harrison and Edward knew they were ready to face whatever challenges lay ahead, as long as they faced them together. With hearts full of hope and love, they embarked on their next adventure, knowing that their bond would guide them through any storm.

And as they walked out of the dark corridor of the laboratory back into the sunlight, their silhouettes blended into one, a testament to the strength of their love and the promise of a future filled with endless possibilities."

"We're so proud of you, Mijo," Carmelo's mother Isabella said sweetly as she closed the book she had been reading from.

The air in Carmelo's downtown Austin home was filled with a mix of celebration and concern as he, his mom, and Tia gathered to celebrate Christmas and mark the completion of his latest novel. The room echoed with laughter and clinking glasses, the sounds of Christmas classics played in the background, yet beneath the surface, his mother and aunt couldn't shake the worry etched on their faces.

"Thanks, Mama," Carmelo said as he took a long sip from his wine glass.

Carmelo was a striking figure, embodying a unique blend of rugged charm and artistic sensitivity. He had a sturdy build with broad shoulders, indicative of strength and resilience, yet there was a graceful fluidity in his movements that spoke of elegance and refinement. His features were expressive, with warm, inviting eyes that reflected a depth of emotion and intelligence.

Carmelo's hair was a dark, rich shade, often tousled in a way that suggested a carefree spirit. He had a well-groomed beard that added to his rugged appeal, framing a warm smile that could light up a room. There was an air of confidence about him, tempered with humility and a genuine kindness that drew people to him effortlessly.

Carmelo exuded an aura of dark sophistication, clad in a fitted black turtleneck sweater that accentuated his sturdy build and highlighted his warm, expressive eyes. His choice of attire continued with tailored charcoal trousers, adding a touch of sleekness and edginess to his look. He wore thick black-framed glasses, adding to his intellectual and artistic appeal. Completing his outfit were polished black leather shoes, a subtle yet distinct statement of his refined taste and attention to detail.

As Carmelo's mother read aloud the excerpt from his book, capturing the essence of the dramatic climax, there was a lingering tension. His aunt couldn't resist voicing her concern, "You're such a romantic, Carmelo. When are you going to stop writing this nonsense and experience a real romance?"

"Tia Paloma, don't start with that please," Carmelo hissed as he rolled his eyes. "Can't we just celebrate the holiday, and that I finished my book?"

His mom chimed in, "Of course, Mijo! We just want you to find a nice man, in the real world, and for you not to live only in this fantasy world full of these 'cuerpos musculosos.' That's all, Mijo. Life is short and you never know what is going to happen. Look at your sister! They found her husband dead in the mountains, God bless them! You have to live your life, Mijo. You are not getting any younger or thinner."

Isabella Quiñones, Carmelo's mother, was an elegant and refined woman with a warm and nurturing presence. She exuded a sense of grace and sophistication, carrying herself with poise and dignity. Isabella had a timeless beauty and a classic, tasteful style, with a touch of old-fashioned values reflecting her stern Catholic upbringing. Despite this, she had become very accepting of her son, making her a figure of stability and support in Carmelo's life.

Carmelo also had a great relationship with his Tia, Paloma. Paloma was a vibrant and spirited woman with a warm and welcoming demeanor. She had a generous smile that could light up a room and expressive eyes that conveyed her lively personality. Paloma had a flair for fashion, often seen in colorful outfits that reflected her joyful spirit. Despite her vibrant exterior, she was also known for her wisdom and nurturing nature, offering guidance and support to Carmelo and others in their family. Her presence brought a sense of joy and comfort to those around her, making her a beloved figure in their lives.

"And who is this Cameron Quinn?" Isabella added with a hint of resentment. "Sounds like a fancy gringo! What's wrong with your real name, Carmelo Quiñones de la Cruz from San Antonio, Texas? That's who you are, Mijo! Not this Cameron Quinn! Come back to San Antonio with me, Mijo. We will find you a nice man and I will feed both of you. You look hungry, Mijo. Do you want some more ceviche?"

He snatched the book out of his mother's hands and stuffed it into the messenger bag on top of the bar. "No Mama! I'm not hungry!"

Carmelo, slightly annoyed, closed his eyes, took a deep breath, and said, "I'm not single; I'm independently owned and operated. It's like being a limited edition—rare, valuable, and definitely not on sale! Besides, who needs a boyfriend when you have pizza delivery and Netflix at the click of a button? They never disappoint, unlike some dates I've been on. Who wants more wine?" They all three raised their glasses in unison. Relieved though he was to have managed to change the subject for now, the undertone of worry persisted.

The following morning Carmelo, battling the remnants of a hangover, hurried through his morning routine. The promise of a meeting with his book marketing manager added urgency to his steps.

As he rushed out, a mailman intercepted him with a package too large for the mailbox. Carmelo, preoccupied, tucked it into his messenger bag without a second glance.

"Your car is waiting for you Mr. Quiñones," said the doorman as he stepped out onto the sidewalk.

Carmelo's Uber pulled up to the corner of West Mary and South First Streets and he stepped out of the car. It was a cold December morning at about 8:30 AM and the wind was whipping the Pride flag hanging above the entrance to Bouldin Creek Cafe, one of his favorite breakfast spots where he often took meetings with his book marketing manager and friend, Gale. Despite it being early, windy, cold and the day after Christmas, the restaurant was packed and positively electric.

As soon as he entered the restaurant he saw Gale from across the room, sitting at a table. He quickly ordered a coffee from the bar and went to meet her there.

Gale was a seasoned professional with a sharp eye for detail and a knack for strategic planning. She exuded confidence and professionalism in every interaction, with a commanding presence that made her a respected figure in the industry. Gale had a keen understanding of market trends and consumer behavior, which she leveraged to create effective marketing campaigns for Carmelo's projects. Her communication skills were top-notch, allowing her to articulate complex ideas and strategies with clarity and persuasiveness. Despite her business-oriented demeanor, Gale also had a personable side, often engaging with clients and colleagues in a friendly and approachable manner. Overall, she was a valuable asset to Carmelo's team, contributing significantly to the success of his endeavors in the publishing industry.

Gale was a striking woman with vibrant red hair that cascaded down her shoulders in loose waves, framing her heart-shaped face. Her hazel eyes sparkled with intelligence and warmth, adding depth to her engaging personality. She often dressed in stylish yet professional attire, favoring tailored blazers and chic blouses that accentuated her slender figure. Gale's fashion sense reflected her confident and dynamic character, making her a standout presence in any business setting.

"Carmelo," Gale said with a smile as he walked up to the table.

"Gale, how are you? Good to see you!" Carmelo set his messenger bag down beside his chair and gave her a brief hug.

"I'm well! How are you, Carmelo?" She asked warmly.

"Well, I finally finished it!" He said as he sat down across from her.

"Yes!" Gale exclaimed, clapping her hands together delightfully. "I've already finished reading it, my love. It is brilliant..as usual!"

As they delved into discussions about Carmelo's latest book, their meals arrived and vanished unceremoniously, along with several cups of coffee. Suddenly Gale took on a more somber expression. "I do want to point something out, and it's because I love you."

Carmelo gave her a sharp look and said "Oh don't you start this too! If I had a dollar for every time I received unsolicited relationship advice, I'd have enough to buy a private island and live happily ever after—alone."

"That's not what I was going to say, Carmelo," she interjected. "While I do want you to be happy, I'm more troubled about your writing. It's just that I'm concerned about how long it took you to finish this one."

Carmelo exhaled heavily. "The inspiration comes when it chooses to. I can't control it any more than I can control the weather. If I could I would make it rain on you right now," he quipped.

Gale gave Carmelo a cheeky glance, replying, "I know that darling, what I mean is your pace. It's slowing down. This book took you twice as long as the last two, and those took almost twice as long as the one before that. And there's no reason to get bitchy!"

Carmelo diverted his gaze.

"Perhaps you should take some time off to relax, reset, take a sabbatical! Take a break from writing! Go to Tibet and clear your mind of your breakup with, what's his name—and this horribleness with your sister. How is your sister by the way? Have you heard from her recently?"

"Not since the funeral," he said as he gripped his coffee mug tightly.

"Do they know anything? Do they have any suspects?" Gale inquired with genuine concern.

"I don't know. I don't think so. You know, it's Argentina. They aren't exactly forthcoming with information there. It has only been a couple of months since the investigators positively identified Lorenzo's remains."

Carmelo closed his eyes and sighed. "Eloisa said she would call me when she got more information. She is staying there until the police finish their investigation. They don't want her to leave the country while the case is still ongoing. She told me as soon as that business is taken care of, and Lorenzo's will is settled, she wants to sell her house in Buenos Aires and come back home to Texas."

"That poor girl! Getting married to a handsome, exotic archaeologist and moving to Argentina!" Gale's eyes widened. "It sounds so romantic like the beginning of one of your novels, until her husband's body was found floating in the bay. It's just so tragic." She blotted a teardrop from the corner of her eye.

"Yes, well Eloisa is very strong, probably more so than me. She will get through this. We all will get through it eventually, la familia, together." Carmelo stared blankly at the empty coffee mug in his hands. The shadows of personal struggles began to cast a pall over their professional lunch. "Maybe we should order some mimosas," he said forcing a smile.

"Brilliant idea!" Gale cheered enthusiastically.

A few hours later when Carmelo arrived home, he noticed the front door slightly ajar, a feeling of unease crept over him. He stood there wide-eyed for a moment. His heart pounded in his chest.

"What the hell!?" Carmelo whispered.

Stepping cautiously inside, his heart sank as he saw the chaos: furniture overturned, drawers pulled out, and belongings scattered across the floor. Panic arose within him as he realized the severity of the situation. Trembling, he reached into his messenger bag for his smartphone and dialed 911.

Carmelo paced anxiously in his living room, the remnants of the break-in still scattered around him. The sound of approaching footsteps outside signaled the arrival of the police. Taking a deep breath to steady his nerves, he opened the door to find a uniformed police officer standing on his doorstep, a look of concern etched on the man's face.

"Good day, Sir. "My name is Officer Rodriguez. I am responding to a call about a home invasion."

Officer Rodriguez was a striking figure, standing tall with an athletic build that spoke of discipline and strength. His dark hair was impeccably styled, framing a chiseled jawline and piercing brown eyes that seemed to hold a hint of mystery. Every movement exuded confidence, from the way he carried himself to the commanding presence in his voice. Despite the seriousness of his profession, there was a warmth in his smile that instantly put Carmelo at ease, adding to his undeniable charm.

"Mr. Rodriguez, thank you for coming," Carmelo said, his voice betraying his anxiety.

Officer Rodriguez nodded solemnly, his dark eyes scanning the disarrayed room. "What happened here, Mr. Quiñones?" he asked, his tone professional but empathetic.

Carmelo recounted the events of the break-in, his words tumbling out in a rush as he described the chaos he had come home to. "And then I found this," he said, gesturing towards the overturned furniture and scattered belongings.

The officer listened attentively, jotting down notes on his pad. "I'm sorry you had to go through this, Mr. Quiñones," he said, his voice tinged with sympathy. "Do you have any idea who might have done this?"

Carmelo shook his head, frustration evident in his expression. "I have no idea. Nothing was stolen, so I don't understand why someone would break in like this. I mean, what would anyone be interested in stealing from me anyway, my collection of empty wine bottles?"

Officer Rodriguez nodded, his brow furrowed in thought. "We'll do everything we can to find out who's responsible," he assured Carmelo. "In the meantime, I'll need you to come down to the station to make a formal statement."

Carmelo nodded, relieved to have the support of the police. "Thank you, Officer Rodriguez. I'll do whatever I can to help."

As they left the apartment together, Carmelo couldn't shake the feeling of unease that lingered in the air. But with Officer Rodriguez by his side, he felt a glimmer of hope that justice would soon be served.

As the officer escorted Carmelo home from the police station, they engaged in small talk, discussing the neighborhood and recent events in the area. Carmelo expressed his gratitude for Rodriguez's help and reassured him that he'd be okay.

Upon arriving at Carmelo's condo, they found his mother and Tia inside, tidying up the mess left behind by the intruders. Carmelo's mother rushed over to him, relieved to see him safe, while Tia Paloma offered a sympathetic smile.

Carmelo thanked Officer Rodriguez once again before bidding him farewell. As Rodriguez left, Carmelo turned to his mother and Tia, feeling a mixture of emotions—gratitude for their presence and the unsettling horror of knowing that someone had been inside his home. Together, they began to assess the damage and discussed what steps to take next.

"I think you should come back to San Antonio with me for a while," his mother offered consolingly. "You don't need to be here by yourself right now, mijo. You've finished your book and you can afford to take some time off. Tia Paloma was going to take me home the day after tomorrow, pero you can take me so she doesn't have to."

Just then, Carmelo's phone rang, the screen displaying an unfamiliar number.

"It's a foreign number," he said with a look of confusion on his face. A feeling of trepidation washed over him. With trembling hands, Carmelo answered, "Hello."

His sister's frantic voice came through the line. "Carmelo? Carmelo!" She cried. Her distress was palpable.

"Eloisa, it's me. Are you okay?" Carmelo gripped the phone tightly.

"Carmelo, I'm so scared. They took me, and I don't know where I am," she sobbed.

"Try to stay calm, okay? Tell me, did they hurt you?" A wave of panic flooded through him.

"No, not yet. But they keep asking me about a package. A package from Lorenzo." Eloisa breathed heavily in between words.

"Who are they? Lorenzo? But he's…he's gone. What package are they talking about?" Carmelo's voice betrayed the growing panic he felt.

"I don't know, Carmelo. They keep saying that I have it, or that you or Mama have it," she whimpered.

Suddenly, Carmelo remembered the package the mailman had given him earlier that morning. He frantically ripped open his messenger bag and pulled out a thick envelope. "It's from Argentina," he exhaled.

"Carmelo, you have to help me! You have to bring that package.." Eloisa's voice was suddenly cut off and replaced by a deeper, more sinister voice with a thick accent. It was a man's voice.

"Listen to me, Carmelo. If you want to see your beautiful sister alive ever again, you will bring the package to me immediately in Argentina. Go to the Hotel Gran Mendoza in Mendoza. Come alone. You will give me the package. I will give you your sister. Write down this number. When you arrive at the Hotel Gran Mendoza, call this number. Don't do anything estúpido."

Suddenly Eloisa's voice returned to the line, "Carmelo, please hurry!"

"Okay, listen to me. I'm coming to get you, okay? Just hold on a little longer."

"Be careful, Carmelo. Please!" The call crackled and went dead.

Holding the mysterious package sent shivers down Carmelo's spine, realizing its connection to the unfolding nightmare. His mother and Tia were close beside him, crying.

"What are we going to do, Carmelo?" His mother squeaked out in between a series of sobs and panicked breathing. "You can't go to Argentina all by yourself!"

"I have to, Mama! The man said that I have to go alone." Carmelo's mind raced with uncertainty.

Isabella reached out, her hand trembling as she grasped Carmelo's arm. "But it's dangerous, mijo. How can you face this alone?"

Carmelo turned to her, his eyes reflecting a mix of resolve and vulnerability. "I know it's risky, Mama. But I can't let fear paralyze me. I have to try, for Eloisa's sake."

Tia Paloma, her voice filled with concern, interjected, "But what if something happens to you, Carmelo? We can't lose you too."

Carmelo took a deep breath, his gaze unwavering. "I'll be careful, Tia. I promise. I won't let anything happen to me. I have to believe that I can bring Eloisa back."

"Then we will go with you," Isabella insisted.

"No, Mama!" Carmelo protested, determined to keep everyone safe. "The more people who get involved, the greater the potential of someone getting hurt. It's best if only I go."

Isabella squeezed his arm tightly, her eyes pleading. "Please be safe, Carmelo. We will be praying for you every day."

Carmelo nodded, a determined expression settling on his face. "I'll do everything I can to bring Eloisa home. I won't give up on her."

Despite his mother's concerns, Carmelo knew he must act swiftly, propelled by love and a fierce determination to rescue his sister, even if it meant venturing into the unknown alone.

Chapter Two

Carmelo stepped off the plane into the bustling Córdoba terminal, greeted by a wave of heat that contrasted sharply with the weather he had left behind. The lack of air conditioning amplified his discomfort, causing beads of sweat to form across his forehead almost instantly. He was dressed in layers more suitable for a Texan winter than an Argentine summer, and the discrepancy in temperature became glaringly apparent as he began to feel the heat seeping through his clothes.

"In today's episode of 'What Not to Wear at the Córdoba Airport,' I proudly present Exhibit A: Me, melting faster than an ice cream cone in July." Carmelo wiped the sweat off his brow with the sleeve of his sweater. "Who knew airports could double as tropical rainforests? If I survive this heatwave, I'm writing a survival guide for overdressed travelers."

Navigating through the throngs of people, Carmelo tried to find his bearings, his eyes scanning for familiar signs or symbols amidst the sea of Spanish signage. With each step, he realized the extent of the language barrier, feeling a sense of isolation in the crowded terminal.

Before leaving Austin, he had attempted to book a connecting flight directly to Mendoza from Córdoba, but there were no connecting flights available until the following Monday, so he decided to book a taxi service through DayTrip. Traveling by car would take approximately six hours longer, but he was relieved that, at least, he would arrive later that evening.

As he approached the information desk, Carmelo mustered the courage to ask for directions to the taxi stand, mentally preparing himself for the challenges that lay ahead in this unfamiliar environment.

At the taxi stand, amidst the hustle and bustle of travelers coming and going, Carmelo's gaze swept across the chaotic scene. Among the throng of people waving signs and navigating their luggage, one figure stood out—a short man sporting a chauffeur's hat, sunglasses, and a beard.

Instinctively, Carmelo's eyes locked onto the man, his heart rate quickening with a mix of anticipation and uncertainty. Could this be his ride, the driver he had arranged through the DayTrip app? He approached cautiously. The image of the driver matching the description he had been given, but doubt lingered in the back of his mind.

With a mixture of hope and apprehension, Carmelo closed the distance, ready to embark on the next leg of his journey through the unfamiliar streets of Córdoba.

"Señor Quiñones?" The man held up a white card with Carmelo's name written on it.

"Sí, Buenos días. Soy Carmelo Quiñones." Carmelo shook the driver's hand and smiled nervously. "¿Hablas inglés?"

"Little," the man replied blankly. "The car is aqui." He pointed to the black Lincoln parked behind him. The man took Carmelo's carry-on luggage and stowed it in the car's trunk.

"Por favor," he said as he opened the rear passenger door.

As Carmelo settled into the car, the heavy thud of the door closing behind him echoed through the vehicle. The sudden sound served as a stark reminder of his current vulnerability, trapped within the confines of this unfamiliar vehicle, his fate now in the hands of a stranger.

He glanced around, taking in his surroundings with a mixture of curiosity and trepidation. The interior of the car felt oppressive, the air thick with tension as silence hung heavy in the space between them. Carmelo's mind raced with questions, his senses heightened as he braced himself for whatever lay ahead on the road to Mendoza.

As the car pulled away from the bustling chaos of the airport, the landscape gradually transitioned from urban sprawl to serene countryside. The city's frenetic energy gave way to rolling hills and vast expanses of greenery, stretching out into the distance in every direction.

Carmelo watched through the window for hours as quaint villages and charming farmhouses dotted the roadside, their rustic charm a stark contrast to the modernity of the city he had just left behind. The sun beat down mercilessly, casting a golden hue over the landscape and bathing everything in its warm embrace.

Occasionally, they would pass by fields of vibrant crops swaying gently in the breeze, their verdant hues painting a picture of agricultural abundance. The air carried the earthy scent of soil and vegetation, mingling with the faint aroma of wildflowers that danced on the breeze.

As they ventured further into the countryside, the roads grew narrower and less traveled, winding their way through picturesque valleys and meandering rivers. The driver navigated with practiced ease, his expression inscrutable behind mirrored sunglasses as they pressed onward into the unknown.

The car suddenly veered off the main road and Carmelo's heart began to race. Panic seized him as he realized they were heading in the wrong direction. His mind raced, trying to make sense of the situation. Was this a mistake? A detour? Or something far more sinister? Fear gripped him as the driver remained silent, his hands clenched on the steering wheel. A sinking feeling settled in Carmelo's stomach as he contemplated the implications of their unexpected route.

"Excuse me, driver, pero I think we might be going the wrong way. We're supposed to be heading to Mendoza, not south."

The driver remained silent, his eyes fixed on the road ahead.

Growing more anxious, Carmelo said with an elevated tone, "Did you hear me? I said we need to turn around. I have an important meeting in Mendoza!"

The driver, still silent, continued driving.

Carmelo's voice rose with panic, "Stop the car! Let me out! This isn't where I need to be heading."

The driver finally spoke, in a cold, menacing tone, "You're not going to Mendoza, señor."

Carmelo's heart pounded in his chest as the realization dawned on him like a sudden storm. Panic surged through him, adrenaline coursing through his veins as he assessed the situation.

With a surge of determination, Carmelo lunged forward from the back seat, his hands grasping for anything within reach. He seized the driver's shoulder, his fingers digging into fabric and flesh as he fought to wrest control of the vehicle.

The driver reacted with surprising speed, swerving to evade Carmelo's grasp. The car lurched violently, tires screeching against the asphalt as it careened around a sharp bend. Carmelo braced himself against the impact, his knuckles white with tension as he fought to maintain his grip.

Desperation lent him strength as he grappled with the driver, clawing at the man's eyes, each movement fueled by a primal instinct for survival. He knew he had to act fast, to find a way to stop the car before it was too late.

Through the chaos, Carmelo's mind raced, searching for any possible means of escape. With every passing moment, the gravity of his situation became more apparent, driving him to fight with a fierce determination born of sheer necessity.

He managed to get a hand onto the steering wheel and he pulled it hard with all of his strength. The car lurched to the left, jumping the embankment and smashing hard into an ombú tree.

The driver's face slammed into the steering wheel with lethal force. Carmelo flew over the seat and ended up belly down on the passenger side, his chin scraping the floorboard.

The car's engine immediately stalled on impact with the ombú tree. The engine hood was bent upward and a spray of steaming hot mist shot up out of the car's radiator like a geyser.

Minutes passed before Carmelo was able to pull himself out of the floorboard and get out of the vehicle. He looked back at the driver, still slumped over the steering wheel, a stream of blood dripping from his nose.

"Oh my God," he thought to himself. "Is he dead? Did I kill him? Did I just kill somebody?" Suddenly a wave of nausea flooded his senses and he doubled over, retching violently. His ears were buzzing from the impact.

Carmelo's heart raced as he stumbled away from the wreckage, his breath coming in ragged gasps. The air hung heavily with the scent of scorched metal and burning rubber, a stark reminder of the chaos that had unfolded moments before.

As he surveyed the desolate landscape, a sense of dread settled over him like a shroud. The road stretched out before him, a narrow ribbon of asphalt and caliche winding its way through the rugged terrain. There was no sign of civilization in sight, no comforting lights on the horizon to guide his way.

With a sinking feeling in the pit of his stomach, Carmelo reached for his cell phone, fingers trembling as he fumbled with the device. He cursed under his breath as he realized there was no signal, no lifeline to connect him to the outside world.

"Well, I've always dreamed of exploring the great outdoors," Carmelo remarked dryly, "but I never imagined it would include a near-death experience and getting stranded in the middle of nowhere. I guess I can check those off my bucket list now."

For a moment, he stood frozen in indecision, torn between the instinct to stay put and wait for help to arrive, and the desperate urge to flee from that desolate place. Every fiber of his being screamed at him to run, to escape from the looming shadows that seemed to close in around him.

But as he weighed his options, a glimmer of hope sparked within him. Perhaps there was still a chance that someone would come along, a Good Samaritan willing to lend a helping hand in his time of need. With a shaky breath, Carmelo made his decision, steeling himself for the long wait ahead.

As Carmelo sat by the side of the road, the minutes stretched into hours, each passing moment feeling like an eternity. Panic gnawed at the edges of his mind, threatening to consume him whole.

Thoughts raced through his head in a chaotic jumble, a whirlwind of fear and uncertainty. He berated himself for ever getting into that car, for trusting a stranger in a foreign land. What if help never came? What if he was doomed to spend the rest of his days stranded in this foreign wilderness?

His mind conjured up vivid images of worst-case scenarios, each one more terrifying than the last. What if wild animals were lurking in the shadows, waiting to pounce? What if he stumbled upon some hidden danger, some unseen threat lying in wait?

With each passing moment, his anxiety grew, a relentless tide that threatened to overwhelm him. He felt utterly powerless, a mere pawn at the mercy of fate. As the sun dipped below the horizon, casting long shadows across the barren landscape, Carmelo couldn't help but feel a creeping sense of dread settle over him like a suffocating blanket.

Carmelo's heart leaped with a surge of hope as he spotted an approaching headlight cutting through the darkness like a beacon of salvation. The buzzing in his ears seemed to intensify, drowned out now by the roar of the motorcycle engine drawing nearer.

As the figure on the motorcycle drew closer, Carmelo could make out the silhouette of a man, his features obscured by the glare of the headlight. Relief flooded through him, washing away some of the fear and uncertainty that had gripped him for so long.

Desperation lent wings to his voice as he waved frantically, hoping against hope that this stranger would see him, would stop, would offer him the lifeline he so desperately needed. His throat felt raw with the effort, his cries lost in the vast expanse of the night.

"¡Ayuda!" Carmelo cried out, his voice tinged with relief and gratitude. "Please, help me!"

Then, miraculously, the motorcycle slowed to a stop, the engine growling its protest as the rider dismounted. Carmelo's heart soared as the man approached, his features finally coming into focus in the dim glow of the headlight.

With one hand raised against the blinding glare, Carmelo squinted to get a better look at the approaching figure.

The man was tall and lean, his silhouette, outlined against the backdrop of the Argentine night, exuded confidence and strength. With chiseled features and piercing green eyes that seemed to hold a world of secrets, he commanded attention.

His hair, the color of sun-kissed chestnuts, fell in unruly waves, framing his ruggedly handsome face with an air of casual elegance. There was a hint of stubble along his jawline, adding to his rough-hewn allure.

Dressed in worn jeans and a faded leather jacket, the man embodied a rough, exotic charm that spoke of a life lived on the edge. Despite the casual attire, there was an air of understated sophistication about him, a sense that he was not just an ordinary local.

His movements were fluid and purposeful, betraying the athleticism and grace of someone accustomed to navigating the wild terrain of the Andes. Yet, beneath the veneer of confidence and strength, there lurked a hint of vulnerability, a shadow that flickered in the depths of his emerald eyes, hinting at a past marked by pain and loss.

The man's voice cut through the night air, his concern evident as he approached Carmelo. "¿Estás herido?" he inquired, his tone filled with genuine worry.

Carmelo shook his head, the relief evident in his response. "No, I'm okay. Just a bit shaken up," he replied, his voice wavering slightly as he took in the gravity of the situation.

"You are American," the man said in English, his accent carrying the melodic cadence of his native Spanish, infused with a subtle charm and warmth. His pronunciation was precise yet tinged with a faint hint of his Argentine roots, adding a touch of exotic flair to his words. Carmelo gave a confirming nod.

As the man moved to inspect the wreckage, Carmelo remained rooted to the spot, his gaze fixed on the twisted metal and shattered glass that littered the roadside.

"That man is dead," the man said with a blended expression of sadness and curiosity. Carmelo felt a shiver run down his spine. "Did you know him?"

"No, I didn't know him," Carmelo answered, his voice barely above a whisper. "I...I don't know what happened. One moment we were driving, and the next..." His words trailed off, lost in the darkness that enveloped them.

With a heavy sigh, Carmelo turned his attention back to the man, his expression one of desperation mingled with gratitude. "Thank you for stopping," he said, his voice choked with emotion. "I don't know what I would have done if you hadn't come along. My name is Carmelo. Can I ask your name?"

"You can ask," the man returned flatly. His tone was guarded, his eyes scanning Carmelo's face with a hint of apprehension.

"Alejandro," he finally replied, his voice tinged with wariness. "If you like, you can call me Alex. It feels more American, yes?" Alex's smile was warm yet guarded as if he were accustomed to maintaining a certain level of reserve even in moments of friendliness. His lips curved gently, revealing a flash of white teeth against his tanned skin. There was a hint of mystery in his gaze, adding depth to his otherwise friendly expression.

Carmelo nodded, offering a tentative smile in return. "Nice to meet you, Alex."

"I'll take you to the nearest town," Alex assured him, his voice steady and reassuring. "But it's not going to be an easy journey. These mountains can be treacherous, especially at night. When we reach the town you will be able to call someone."

Carmelo nods, grateful for Alex's willingness to help. "I should report this to the authorities."

"Trust me, you don't want to do that." Alex's voice carried a note of caution, his tone tinged with a hint of seriousness. He leaned slightly closer to Carmelo, his eyes betraying a sense of urgency as he spoke. "The police around here are not exactly the most honest. Most of them work for one man. This man you don't want to deal with. Come! Let's go!"

Alex turned toward his motorcycle again just as Carmelo cried out, "Wait, my messenger bag is still in the car and my suitcase is in the trunk!"

"A suitcase?" Alex's forehead wrinkled. "I am driving a motorcycle."

"I know, but it has all of my things in there. I can't live without it. Just…" Carmelo's voice trailed off as he opened the trunk, revealing the gruesome sight inside. His gasp was audible, his eyes widening in shock and horror at the unexpected discovery. There was another dead body stuffed inside the trunk.

Alex approached, his curiosity piqued by Carmelo's reaction. "Who is that?" He asked, his tone tinged with concern and suspicion.

Carmelo's voice wavered as he admitted, "I think...that was supposed to be my driver." He couldn't shake off the weight of guilt that settled on his shoulders. "Unless this is the standard welcoming gift for first time travelers to Argentina."

"Your driver?" Alex's eyes shifted from the dead body in the trunk to the one in the driver's seat. "You mean the man who was driving killed this man and took his place?"

"I think so, unless this is the start of a murder mystery vacation that I didn't sign up for," Carmelo quipped.

"We need to get out of here," Alex insisted urgently.

"But what about my suitcase?" Carmelo protested, his tone tinged with panic.

"Leave it," Alex repeated firmly.

"Leave it? Are you kidding me? I have thousands of dollars worth of clothes in there, and all of my shoes! I can hold onto it while you drive," Carmelo argued, his voice rising in desperation.

"You will need both hands to hold on so you won't fall off the motorcycle. It's not possible."

"Ok, well then…in one of the novels that I wrote, the main character, Ridley, built a sled out of tree branches, and…"

"We don't have time for that. Listen, the man who killed this man was working for somebody. Now that man is also dead. Whoever he was working for will want to know why he did not return with you. Do you want to wait until that man arrives?" Alex explained urgently, his voice low but intense.

Carmelo was silent. Alex took the suitcase from Carmelo's hands and threw it into the darkness as hard as he could. "There! It is done. We must go now."

Carmelo erupted in a fit of rage. "You asshole!" He spat, his voice tinged with anger and frustration. "My Louboutin's were in there," he whimpered.

"Get on the motorcycle, or I will leave you here and let you take your chances," Alex stated firmly, his tone leaving no room for argument.

Carmelo reluctantly climbed onto the motorcycle behind Alex. As they sped off into the night, Carmelo seethed with anger as he clung to Alex's back, his thoughts consumed by the audacity of Alex's actions. How could someone be so callous, so arrogant? He stewed in silent resentment, the roar of the motorcycle engine drowning out his inner turmoil.

Carmelo's frustration grew as raindrops began to fall, soaking them both. He shot Alex a glare, but Alex remained unfazed, focusing his attention on the rough road and ominous weather ahead.

As the rain continued to pour, Alex pressed on, determined to make progress despite the worsening conditions. However, it soon became evident that the muddy and treacherous roads posed a significant risk to their safety. With each passing moment, the journey became more precarious, prompting Alex to finally concede that they needed to seek shelter before the situation escalated further. Adjusting their course, he guided the motorcycle to a stop, signaling to Carmelo that they needed to find refuge from the storm.

"There!" Alex pointed toward a narrow trail that branched off the road and disappeared up a hill into the darkness. "We will walk the motorcycle up this trail and around that rocky outcrop over there. That way nobody will see us if they come by looking for you."

"Will there be shelter there? I am soaked!" Carmelo wrung the water out of his shirt in futility.

"Don't worry, there should be enough space to set up my tent. That rock overhang will help block the wind. If we are lucky, we can build a fire," Alex assured, his voice barely audible over the pounding rain. "It won't be luxurious, but it'll keep us dry. Let's get moving."

Carmelo nodded, grateful for any form of refuge. They dismounted the motorcycle and began the trek up the trail, their footsteps muffled by the relentless drumming of rain on the earth.

As the fire crackled, casting dancing shadows on the tent walls, Carmelo turned to Alex, who was lying close to him. "Nice digs," Carmelo remarked with a grin.

"It has come in handy on more than one occasion. It's not very spacious though," Alex replied, smirking. "I am sorry about your suitcase, but I have another surprise for you to make you feel better." He whipped out a thick brown bottle of liquor.

"La Alazana," Carmelo read curiously off the bottle's label. "Whiskey?"

"Made in Argentina! Would you like some?" Alex offered, extending the bottle toward Carmelo.

Carmelo snatched the bottle and took a deep swig, choking it down. "Yes, please!"

Alex turned to Carmelo, his gaze piercing. "Tell me, Carmelo," he said, his voice steady. "We hat's your story?

Why were you out here in the middle of nowhere, and why did those guys want to grab you?"

Carmelo hesitated for a moment, the crackling of the fire the only sound between them. "I...I don't know," he admitted, his voice barely above a whisper. "I was just on my way to Mendoza when the driver suddenly veered off course. Next thing I knew, we crashed, and I found myself stuck in the middle of nowhere with a dead man and no idea what was happening."

"Earlier you said you had written novels. You are a writer? A famous one?" Alex smiled teasingly, his eyes glinting with amusement.

Carmelo nodded slowly, his gaze fixed on the flickering flames. "Yes, I am. Well, I don't claim to be famous, but I write romance novels," he confessed, a hint of embarrassment coloring his cheeks. "It's not exactly a glamorous profession, but it pays the bills…most of the time." He took another swig and then handed the bottle back to Alex.

"Could that be why they wanted to grab you, for ransom?" Alex's tone was thoughtful, his expression pensive as he considered the possibilities.

Carmelo shook his head, a hint of disbelief coloring his expression. "No, that doesn't make sense. I'm not that famous or wealthy. My novels sell decently, but I'm hardly a household name."

"I don't mean to pry, but what brought you to Argentina? Are you writing a novel about Mendoza?" Alex asked, his tone casual yet curious.

"I wish it were something that exciting," Carmelo replied with a wry smile. "No, I'm not here for work. My sister...she's in trouble, and I came to help her."

"You came to help your sister and you ended up almost being kidnapped?" Alex asked, his tone a mix of curiosity and playfulness.

Carmelo quipped, "Just another day in the life of the family hero, I suppose. Do you think I look bad? Wait until you see the other guy." They both shared a chuckle, though the levity was tinged with the seriousness of their situation.

Carmelo took another swig from the bottle, handing it back to Alex with a grateful nod. "Thanks. And yeah, it's been a bit of a wild ride since I got here. Definitely not what I had planned."

Alex nodded, his expression serious. "It seems like you've stumbled into something bigger than you expected."

"Yeah, no kidding," Carmelo replied, grabbing his messenger bag and pulling it closer. "I never imagined my trip to Argentina would turn into a suspense thriller."

"Life has a way of throwing us curveballs," Alex said, his voice tinged with empathy. "But hey, at least you're still in one piece."

Carmelo chuckled weakly. "Yeah, there's that."

They fell into a comfortable silence, the crackling of the fire providing a soothing backdrop to their conversation. Despite the chaos of the situation, Carmelo couldn't help but feel a sense of camaraderie with Alex, as if they were in this together against the odds.

"So, what's your story, Alex?" Carmelo asked, breaking the silence. "What brings you out here in the middle of nowhere?"

Alex hesitated for a moment before answering, his gaze distant as if lost in thought. "Well, believe it or not, I'm a zoologist," he said with a wry smile. "I'm here studying the local wildlife, particularly the elusive mountain cat that roams these parts."

Carmelo's eyebrows shot up in surprise. "A zoologist? That's fascinating! I never would have guessed."

Alex shrugged modestly. "Yeah, it's not your typical career choice, but I've always had a passion for animals. And hey, it certainly keeps life interesting."

Carmelo nodded, intrigued by Alex's unexpected profession. Despite the danger and uncertainty surrounding them, he found himself oddly comforted by the thought of spending more time in the company of this enigmatic stranger.

"There's more to the story," Carmelo blurted out suddenly.

Alex raised an eyebrow, a curious expression on his face. "Oh? Do tell."

Carmelo hesitated, unsure of where to begin. "Well, it's just...My sister, she's the reason I came to Argentina in the first place."

Alex nodded, his interest piqued. "Go on."

Carmelo took a deep breath, steeling himself to share the details of his sister's ordeal. "She called me a few days ago, frantic. Said she was being held captive, that her husband had been murdered, and that I was her only hope."

Alex's expression softened with empathy. "I'm sorry to hear that, Carmelo. That sounds like a nightmare."

"Yeah, it's been a nightmare, all right," Carmelo replied, his voice tinged with bitterness. "I'm supposed to be in Austin right now celebrating my new book." He reached into his bag again and pulled out the book his mother had read just days before. "And now, here I am, stuck in the middle of nowhere with no clue how to help her."

Alex reached out, taking the book for closer examination. He rested a comforting hand on Carmelo's shoulder. "What is it that you are supposed to do?"

Carmelo's voice faltered as he recounted the instructions laid out by his sister's abductor. "I'm supposed to go to the Hotel Gran in Mendoza," he explained, his words tinged with frustration and uncertainty. "The man said he'd send a car to pick me up later tonight. That clearly didn't happen."

Alex nodded thoughtfully, absorbing the information. "And then what?"

Carmelo shrugged helplessly. "I don't know. They didn't say. But I still have to go. It's the only chance I have of seeing my sister again. They gave me a number to call after I checked into the hotel. I need to call that number and explain to them what happened and tell them that I am still coming for her."

Alex's gaze softened with understanding. "I'll help you get to a telephone as soon as it dries up a bit."

"What do they want from you?" Alex asked, his voice gentle but insistent.

"They want me to bring a package to them in Mendoza," Carmelo replied, his voice tinged with uncertainty, his gaze drifting to the ground where his messenger bag was lying. He reached inside the bag and pulled out the contents. "This package."

"What is it? Alex leaned in closer to get a better look.

Carmelo hesitated, unsure how much to reveal. "I don't know," he admitted. "It's from my sister's late husband, Lorenzo. He sent it to me just before he was murdered." As he spoke, Alex leaned in closer, his hair brushing against Carmelo's face, and a scent of earth and rain filling Carmelo's senses.

Alex's voice softened with concern. "Are you sure you want to get involved in this, Carmelo? It sounds dangerous."

Carmelo sighed heavily, running a hand through his hair. "I don't have a choice, Alex. My sister's life is on the line."

Alex nodded understandingly. "Okay, then. So you are supposed to give them this package and then they will just let you and your sister go?"

"As far as I know, that's the plan." Carmelo chuckled nervously.

Alex frowned, concern evident in his expression. "That sounds too simple. You need to be cautious. Things might not be as straightforward as they seem."

Carmelo nodded in agreement. "I know. But right now, I don't see any other option. I have to do whatever it takes to save my sister."

"What is it they want so badly?" Alex asked cautiously, hoping not to overstep.

Carmelo hesitated before responding, weighing his words carefully. "I'm not entirely sure. It could be something to do with why my sister's husband was murdered. He was an archaeologist. I think he was involved in some things that…well, let's just say they weren't exactly legal."

Alex's eyebrows shot up in surprise. "So you think this package might contain something incriminating?"

"It's possible," Carmelo admitted. "But I won't know for sure until I deliver it."

Alex's curiosity was evident in his voice. "You haven't opened it?"

Carmelo shook his head. "No, I've been too afraid to. It feels…ominous."

Understanding, Alex nodded thoughtfully. "I get it. Sometimes it's better not to know until you absolutely have to."

Carmelo sighed, his gaze lingering on the package. "Yeah, but it's driving me crazy not knowing what's inside."

"Well, it is addressed to you," Alex offered with a wily grin.

Alex's observation hung in the air, adding to the tension. Carmelo's gaze flickered to the package, a knot forming in his stomach. "Yeah... it is," he muttered, feeling a wave of nervousness wash over him.

"Who is Cameron Quinn?" Alex asked as he held the book up, a look of confusion flashing across his face.

Carmelo's cheeks blushed. "That's my pseudonym, my pen name."

"I see," Alex replied with a smirk, giving the book a thorough examination. "It looks…interesting."

Chapter Three

As the morning sun pierced through the dissipating rain clouds, Carmelo stirred from his restless slumber, a faint rustling sound catching his attention. Blinking sleep from his eyes, he was met with the sight of Alex leaning over him, his breath warm against Carmelo's cheek.

Instinctively, Carmelo shifted, only to freeze as Alex's hushed whisper reached his ears, urging him not to move a muscle. Panic seized Carmelo's heart as he lay perfectly still, his senses heightened.

In the dim light, Carmelo's gaze darted downward, and his heart skipped a beat as he realized the truth—what he had mistaken for Alex's leg brushing against his own was, in reality, the sinuous form of a giant snake slithering across his leg.

The snake was an impressive, if not fearsome, sight, with its sleek and muscular body coiling gracefully in the corner of the tent. Its scales shimmered with an iridescent sheen, reflecting the dappled light filtering in through the tent opening. The patterns on its scales were a mesmerizing mixture of black and white blended with earth tones ranging from rich browns to vibrant reds, creating a camouflage that blended seamlessly with its surroundings. Its body stretched nearly three meters in length, conveying a sense of power and strength, yet there was a certain elegance to its posture as it rested, belying its potential for swift and decisive action.

Every muscle in Carmelo's body tensed as he fought the urge to flee, his heart pounding in his chest.

With a steady hand and unwavering focus, Alex carefully reached for Carmelo's arm, guiding him with a gentle touch as he inched away from the snake which was coiling itself in the corner of the tent. Keeping their movements slow and deliberate, they managed to retreat without disturbing the reptile, their hearts pounding in unison with each cautious step. Once they were safely out of the tent and out of harm's way, Alex exhaled a quiet sigh of relief, his gaze meeting Carmelo's in silent acknowledgment of their narrow escape.

"It's not the first time I've spent the night with a man who wanted to inappropriately whip his snake out in front of me, but never has it been an actual snake," Carmelo jested with a nervous chuckle.

"That is an Argentine Boa," Alex said coolly, a sense of experience present in his voice. "It looks like a female. They are relatively docile unless provoked, but you don't want to get bitten by one and you certainly don't want it to get wrapped around you. They are not poisonous, but their teeth are very long and sharp. ¡Duele como la puta madre!" Alex flashed a smile, his shiny white teeth glistening in the morning sunlight. "They are mostly nocturnal, but the recent rain has probably stirred it from its usual hiding place."

Carmelo chuckled nervously, a playful glint in his eyes. "Ah, so this is the exotic wake-up call package, huh? I'll give this place a four star rating, but next time, can we upgrade to breakfast in bed instead?" He feigned dissatisfaction, his humor cutting through the tension of the moment.

Alex grinned, his eyes sparkling with amusement. "Thanks for the feedback. I'll go with that next time. But for now, let's focus on getting out of here in one piece," he replied, his tone lighthearted yet filled with determination.

As Alex scanned their surroundings, his eyes widened in alarm. "Carmelo, I think we have a problem," he said, his voice tinged with concern. "The motorcycle...it's gone." He gestured toward the spot where the bike should have been, his heart sinking as he realized what had happened.

Carmelo followed Alex's gaze, his expression turning from confusion to disbelief. "Gone? How is that even possible?" He exclaimed, moving closer to the edge of the cliff to get a better look.

As they peered over the precipice, they were met with the sight of Alex's motorcycle lying at the bottom of the cliff, battered and broken from the fall. The once sleek and formidable machine now lay in a crumpled heap, its metal frame twisted and mangled from the impact.

Alex let out a frustrated sigh, running a hand through his hair in frustration. "¡Me cago en Dios! All of the rain! It has eroded the hillside! Look over there." He pointed to a section of the trail that had broken off and fallen down the cliff. "Looks like there was a landslide. I should not have left the motorcycle there."

Examining the wreckage, Alex shook his head in dismay. "It's beyond repair," he muttered, frustration evident in his voice. "We'll have to leave it here and find another way to reach our destination. I'm so sorry Carmelo. I'm afraid we're on foot from here," he said, his tone a mixture of frustration, anger, and determination.

With their mode of transportation rendered useless, Carmelo and Alex knew they had no choice but to continue their journey on foot. After carefully navigating their way down the hillside, they reached the bottom and approached the damaged motorcycle.

Carmelo nodded in agreement, though disappointment weighed heavily on him. "At least we're both okay," he said, trying to find a silver lining in their predicament.

They began to trek along the muddy path, their footsteps squelching in the damp earth. The landscape stretched out before them, a vast expanse of wilderness punctuated by rugged terrain and dense vegetation.

As they walked, Alex took the lead, guiding them along the trail with a sense of purpose. Despite the setback, he remained determined to press on, his resolve unwavering in the face of adversity.

Carmelo followed close behind, his thoughts consumed by their uncertain future. Despite the challenges ahead, he found solace in the company of his companion, their bond growing stronger with each step they took together.

"Wouldn't it be easier to follow the road?" Carmelo asked as he struggled to walk over the rocky path in his Oxford dress shoes. "I should have packed a better pair of shoes." He shot Alex a cool glance. "Oh wait, I did," he added sarcastically, unable to resist the jab.

Alex rolled his eyes, a smile peeking through his lips. "We must stay off the roads. They will be patrolling all of the roads looking for you."

Carmelo's eyes widened, but he remained silent as he carefully stepped over a patch of loose rocks.

As they reached the edge of a small village hidden in the mountains, tall rows of lush greenery dominated the landscape, casting a surreal glow over the surroundings. The villa, standing prominently at the heart of the village, exuded an air of opulence amidst the rugged terrain and dilapidated structures surrounding it.

Initially drawn by curiosity, they approached cautiously, their senses alert to the unfamiliar sights and sounds. However, their fascination quickly turned to unease as they realized the true nature of the village. Shock set in as they comprehended the scale of the operation—a sprawling cannabis plantation concealed within the tranquil mountains.

Carmelo's eyes lit up in utter amazement as he stood before the rows of cannabis plants, their flowery buds glistening in the sunlight like precious jewels. Unable to resist the temptation, he stepped up close to one of the plants, his fingers itching to pluck a single bud from its lush foliage. With a mischievous grin spreading across his face, he turned to Alex and joked, "You don't think they would miss it if I picked just one of those, do you?" His expression mirrored that of a kid in a candy store, filled with excitement and anticipation at the prospect of indulging in a forbidden delight.

His words hung in the air, laced with a hint of mischief and reckless abandon, as he toyed with the idea of seizing a small memento from this surreal landscape. Yet, beneath his playful demeanor lurked a sense of nervous vigilance and thickening apprehension.

As they cautiously entered the village, their eyes darted nervously from side to side, they noticed the villagers casting wary glances their way. Suspicion hung heavily in the air, more palpable with every step they took. Suddenly, the villagers began to emerge from the shadows, their presence closing in around them. Heartbeats quickened as the gravity of the situation sank in—trapped amid a clandestine operation, with nowhere to run and no one to turn to for help.

Before they could even begin to process their predicament, they found themselves surrounded. The clicking of guns cocking sent a chill down their spines. Fear gripped them as they stood frozen, their minds racing with the realization that they were at the mercy of these unknown assailants. Caught in a moment suspended between disbelief and terror, they summoned every ounce of courage and resourcefulness within themselves to navigate this perilous encounter and emerge unscathed from the jaws of danger.

""Well, this is quite the welcoming committee. Did I miss the 'bring your own weapon' memo?" Carmelo quipped, his tone conveying panic.

"Stay calm," Alex directed, putting his hand on Carmelo's shoulder to comfort him. "They probably just want to know what we're doing here."

"Disculpe, señores, ¡Esto es propiedad privada! ¿Qué haces aquí?" An older man wearing western clothing, boots, and a dirty cowboy hat said while taking a few steps toward them, his gun fixed on Alex's abdomen. He wore an unwelcoming expression that warned of danger if he did not like the response to his question.

Alex flashed his most perfect smile. His green eyes shined like freshly polished malachite in the summer sun. "Perdónanos, señor. No queríamos invadir o entrometernos en su operación aquí. Nuestro automóvil se averió y estamos perdidos. ¿Tienes un teléfono que podamos usar, o tal vez un coche?"

The man stood there silently, his gun still trained on Alex's midsection.

"¿Alguien tiene teléfono?" Alex asked again with more enthusiasm.

"¡Tú vendrás conmigo!" The man with the hat stepped even closer, jabbing the barrel of his pistol into Alex's abdomen. Carmelo gasped audibly.

Alex flashed Carmelo a concerned look, panic beginning to wash over him. "If you've got any clever escape plans from your novels that we could use to get us out of this, right now would be the perfect time Mr. Cameron Quinn, romance novelist."

"Que?" The man sticking the gun into Alex's belly suddenly stopped and turned toward Carmelo. "¿Cameron Quinn? ¿El novelista romántico? ¿Aquí? ¿Eres él?"

Carmelo's wide eyes darted back and forth between Alex and the man with the gun, a look of utter confusion betraying his calm facade. "Yes, I am!"

The man suddenly relaxed, releasing Alex from his grasp and re-holstering his revolver. He turned to the other villagers, who seemed to be sharing the same confusion as Carmelo. "¡Aye, mira! ¡Mis amigos, este hombre es Cameron Quinn, famoso novelista de romance de los Estados Unidos!" He continued enthusiastically, "¡Este es el tipo que escribe los libros que El Sastre nos lee por las noches!"

The townspeople, their weapons still raised, exchanged uncertain glances, their confusion palpable in the air. Slowly, one by one, they began to lower their firearms, their expressions wavering between suspicion and curiosity.

Some of them cast wary looks at Carmelo and his companion, unsure of what to make of these unexpected visitors who had stumbled upon their hidden operation. Others exchanged murmurs and whispers, their voices a hushed chorus of uncertainty as they tried to make sense of the situation unfolding before them.

The man with the hat suddenly turned away from Alex as if he were no longer interested in him. "Forgive me for asking, but what are you doing here in these parts of the Andes, señor Quinn?" The man spoke slowly in English. His pronunciation was a bit unusual to Carmelo but he had no trouble understanding.

Cameron stumbled briefly for an appropriate response. "I'm writing a new novel that takes place here in Argentina! This man was taking me for a tour of your beautiful country when our automobile broke down. Now here we are. Perhaps I will make you a character in my next book!"

"¡Qué maravilloso! We must take you to meet El Sastre. ¡El sorprenderá mucho!" The man put his arm over Carmelo's shoulder and began leading him toward the opulent villa.

"Does El Sastre have a telephone?" Alex asked with a hint of annoyance at being left behind.

"Yes! Most certainly!" The man replied confidently, gesturing toward the gates of the villa. "Aqui, por favor."

The villa stood as a grandiose centerpiece of the village, its imposing facade a testament to the wealth and power of its owner. Surrounded by a lush garden of vibrant flowers and towering trees, the villa exuded an aura of elegance and refinement, in stark contrast to the rugged landscape that enveloped it.

With its intricately carved wooden doors and ornate ironwork adorning the windows, the villa bore the marks of meticulous craftsmanship, each detail a testament to the artisanal skill that had gone into its construction. Tall columns flanked the entrance, their weathered surfaces bearing witness to the passage of time, while a sweeping staircase led up to the grand double doors, inviting visitors into its opulent interior.

As Carmelo approached, he couldn't help but marvel at the villa's beauty, its whitewashed walls gleaming in the sunlight and casting a dazzling reflection against the surrounding greenery. Yet, beneath its facade of luxury lurked an air of secrecy, hinting at the hidden truths that lay concealed within its walls.

As they stood before the villa, his gaze lingering on its imposing silhouette, he couldn't shake the feeling of unease that gnawed at his insides. What secrets lay hidden behind those elegant walls, and what dangers awaited them within the heart of this enigmatic village? Only time would tell as he braced himself to uncover the mysteries that lay shrouded in the shadows of the villa's grandeur.

As they approached the grand entrance of the villa, Carmelo and Alex exchanged a perplexed glance. The villagers, their faces etched with anticipation, halted a few paces behind, their presence a silent reminder of the precariousness of the situation.

An awkward silence descended upon the group, broken only by the soft rustle of leaves in the breeze. Carmelo shifted uncomfortably, his gaze darting between the closed door and the expectant faces of the villagers. Alex cleared his throat, a nervous gesture betraying his uncertainty.

With a hesitant gesture, Carmelo reached out to ring the doorbell, his hand hovering uncertainly over the polished brass. The villagers held their breath, their collective anxiety hanging heavily in the air as if waiting for the inevitable revelation that lay beyond the threshold.

As Carmelo pressed the doorbell, the familiar chime of "Funky Town" filled the air, breaking the silence with a touch of unexpected amusement. Carmelo and Alex exchanged a glance, a subtle smirk playing on their lips as they registered the quirky choice of doorbell melody. Without missing a beat, Carmelo pressed the button a second time, setting off the funky tune once more. The villagers broke out into wide-smiled applause and approval at the doorbell's whimsical theme.

A moment passed until suddenly the entryway rumbled with the clacking sounds of large locks being disengaged.

As the heavy wooden doors of the villa creaked open, a figure emerged from the shadows within. Tall and impeccably dressed, El Sastre cut an imposing figure. His sharply tailored suit accentuated his lean frame, and his perfectly coiffed hair shimmered under the soft glow of the foyer's chandelier.

With a flourish, the man stepped forward to greet Carmelo and Alex, his piercing blue eyes assessing them with a mix of curiosity and vexation. "To what do I owe this displeasure," he said, his voice sharp as a razor blade with a distinct German accent.

Carmelo and Alex exchanged a glance, taking in the opulent surroundings of the villa's foyer. They could sense that this man was not your average host, and they braced themselves for whatever was to come next.

Carmelo took a deep breath, his eyes scanning the foyer nervously. "Excuse us, sir," he began, his voice respectful yet firm. "Our motorcycle broke down, and we were hoping to use your telephone to call for assistance. We also would like to inquire about any transportation assistance that you might have available to loan us or temporarily rent to us so that we might continue on our journey."

Alex nodded in agreement, adding, "We apologize for the inconvenience, but we're in a bit of a bind and would greatly appreciate your help."

El Sastre stared at them coldly. "What does this place look like to you, a rental car lot? Get off my property. You are trespassing!" He quickly pivoted, retreating back into the foyer to close the doors.

In the brief moment before the doors slammed shut in his face, Carmelo yelled out, "My name is Cameron Quinn, I'm a g-gay romance novelist from the United States! I'm begging you to please help us. Our lives are in danger!"

El Sastre froze suddenly. "What did you say?" His face twisted in disbelief.

"Our motorcycle broke down and we are stranded and lost, and.." Carmelo stuttered.

"What did you say your name was?" The man asked insistently.

My name is Cameron Quinn. I am a gay romance novelist." The desperation showed plainly on his face.

"Cameron Quinn? THE Cameron Quinn? Author of "The Heat Between Us", "The Wild West Whispers", "Passion's Embrace", "The Sultan's Secret Oasis", "The Seamen Came To Port", "Midnight Rendezvous"…that's my favorite one…"Back Door Lover?"

Carmelo's cheeks turned red. "Yes, and the soon-to-be-released "The Spy Who Loved Him." He pulled out the book he had been carrying in his messenger bag, his eyes diverted downward in modesty.

El Sastre studied Carmelo silently for a minute, his facial expression revealing none of his thoughts. "Cameron Quinn! Please, please do come inside! Entrez! Mi casa es tu casa! Willkommen bei mir zu hause! "

As Carmelo and Alex stepped over the threshold, they were enveloped by the opulence of El Sastre's villa. The air was heavy with the scent of expensive perfumes and the faint aroma of cigarettes. Intricate tapestries adorned the walls, while plush carpets cushioned their every step.

El Sastre led them through the grand foyer, his confident stride echoing in the cavernous space. Carmelo and Alex exchanged glances, both feeling a sense of awe and apprehension at the lavish surroundings.

"Please, make yourselves comfortable," El Sastre said, gesturing toward a luxurious sitting area. "You look famished. I will arrange for someone to bring you something to eat. In the meantime, would you care for a drink?"

Carmelo and Alex exchanged a brief nod of gratitude before settling into the sumptuous furnishings. As they awaited their host's return, they couldn't shake the feeling that there was more to El Sastre than met the eye.

As El Sastre returned with the cart laden with decanters and glasses, Carmelo and Alex watched in fascination as he expertly mixed cocktails with a flourish. The clink of ice against crystal echoed in the opulent room as he handed each of them a drink, including himself.

Settling into a tall-backed armchair, El Sastre regarded them with keen interest, his piercing blue eyes glinting with curiosity. "Tell me, what brings the famous gay romance novelist Cameron Quinn to my humble doorstep?" He inquired, his tone tinged with a hint of intrigue as if expecting them to share some juicy gossip.

Carmelo and Alex exchanged a glance, sensing that there was more to El Sastre's question than was conveyed with words. With a knowing smile, Carmelo leaned forward, his interest piqued by the enigmatic figure before them. "Well, Mr. Sastre," he began, "let's just say we find ourselves in need of a bit of assistance."

El Sastre winced slightly at the mention of the name, a flicker of annoyance crossing his features. "Please, don't call me that," he said with a brief smile. "You see, the local townspeople here, whom I employ, call me that name because I make, and sometimes repair, their garments. But I am not a tailor, my friends. I am a fashion designer!"

His tone was laced with pride as he emphasized his true profession, his posture straightening imperceptibly. It was clear that he took great pride in his work, and he was eager to set the record straight. "My name is Klaus von Schönfeld," he proclaimed, "but we are friends, yes? So, you can call me Klaus," he added with a disarming wink.

"Of course, Klaus. I love that name!" Carmelo said warmly, feeling strangely comfortable in Klaus' presence. Sensing the need for honesty, he decided to properly introduce himself. "I must confess, my name is not actually Cameron Quinn either."

Klaus looked at him with curiosity, prompting Carmelo to continue. "My name is actually Carmelo Quiñones de la Cruz. Cameron Quinn is my pseudonym."

There was a moment of understanding that passed between them as if they both recognized the power of hidden identity in their respective worlds.

"Can I call you Carmelo then?" Klaus asked playfully. He reached out and took Carmelo's hand in his.

"Yes, of course!" Carmelo smiled warmly.

"Wunderbar!" Klaus released Carmelo's hand and took a sip of his cocktail.

Alex, who had been sitting there quietly, felt the need to chime in. "You have such an impressive and beautiful home! It's quite the departure from its surroundings."

Klaus turned his gaze toward Alex. "Yes…well you see I inherited a substantial fortune from my grandfather. This house, in fact, was built by my grandfather," he said unashamedly. "He was a Nazi…a high-ranking officer of the Third Reich. He fled to Argentina after the war. It's ironic, don't you think, that a man who fought so brutally to irradiate homosexuality from his country would have a homosexual grandson." Klaus paused for a moment to sip his cocktail, "He didn't know, of course, but…all the same."

There was a heavy silence in the room as Klaus' revelation hung in the air, casting a shadow over the elegant surroundings. Carmelo and Alex exchanged a glance, unsure of how to respond to this unexpected disclosure.

"Friends," Klaus offered a comforting explanation, "there's no need to feel uncomfortable about my family's history. I was born here in Argentina and raised mostly by my mother who kept me away from most of my grandparents' ideologies. Also, I have worked very hard to make amends for my family's unsavory past."

Carmelo gave Klaus a sympathetic smile. "That's quite admirable. It sounds like you've become an integral part of this community.   The townspeople seem quite fond of you."

Klaus nodded, a bittersweet smile touching his lips. "Yes, they are," he replied, his voice tinged with a hint of sadness. "They appreciate me because I provide for them. I keep them employed, I make sure they have food on their tables, I mend their clothing and I even entertain them by reading your books among others, and sometimes we put on little shows for entertainment."

Alex offered a nod of understanding. "It looks like you've built quite the operation here," he remarked, gesturing toward the fields outside the window.

"Ah, yes. This is my—how do you say—side hustle? With a portion of my inheritance, I decided to venture into the cannabis industry when Argentina legalized the use of cannabis, recognizing its potential for medicinal purposes. On these premises, we have established a large-scale cannabis plantation, and I personally oversee the cultivation, production, and distribution of our high-quality cannabis products. I guess you could say I have become very passionate about de-stigmatizing cannabis use, and a strong advocate for responsible consumption, and the legalization of cannabis for recreational purposes. We are also very proud of our initiatives that promote equality, inclusivity, and environmental sustainability."

"That's quite impressive," Carmelo remarked, genuinely intrigued by Klaus's entrepreneurial spirit. "It's wonderful to see someone so passionate about not just business, but also social issues like equality and sustainability."

Alex nodded in agreement. "It's clear you've put a lot of thought and effort into this venture. It's not just about profits, but also making a positive impact on society."

Klaus smiled gratefully at their words. "Thank you," he said, his voice tinged with pride. "It's important to me to use my resources and platform for good, to make a difference in the world, no matter how small."

"I must admit that when we arrived and I saw the fields, I was so amazed at how beautiful the plants were. I was so tempted to take a little bud as a souvenir, but I didn't want to get shot by your workers." He chuckled nervously.

Klaus laughed and then leaned toward Carmelo with a serious expression and matching tone, "You would have been." He glared at Carmelo for a moment longer and then erupted in laughter again.

Carmelo's cheeks flushed slightly as he watched Klaus's reaction, relieved that his attempt at humor had been well-received. "I'll be sure to remember that for next time," he replied with a sheepish grin.

Alex chuckled, the tension of the moment dissipating. "I guess we'll just stick to admiring the plants from afar," he quipped, raising his glass in a mock toast.

"Would you like to try some? It's very good!" Klaus gestured toward an ornate wooden box on the nearby table, lifting its lid with a flourish.

The room filled with the earthy scent of freshly harvested cannabis, inviting Carmelo and Alex to partake in the moment. "Let's be indulgent," he said with a devilish grin. Klaus reached his long, slender fingers into the box and pulled out a fat pre-rolled joint. "I prefer to smoke it, but if that's not to your liking, I also have edibles."

Carmelo and Alex exchanged a bemused glance as Klaus expertly lit the joint, drawing in a long, deep breath.

"Now, enough about me," Klaus exhaled with a thick puff of smoke. "Tell me more about your predicament and how I might help you." He handed the lit joint to Carmelo who accepted it graciously.

Carmelo took a drag from the joint, feeling a rush of warmth spreading through him. "Well, Klaus, it's quite a long story," he began, exhaling slowly. "I'll give you the short version. You see, we were on our way to meet someone, and our motorcycle broke down. Now, we find ourselves stranded here in need of transportation, and a way to contact our intended destination," Carmelo continues, passing the joint to Alex. "The man outside told us that you have a telephone and that we might be able to use it."

Klaus scowled briefly, "They told you I had a telephone? No, I'm sorry Carmelo. There is no service out here. No telephone wires. No cell phone towers. No telephone."

Carmelo shot a disappointed look at Alex, who was passing the joint back to Klaus. "I see."

"However, I do have a satellite phone," Klaus added with a smile as he took in another big puff.

Chapter Four

Carmelo's fingers trembled slightly as he dialed the familiar number, his heart pounded in his chest. The phone rang once, twice, before a gruff voice answered on the other end.

"¿Hola?" The voice was rough, filled with suspicion.

Carmelo took a deep breath, steeling himself for the conversation ahead. "Hola, soy Carmelo Quiñones de la Cruz. Quiero hablar con el hombre que tiene a mi hermana."

The phone went silent for a minute and then suddenly Carmelo could hear a voice he knew quite well. "Carmelo?"

"Eloisa! Are you okay?" Carmelo's heart pounded in his chest as he heard his sister's voice on the other end of the line.

"Carmelo, I'm so scared," Eloisa's voice trembled with fear. "Where are you? They told me that you were expected yesterday and you didn't come. The man in charge is very mad. He said that if they didn't hear from you soon, they would…cut me into pieces and feed me to the yacares." She whimpered softly. "I can sometimes hear their calls…the yacares."

Carmelo's heart clenched at the sound of his sister's distress. "Eloisa, I'm sorry. Some things happened and it's taking me a little longer than expected to get there, but I'm here now, in Argentina. I'm coming for you! I won't let anything happen to you, I promise."

"Okay, Carmelo," Eloisa's voice wavered. "Please hurry."

There was a moment of silence, then a low chuckle. "Ah, el hermano valiente," the voice replied, dripping with disdain. "¿Dónde está usted, Sr. Quiñones? You were supposed to be here yesterday."

Carmelo's grip tightened on the phone as he fought to keep his emotions in check. "I…I had some difficulties. Some setbacks, but I am still coming! I am in Argentina! I'll bring you what you want, just please don't hurt Eloisa!"

"I don't have time for your excuses," the voice interrupted sharply, a cold edge to its tone. "You have until sunset tomorrow to deliver the map, or your sister will suffer the consequences."

Carmelo's heart sank at the threat, his mind racing with the weight of the situation. "Please, just give me more time," he pleaded desperately. "I…I just need a few more days to get there. Please!"

"I will give you until the end of the week—five more days. ¡No más! If I do not have the map in my hands by midnight on the fifth day, your sister will perish. There are no second chances, Sr. Quiñones," the voice retorted icily before hanging up, leaving Carmelo with a sense of dread gnawing at his soul. He turned to Alex, his expression grave. "We need to act fast. Time is running out."

Carmelo turned to Klaus with urgency in his eyes. "Klaus, is there any way we can get our hands on a vehicle? We need to leave immediately."

Klaus laid a calming hand on Carmelo's shoulder. "Carmelo, there's no need to panic. It'll be dusk soon, and it's safer not to travel at night. Dinner is already underway. Why don't you and Alex join us for a meal, take some rest, and in the morning, I'll personally drive you to San Rafael. It is the closest city with a bus station and car rental. From there, you can arrange for transportation to continue your journey."

Carmelo hesitated, torn between his desire to reach Eloisa as soon as possible and the practicality of Klaus's suggestion. He glanced at Alex, silently weighing their options. Finally, he nodded reluctantly. "Alright, Klaus. We'll take you up on your offer. Thank you," he said, his voice laced with gratitude.

Klaus smiled warmly, patting Carmelo's shoulder reassuringly. "It's settled then. Let's enjoy a good meal and rest for the night. Everything will work out fine, you'll see," he said, leading them toward the dining area with an air of hospitality.

Carmelo and Alex followed, their minds still racing with worry for Eloisa, but grateful for the respite Klaus had offered them.

"After dinner, we'll have a fashion show," Klaus announced with a flourish, his eyes alight with excitement. "I'll unveil some of my latest designs for you both to admire."

Carmelo and Alex exchanged bemused glances, intrigued by the unexpected turn of events. "A fashion show?" Carmelo repeated, a hint of amusement in his voice.

Klaus nodded enthusiastically. "Yes, indeed! Consider it a little diversion to brighten the evening and showcase my talents. You're in for a treat!"

The dining room was adorned with opulent decorations, from the shimmering chandeliers casting a warm glow to the intricately carved wooden furniture that exuded an air of old-world elegance. The long, polished dining table was set with fine china, sparkling silverware, and crystal glasses, creating an inviting atmosphere for the evening ahead.

As the three men took their seats, the aroma of savory dishes wafted through the air, tantalizing their senses. The meal began with a refreshing gazpacho soup, followed by a succulent roasted chicken drizzled with a tangy lemon sauce. Side dishes of buttery mashed potatoes and roasted vegetables accompanied the main course, adding a touch of indulgence to the feast.

For dessert, a decadent chocolate mousse was served, its rich flavor complemented by a garnish of fresh berries. Each bite was a symphony of flavors, a testament to the culinary skill of the chef. As they savored the delicious meal, Carmelo, Alex, and Klaus exchanged stories and laughter, their worries momentarily forgotten in the warmth of good food and companionship.

Carmelo savored the last spoonful of chocolate mousse, a contented smile gracing his lips. "Klaus, my friend, you have truly outdone yourself! That was quite possibly the best meal I've ever had," he exclaimed, his eyes twinkling with delight. Alex nodded in agreement, raising his glass in a toast. "Compliments to the chef!" He chimed in, his voice filled with genuine appreciation.

Klaus chuckled warmly, a glimmer of gratitude in his eyes. "Thank you, thank you. Truly, all the credit belongs to my cook, Catalina. She is a blessing. I couldn't bear the thought of life without her cooking," he confessed, a genuine appreciation evident in his tone. "Now, gentlemen, we will retire to the parlor!" He rose from his seat, gesturing for Carmelo and Alex to follow him to the cozy parlor where they could continue their evening conviviality.

The parlor looked less like a parlor and more like a posh nightclub, exuding an air of sophistication and extravagance. Ornate chandeliers cast a warm glow over the space, illuminating plush velvet couches and armchairs adorned with intricate embroidery. Paintings and tapestries depicting scenes of grandeur adorned the walls, adding to the room's elegant ambiance. In one corner stood a grand piano, its polished surface gleaming under the soft light. Opposite the piano, a well-stocked bar offered an array of fine liquors and spirits.

Situated at the other end of the parlor, there was a dedicated performance space delineated by a raised platform that served as a stage. Flanked by shimmering curtains that could be drawn aside for dramatic effect, the stage boasted professional lighting and sound equipment, setting the scene for captivating performances.

Carmelo and Alex refreshed their cocktails and found a cozy sofa to settle into. Their anticipation mounted, filling the air with excitement and energy.

The show began with a heralding of dramatic music and dimming of lights, setting the stage for a captivating display of Klaus' creations. As the haunting melody filled the air, the room was bathed in a soft, ethereal glow, casting shadows that danced along the walls. Carmelo leaned forward in anticipation, his eyes fixed on the makeshift stage before them.

One by one, members of Klaus' housekeeping and kitchen staff emerged from the shadows, their silhouettes illuminated by spotlights that followed their every move. With a mix of nerves and excitement, they strutted their stuff, an endearing authenticity to their movements. Their smiles were filled with genuine enthusiasm and camaraderie.

Each ensemble was worn with pride and a sense of fun. Laughter filled the air as they navigated the stage, bringing a charming and heartwarming touch to the show.

The music swelled, rising to a crescendo as the first housekeeper reached the end of the stage, striking a pose that exuded confidence and poise. Carmelo and Alex erupted into applause, their enthusiasm fueling the energy of the room.

With each passing moment, the spectacle unfolded, revealing a stunning array of garments that ranged from the whimsical to the avant-garde. In Klaus's innovative collection, vintage military jackets were transformed into chic blazers, their epaulets and brass buttons adding a touch of regal elegance. Cargo pants were reinterpreted as trendy trousers, complete with pockets adorned with intricate embroidery inspired by military insignias.

Camouflage print was masterfully incorporated into flowing skirts and tailored dresses, offering a modern twist on traditional military attire. Accessories such as belts made from repurposed ammunition pouches and handbags crafted from parachute fabric added a unique and edgy finishing touch to each ensemble.

As the models strutted down the runway with confidence and poise, Klaus's unique designs captivated Carmelo with their bold creativity and undeniable style. Each piece was a testament to Klaus' unparalleled talent and creativity.

Carmelo cast a glance at Alex, his expression a mixture of contentment and concern. "I hope all of this extravagance isn't making you feel uncomfortable," he murmured softly, unsure of how Alex was processing the flamboyant atmosphere surrounding them.

Alex offered Carmelo a reassuring smile, his eyes reflecting a sense of appreciation for Carmelo's consideration. "Actually, Carmelo, I'm quite enjoying myself," Alex replied with a genuine smile. "It's refreshing to be in such a lively and welcoming environment. Besides, who wouldn't love a fashion show starring the talented members of Klaus's staff?" He chuckled, his tone light and relaxed. "I'm finding it quite enchanting. Especially in the company of someone as remarkable as you, Carmelo." His eyes twinkled, his voice trailing off slightly as he met Carmelo's gaze.

As the last member of Klaus's staff gracefully completed her walkthrough, a hush fell over the room, anticipation palpable in the air. The lights dimmed, casting a soft glow over the stage, and a spotlight emerged, illuminating a glittering curtain at the center.

With the resumption of the music, the curtain slowly lifted, unveiling Klaus standing proudly, in full drag, the embodiment of his show's pièce de résistance. He wore a dress crafted from meticulously cut pieces of his grandfather's Nazi uniforms, the fabric intricately arranged to form a stunning and provocative ensemble.

Klaus exuded an aura of captivating glamor and confidence. His hair was a masterpiece of styling, meticulously teased and styled into glamorous waves that framed his face with effortless elegance. Each strand seemed to catch the light, shimmering with a hint of sparkle, adding a touch of enchantment to his overall look.

His makeup was expertly applied, with a flawless complexion serving as the canvas for his artistry. His eyes were the focal point, adorned with dramatic winged eyeliner and smoky eyeshadow that accentuated their mesmerizing blue glow. Long, fluttering false lashes added depth and drama, while his lips were painted in a vibrant shade of red, drawing attention to his captivating smile.

As Klaus stood tall in his breathtaking creation, his physique radiated confidence and allure. The gown hugged his curves in all the right places, accentuating his statuesque figure with its form-fitting silhouette. With each step, he moved with grace and poise, commanding the attention of all who beheld him with an air of undeniable charisma and sophistication.

Carmelo and Alex were visibly struck by the audacity and boldness of Klaus's creation, the dress serving as a powerful statement that challenges perceptions and ignites conversation. Klaus's expression radiated both defiance and pride as he commanded the stage, his creation captivating all who beheld it.

As the final performance ended, Klaus took his bow and the last notes of music faded into the air, the room erupted into applause once more, the sound reverberating off the walls in a symphony of appreciation. Klaus smiled, his heart swelling with pride as he basked in the adulation of his small but adoring audience, knowing that he had succeeded in creating a moment of pure magic.

The lights flickered and went out as the curtain fell with a whoosh. By the time Klaus returned to the parlor, the staff had already redonned their own clothes and returned to their duties. Carmelo and Alex returned to the bar to refill their empty glasses.

As Klaus made his grand return to the parlor, he surprised everyone by appearing in a rather unexpected ensemble. Clad in nothing but a snug speedo, his thin athletic physique on full display, he sported a pair of comically oversized goggles perched atop his head. With a mischievous twinkle in his eye, he addressed the room with a playful grin. "Anyone up for a swim?"

By the time Carmelo and Alex were introduced to their rooms, the mansion was cast in the gentle glow of evening. Their accommodations were luxurious yet cozy, each room exuding its own unique charm. Carmelo's room boasted rich mahogany furnishings and plush velvet drapes, while Alex's room was adorned with intricate tapestries and a grand four-poster bed.

"Klaus, thank you so much for such an amazing evening! It was such a wonderful experience and a welcome distraction from this horrible situation," Carmelo said with genuine gratitude.

"Yes, thank you, Klaus," Alex added, sincerity coloring his voice. "Your hospitality and generosity have been truly remarkable. It's been an unforgettable evening. And thank you for helping us get to San Rafael tomorrow!" Alex said, his gaze turning to Carmelo with a warm smile. "I know how much it means to Carmelo to get his sister back safely."

"Oh, thank you, Carmelo and Alex. It has been my supreme honor to entertain my new friends!" Klaus replied, his eyes sparkling with delight. "I just have one question." Carmelo looked at him curiously. "What did you think of the dress?"

"It was quite the statement piece," Alex replied diplomatically, his tone carrying a hint of admiration. "Definitely unforgettable."

Carmelo paused for a moment, his eyes reflecting a mixture of emotions. "It was...bold," he finally said, choosing his words carefully. "The use of the Nazi uniforms. You took something horrible and ugly and turned it into something beautiful."

"Those uniforms belonged to my grandfather. I stumbled upon them in the attic when I was just a boy. My mother used to regale me with tales of his bravery and heroism for his country. It wasn't until I grew older and learned about the horrors of the Second World War and the Nazi regime that I realized who my grandfather truly was. I understood why my mother kept him distant from me during my childhood. Discovering my own identity as a gay man was a tumultuous journey. Learning that my grandfather was affiliated with a party that deemed people like me unworthy of life was a harsh reality to swallow.

One night, fueled by a mix of emotions, I found myself in the attic once more. I reached for a pair of fabric scissors and, in a moment of catharsis, I destroyed those remnants of my grandfather's past. I sealed them away, never to be reopened until last year. It was then that I decided to take a stand against the hateful ideology that once consumed my family. What better way to defy his legacy than to create something beautiful from the remnants of his hatred? This dress represents my defiance, my reclaiming of identity, and my unwavering stance against bigotry and intolerance.

Anyway, I'm sure the two of you are very tired and would like to settle in. I took the liberty of providing each of you with some pajamas to sleep in. You can put your clothes in this basket over here and they will be laundered for you by tomorrow morning. Goodnight! I will see you both in the morning." With a warm smile, Klaus disappeared down the hallway, leaving Carmelo and Alex to retire for the night.

As Carmelo turned down his bed, the soft strains of classical music filled the room, offering a comforting backdrop to the day's tumultuous events. With a sigh, he slipped into the luxurious pajamas thoughtfully provided by Klaus, relishing the softness against his skin. Nestling into the plush bedding, he allowed his thoughts to wander, replaying the phone conversation with his sister's kidnapper in his mind.

The callousness of the kidnapper's words echoed in Carmelo's thoughts, stirring a mix of anger and determination within him. What did the kidnapper mean by "the map"? Was it truly a map, and if so, to what? His gaze drifted to the messenger bag resting nearby, the package inside it teasingly visible. A surge of curiosity swept over him, urging him to seek answers. Tonight, he resolved, he would uncover the truth.

Chapter Five

As Carmelo awakened from his slumber, the events of the previous day lingered in his mind like fragments of a vivid dream. He stretched, feeling the weight of the day ahead pressing upon him. He noticed his clothes neatly washed, folded, and placed on the small table by the doorway. Grateful for the gesture, he quickly gathered his belongings and began changing.

As Carmelo emerged from his room, the aroma of freshly brewed coffee greeted him, leading him to the villa's kitchen where Alex stood by the counter, a mug in hand.

"Good morning," Alex greeted with a sleepy smile, gesturing towards the coffee pot. He, too, was already dressed for the day. "Help yourself. It's not gourmet, but it'll do the trick."

Carmelo nodded his thanks, pouring himself a cup and taking a grateful sip. The warmth of the liquid spread through him, chasing away the last remnants of sleep.

"Did you sleep okay?" Alex asked, leaning against the counter.

Carmelo nodded, a sense of purpose settling over him. "Yeah, thanks. Hey, can I show you something?"

Alex chuckled, a hint of wry amusement in his eyes. "Certainly! What is it?"

Carmelo glanced towards the window, where the morning sun was just beginning to filter through the trees, and then back to Alex abruptly. "I found a map inside the package. I opened the package." Carmelo pulled out the map and started to unfold it.

Alex blinked as if he had already anticipated the announcement. "A map? What kind of map?" He took another sip of his coffee.

"I don't know. Don't laugh at me, but I think it's a treasure map!" Alex choked, almost spitting out his coffee. Carmelo glared at him, a mix of amusement and annoyance flickering across his features. "Is something funny?" He asked dryly, crossing his arms over his chest.

Alex cleared his throat and composed himself. "Sorry, sorry," he said, a sheepish grin spreading across his face. "It's just…a treasure map? Really?"

Carmelo rolled his eyes, but there was a hint of mischief in them. "I know it sounds ridiculous, but that's what the kidnapper mentioned. He said something about needing it by midnight on Sunday."

Alex raised an eyebrow, curiosity piqued. "And do you have any idea what this treasure might be?"

Carmelo shrugged, a deep crease forming across his forehead. "Your guess is as good as mine. But whatever it is, it's important enough for him to threaten Eloisa's life over."

Alex's expression sobered, a flicker of concern crossing his features. "We need to get some answers from this map, then. And fast."

Carmelo nodded in agreement, the weight of the situation settling over them once more. "Agreed. First, we need to find out more about this map. Then, we'll figure out our next move."

With a shared nod, they finished their coffee and prepared themselves for the day ahead, knowing that whatever challenges awaited them, they would face them together.

"By the way, the map was not the only thing I found inside the package," Carmelo said as he began carefully refolding the delicate map. "There were also some other documents, letters, and a journal belonging to Lorenzo, my sister's dead husband. He was an archaeologist."

Alex's eyes widened with interest, setting his coffee mug down on the counter. "An archaeologist, you say? That's intriguing. What kind of documents did you find? Anything that might shed light on this treasure map?"

Carmelo shook his head, brows furrowed in concentration. "I haven't had a chance to go through them all yet. But if Lorenzo was involved in archaeology, there might be something useful in there. It's worth taking a look."

Alex nodded in agreement. "Absolutely. Let's go through them together. Maybe there's a clue that could help us figure out what this treasure is all about."

Carmelo gave a determined nod, feeling a renewed sense of purpose. "Agreed. Let's see what we can find."

Klaus hurried into the kitchen sporting a trucker hat pulled over his brow with the words "LET'S TRUCK" printed on it, and large, dark mirror-tinted aviator glasses shielding his eyes. He wore a vintage embroidered western pearl-snap shirt, paired with boot-cut jeans and alligator hide boots, giving him a rugged yet stylish appearance. His expression betrayed a sense of urgency. "We seem to have some uninvited breakfast guests," he announced, his voice tinged with concern.

Alex carefully peeked out the window and saw several military vehicles parked outside the villa grounds. "Oh no, this is not good," he said running his hands through his hair nervously.

Carmelo's heart sank as he joined Alex at the window, his stomach churning with unease. "Military vehicles? What on earth are they doing here?" He glanced back at Klaus, his expression mirroring the concern evident in Alex's demeanor.

"Who are these people?" His mind raced with ominous possibilities.

"That's the man I warned you about," Alex whispered urgently, his eyes fixed on the imposing figure outside. "Remember when I told you about the police here? They can't be trusted. Most of them work for one man. And trust me, you don't want to deal with him. That's him out there."

Carmelo's heart raced as he absorbed Alex's words, a chilling realization sinking in. "What does he want?" He asked, tearing his gaze away from the window to meet Alex's eyes. "What do we do now?" His voice was barely above a whisper, tinged with a mixture of fear and urgency.

"I'm guessing he's the one responsible for the driver's murder and your attempted abduction. What does he want?" Alex asked rhetorically, his gaze shifting to the map in Carmelo's hands.

Carmelo looked at the map in his hands, his mind racing with possibilities. "Is this the man who has Eloisa?" He asked urgently.

Alex shook his head, his brow furrowed in thought. "I don't believe so. It doesn't make sense. If he was holding your sister for ransom, why would he then come after you like this? I would think he would have done that to begin with."

"Who is this guy?" Carmelo questioned, his voice tinged with concern and frustration.

"His name is Santiago Vargas. Around here he is called El Torre because he's very tall in stature, his height only being exceeded by his cruelty." Klaus interjected, his voice heavy with gravity as he entered the room. "He's a powerful and dangerous man in these parts. He controls everything, including the local law enforcement. If he's involved, things are bound to get even more complicated. He must have some reason to suspect that you are here. We must flee."

Carmelo and Alex exchanged worried glances as Klaus's words sank in. Santiago Vargas, El Torre, loomed over their plans like a dark cloud. The realization that they were now entangled in a web of danger sent a shiver down Carmelo's spine. They couldn't afford to underestimate El Torre's reach and influence. With a sense of urgency, they knew they had to act quickly to evade his grasp.

The room was suddenly filled with the infectious melody of "Funky Town," the lively tune breaking the tense silence that had settled over them. Its upbeat rhythm seemed out of place amidst the gravity of their situation, yet its presence injected a touch of surrealism into the air, momentarily lifting their spirits and lightening the mood.

Klaus turned to Diego, his footman, who stood nearby, his expression fraught with apprehension. "Diego, answer the door," Klaus instructed, his voice firm but reassuring. "Don't let on that we're here. Tell the man at the door that I'm away on urgent business. Allow him to inspect the house and the grounds thoroughly. He'll only leave when he's satisfied that whatever he's looking for isn't here."

Diego nodded, though his nerves were palpable. Klaus placed a comforting hand on his shoulder. "It'll be alright, Diego. Trust me," he said with a reassuring smile.

As Diego hesitantly made his way to the door, Klaus pulled on a pair of leather driving gloves, a sense of determination evident in his demeanor. "I have an escape plan," he muttered to himself, his mind already racing through the details.

With a final encouraging nod to Diego, Klaus prepared himself for the sudden escalation in urgency and for what was soon to come. He gave Carmelo and Alex a confident smile, "Follow me."

As Klaus led them down the corridor into the west wing of the villa, the atmosphere grew tense with anticipation. He ushered them into the study where they were met with an air of opulence and mystery. A massive wooden desk, crafted from rich, dark wood, commanded attention in the center of the room. Bookshelves lined the walls, filled with leather-bound tomes and ancient manuscripts, hinting at the room's scholarly purpose.

Against one wall stood a panel of surveillance monitors and recording equipment, hinting at the room's dual function as a command center. Nearby, a towering gun cabinet loomed, its metal exterior gleaming under the soft light. Beside it, a large floor safe sat, its imposing presence adding to the room's aura of secrecy and intrigue.

To the side of the massive fireplace, nestled in the corner, stood a large concrete statue of a majestic German shepherd. Its stony gaze seemed to watch over the room with a sense of solemnity, adding an unexpected touch of elegance to the otherwise utilitarian space.

With a determined push, Klaus moved the statue aside, revealing a hidden staircase descending into the darkness beneath. "Down here," he said, gesturing toward the dark, descending steps, his voice echoing faintly against the cold stone walls of the study.

Carmelo felt a shiver run down his spine as he peered down into the dark stairwell, which seemed to lead into an abyss of uncertainty. Despite the flickering light from the study casting eerie shadows on the steps, he knew that venturing into the unknown depths below was their only chance at escaping the looming threat above. With a mixture of apprehension and determination, Carmelo took a deep breath and prepared himself for whatever awaited them in the hidden tunnels below.

As they descended into the dimly lit tunnels, Klaus reached out to close the entrance behind them, ensuring their trail would be difficult to follow. With a steady hand, he carefully manipulated the mechanisms, sealing the passage and returning the concrete statue to its original position with a subtle click. As the echoes of their footsteps faded into the darkness ahead, they pressed on, their escape route now hidden from prying eyes above.

Once they had ventured deeper into the tunnel, Klaus began to explain its origins. "My grandfather commissioned the construction of this tunnel when the villa was built," he recounted solemnly. "He foresaw the possibility of being hunted down by Nazi hunters seeking justice for war crimes. This tunnel served as a last resort escape route, a way to flee from those who sought to hold him accountable for his actions during the war."

Klaus continued, "I found the tunnel not long after I took ownership of the villa. I kept it maintained just as an extra safety measure. As you can imagine, running a large-scale cannabis plantation comes with a fair share of risks."

As Alex stepped further into the tunnel, his expression shifted from one of curiosity to a mixture of apprehension and awe. The dimly lit passageway stretched out before him, its walls seeming to close in with each step. Despite the uncertainty that loomed in the darkness, there was a sense of intrigue that flickered in Alex's eyes, a recognition of the gravity of the situation mingled with a hint of excitement at the unfolding adventure.

Carmelo squinted as he tried to peer further into the tunnel, worried about what creeping critters he might encounter in this dank, wet environment. The musty scent of damp earth filled his nostrils, and the dim lighting cast eerie shadows along the walls. Despite his urban upbringing, he couldn't shake the primal sense of unease that gnawed at him in this subterranean environment. Yet, beneath the surface fear, there was a spark of determination in Carmelo's eyes, a resolve to press forward in the face of the unknown.

They continued further into the tunnel until they reached a large chamber where a truck was parked, its slick, glossy black paint casting a stark contrast against the dank moldiness of the underground passage. The RAM 1500 TRX seemed out of place in such surroundings, its sturdy frame suggesting it was ready for a journey beyond the confines of the hidden tunnels. Klaus approached the truck with purpose, indicating that it was their means of escape from the looming threat aboveground.

Carmelo peered at Klaus with a questioning expression, "You keep a TRX in your escape tunnel? Quite the getaway truck!"

Klaus responded with a casual shrug, "In my line of work, it pays to be prepared for anything." He smiled smartly, his demeanor reflecting a mix of confidence and readiness for whatever challenges lay ahead. Alex shot him an impressed look, acknowledging the practicality and foresight of keeping such a powerful vehicle in an escape tunnel. Klaus continued, "Technically I don't keep it down here. The truck is parked on an elevator that lowers it down from the garage above," he pointed up at the large rectangular hole in the ceiling of the chamber. We will remove the truck and then raise the floor so they will not be aware of our escape."

Carmelo and Alex exchanged a glance, their expressions reflecting a shared sense of speechless amazement at the unexpected sight of the well-equipped escape tunnel.

"Get in!" Klaus said firmly as the doors of the truck unlocked with a clunk, his tone leaving no room for further discussion.

The engine roared, catching air as it lept out of the tunnel exit ramp and into the blinding morning sun. Carmelo and Alex whooped with excitement, their laughter mingling with the rumble of the truck as it rocked, tilted, and bounced over the rough, rocky terrain.

Klaus expertly navigated the powerful vehicle along the rugged, untamed, primitive road that wound its way further up into the mountains. His hands moved with precision on the steering wheel, guiding the truck effortlessly over the uneven terrain. With practiced finesse, he also managed to spark up a joint, taking a long drag as he focused on the road ahead.

Carmelo and Alex exchanged nervous laughs as Klaus took another deep toke, the smoke swirling around him as he continued to steer the truck with ease.

Klaus glanced over with an amused expression as he saw their faces. "It helps me focus," he explained casually, passing the small joint to Carmelo. "It will help calm your nerves. Normally I don't advocate smoking and driving, but we are still on my property and these are extenuating circumstances."

Once the joint reached the end of its circuit and had returned to Klaus, he quickly snuffed it out and tossed it out the window, the remnants disappearing in the rush of wind. "This is the old escape route. I can't take you on the main roads," Klaus said, his tone grave and serious. "El Torre will surely have them barricaded by the police." Carmelo and Alex exchanged nods, silently acknowledging the likelihood of Klaus's warning.

They drove for almost an hour, navigating through narrow mountain passes and around precipitous cliff ledges. They passed by a pristine glacial lake and ascended to the top of the range. Eventually, they reached a plateau overlooking a giant ravine, a huge crack in the earth carved out by a seismic fault.

Klaus slowed the truck to a halt and killed the engine. "This is as far as I can take you," he announced solemnly. "In the next valley is the town of Malargüe. I'm not sure if there's a place that will rent you a car. Unfortunately, I believe the buses don't run through there during the off season, but you can find a hotel and hopefully have luck finding transportation. I'm truly sorry I cannot take you all the way to San Rafael. I will drive in another direction and hopefully act as a decoy. Best of luck to you, Carmelo and Alex."

Carmelo paused, his hand reaching into his bag to retrieve something. "Wait! Before you go, I have something to give you for all of your generosity and kindness," he said, pulling out the copy of his newest, yet-to-be-released book. It was the very book his mother had read from on Christmas Day. "I know it isn't much, but it's all that I have with me. I wrote a little note inside and signed it."

Klaus read the title of the book with an excited grin. "The Spy Who Loved Him," he said, appreciating the gesture. "Thank you, Carmelo. It has truly been my honor to have met you." He received Carmelo's hug warmly and then turned to Alex, extending his hand. "And you as well, Alex. I hope that we will meet again someday."

Carmelo and Alex's attention suddenly turned toward the deep gorge blocking their path into Malargüe. They inspected the deep crag with trepidation. Alex's voice held a hint of desperation as he spoke. "How are we supposed to get across that? It's totally impassable!"

Klaus gave them a devilish smile, his teeth sparkling under his thick sunglasses. "Leave that to me," he said confidently. He reached into the bed of the truck and pulled out a Nazi-era tactical grapnel launcher. "I found this in my grandfather's attic also," he said proudly, a glint of mischief in his eyes. "This is my parting gift to you both!"

Klaus lifted the grapnel gun and took aim at a large tree directly across the ravine. His stance exuded pure masculinity, radiating confidence and determination. Carmelo and Alex exchanged puzzled glances, their expressions mirroring a mix of disbelief and uncertainty. Klaus, undeterred, adjusted his aim with a steady hand, peering down the sight of the launcher. "Don't worry, I'm a gaymer," he said casually. "I've got this."

With a loud burst of air and a resounding boom that sent a wave of sound echoing through the ravine, Klaus fired the grapnel gun. The projectile launched across the chasm, pulling coils of monofilament wire in its wake. With precision, it slammed into the tree beyond, embedding itself firmly into the trunk. "Bullseye!" Klaus said with a celebratory gesture. He quickly anchored the line using the thick steel bumper guard on the front of his truck. Reaching once again into the truck bed, he sat down the spent grapnel gun and retrieved two more objects.

"These are harnesses," Klaus explained, handing one to Carmelo and the other to Alex. "Put them on."

Carmelo's hands trembled as he slipped into the harness, his fingers fumbling with the straps as his mind raced with a mixture of fear, uncertainty, and an underlying determination to see this perilous journey through to its end.

As the two men adjusted their harnesses and secured their safety straps, Klaus deftly attached two EZ clip trolleys onto the monofilament cable. With practiced hands, he then connected each man's harness to a trolley using daisy chain lanyards, ensuring their safety for the daring journey across the gaping ravine.

Carmelo's heart began to pound, fear gripping him like a vice. "Are you sure this is a good idea? Isn't there some other way to cross?" He asked, his voice tinged with anxiety. Alex's expression was one of full excitement.

Klaus ignored his question and continued with his instructions. "Alex can go first to show you how it's done," he replied.

"Heck yeah!" Alex exclaimed with enthusiasm. He eagerly sat down on the ledge and pushed away, embracing the adrenaline rush. Off he went, propelled by the tension of the monofilament wire, zipping across the ravine with a mix of excitement and concern for Carmelo.

"So, what you're going to do is sit down on the ledge there, and when you feel ready, just lean back like you're reclining in front of the television," Klaus instructed Carmelo, laying a comforting hand on his shoulder.

Alex reached the other side and came in for a smooth landing. He quickly unfastened his lanyard and yelled back across the ravine, "Woohoo! What a rush! It's your turn, Carmelo!"

With a nervous groan, Carmelo sat down on the edge of the ravine. "Sure, let's do this. How hard could it be? Famous last words, right?" He closed his eyes and counted to ten, trying to calm his racing heart. At ten he did just as Klaus had instructed. With his eyes closed, he slowly leaned back, remembering the previous night's poolside fun at the villa. In his mind, he pictured himself lying back in a chaise lounge next to the pool with an ice-cold beverage in hand.

Suddenly, he was swept away by the forces of gravity. As Carmelo zipped across the ravine, his initial panic gave way to exhilaration. With the wind rushing past him and the breathtaking scenery below, he couldn't help but feel a surge of adrenaline coursing through his veins. A sudden wave of emotion hit him and he started to laugh and cry simultaneously, each tear one of pure euphoria.

Before he knew it, he had reached the other side. He came in fast, but as he touched down on terra firma, he was caught in Alex's warm muscular grasp. He looked up and met Alex's friendly eyes with his. For a moment, all of his surroundings faded into a blurry patchwork of shapes and colors, and the only thing clearly visible was Alex's deep green eyes. He wanted nothing more than to burrow himself deeper into those warm, bulging arms and never let go. He felt Alex's soft breath on his neck.

The moment was broken by a call from the other side of the ravine. "Auf Wiedersehen!" Klaus exclaimed as he waved from the other ledge. "Be careful!"

Carmelo managed a wave back, a mix of gratitude and nervousness evident in his gesture. "Thank you, Klaus! We'll see you again, I promise!" Alex waved his goodbye as Klaus turned to climb back into the truck.

Chapter Six

By the time Carmelo and Alex reached the edge of the city of
Malargüe, it was already mid-afternoon and the sun was
beating down relentlessly.

Malargüe was a picturesque town nestled amidst the rugged
beauty of the Argentine Andes. As Carmelo and Alex
approached, they were greeted by the sight of quaint, colorful
buildings lining the streets, their facades adorned with vibrant
murals depicting scenes of local life and culture. The town
square bustled with activity, with vendors selling fresh
produce and handicrafts, and locals going about their daily
routines.

In the distance, the snow-capped peaks of the Andes loomed
majestically, casting a breathtaking backdrop against the
azure sky. The air was crisp and invigorating, carrying with it
the scent of pine and mountain wildflowers.

Despite its remote location, Malargüe exuded a sense of
warmth and hospitality, welcoming visitors with open arms. It
was a place where time seemed to slow down, allowing one
to immerse themselves in the natural beauty and laid-back
charm of the Andean foothills.

Carmelo, noticing how confidently Alex seemed to stroll through town, asked, "Have you ever been to Malargüe before?"

Alex responded with a wistful smile, "Yes. Many times. My family used to vacation here when I was younger. It holds a special place in my heart."

He pointed out towards the mountains, "Up that way, there are ski resorts with some of the best skiing in Argentina. Many people choose to stay here in Malargüe to save money, also there are a lot of shops and boutiques, and restaurants here. It can be quite the winter destination!"

Hearing something about Alex's childhood sent Carmelo's curiosity swirling within him like a whirlwind, catching him off guard. He had always assumed Alex's origins were distant and nebulous, yet here he was, speaking with a familiarity that hinted at deeper connections. "I never asked you," Carmelo ventured tentatively, his voice carrying the weight of his newfound intrigue, "what part of Argentina are you from?"

Alex's response carried a hint of guardedness as if he were choosing his words carefully. "Believe it or not," he began, his voice tinged with a touch of vulnerability, "I grew up near the city of Mendoza."

Carmelo's eyes widened in surprise, a flicker of realization crossing his features. "Mendoza?" he repeated, his voice tinged with curiosity. "That's where I'm heading. What are the odds?"

Alex's voice trailed off, a hint of melancholy coloring his words. "Yes, it is a coincidence," he agreed softly. "Though, I haven't lived there in years. It's not a place with many fond memories for me..."

Sensing the discomfort in the air, Carmelo shifted gears, changing the subject to lighter matters. "If you've been to Malargüe before, there must surely be a restaurant here that you have fond memories of, perhaps even a hotel for the night. I'm exhausted and sweaty. I could use a shower and something to eat. I'm feeling famished. My treat!"

Carmelo's thoughtful redirection lifted the tension in the air, prompting Alex to respond with a grateful smile. "That sounds wonderful!" He exclaimed, appreciating Carmelo's offer for a much-needed break.

With a hint of concern in his voice, Alex suggested, "I think I know a place. There's a reputable hotel near the Plaza San Martin. I believe we'll be safer there. Once we check-in, you can freshen up and I will see about securing us a vehicle for tomorrow." Carmelo nodded in approval.

They reached the Hotel Terra Patagonia shortly before the sun began to set behind the snow-capped Andes. The hotel stood as a beacon of rustic elegance against the backdrop of the rugged Argentine landscape. Its exterior, constructed from locally sourced stone and timber, blended seamlessly with the natural surroundings, offering a warm and inviting atmosphere. As Carmelo and Alex stepped through the entrance, they were greeted by a spacious lobby adorned with handcrafted wooden furniture, plush leather sofas, and intricate indigenous artwork, reflecting the rich cultural heritage of the region.

The interior design featured earthy tones and natural textures, creating a sense of harmony with the surrounding landscape. Large windows allowed ample natural light to filter in, offering breathtaking views of the majestic Andes mountains.

As they approached the reception desk, Carmelo and Alex exchanged hopeful glances. Their anticipation quickly dissipated as the concierge delivered unwelcome news.

"We're fully booked," the concierge announced apologetically. The man was a weathered and stoic figure. His chiseled features spoke of a life lived with purpose, and his intense gaze held a hint of underlying warmth beneath its hardened exterior. Despite his formidable appearance, there was an air of professionalism and efficiency about him as he attended to the guests' inquiries. He had a strong, square jawline, prominent facial features, and a thick, black mustache. His dark eyes exuded intensity and determination, adding to his tough and imposing demeanor.

Disappointment etched across Alex's face as he ventured, "Is there any possibility of securing a room with two beds?"

Regrettably, the concierge shook his head, a stern, yet sympathetic expression on his face. "I'm afraid not. We don't have any rooms with two beds available at the moment."

Alex took a diplomatic approach. "I understand the situation, and we don't wish to inconvenience you. However, this gentleman here," he said, placing a hand on Carmelo's shoulder, "is Señor Cameron Quinn, a renowned novelist from the United States, here to pen his latest masterpiece." Carmelo's face was flushed, his cheeks warm and red.

Alex turned his gaze towards the concierge, his expression earnest and his voice slightly hushed. "As for myself, I am Alejandro Thiago Mendoza. My family has frequented this establishment for many years, spanning my entire childhood. I am Señior Quinn's guide while he is here in Mendoza Province. I was sincerely hoping that you could make an exception for us, just for one night."

The concierge glanced at the two men with wide eyes and uttered, "Let me see what I can do if you will excuse me." He disappeared into a back room momentarily before reemerging with a grin stretching across his weathered face.

"You're in luck! A room has suddenly become available. It is our finest suite!" His enthusiasm was palpable as he addressed Alex and Carmelo. "If you could just give us an hour to get the room ready for you, I think you will be most comfortable there. Welcome to the Hotel Terra Patagonia."

"Gracias, señor," Alex exhaled with relief.

Carmelo's gaze shifted between Alex and the concierge, his expression a blend of amusement and disbelief upon realizing the concierge's seeming familiarity with his work. A smile tugged at the corners of his mouth as he remarked, "I guess we really do come in all shapes and sizes. I never realized my writing was this popular in Argentina." Chuckling quietly to himself, he gave the concierge an appreciative smile. The concierge returned the expression, his teeth gleaming under the light of the chandeliers, his eyebrows raised with a coy flash as their eyes met.

Alex gave Carmelo a playful smirk and replied, "Indeed, it seems you are famous even in Malargüe, Carmelo." Together they turned to walk away hoping to find a nearby distraction to kill time.

As they strolled around the Plaza San Martin, the heart of Malargüe, they were greeted by the vibrant energy of the bustling town square. Tall trees provided welcome shade, their branches swaying gently in the breeze. Colorful flowers adorned the well-maintained gardens, adding a touch of natural beauty to the urban landscape.

Around the plaza, quaint cafes and artisanal shops lined the cobblestone streets, their inviting facades beckoning passersby to explore their offerings. The sound of lively conversations and laughter filled the air, accompanied by the occasional notes of street musicians performing nearby.

In the center of the plaza stood a majestic statue of General José de San Martín, a revered figure in Argentine history, mounted on his horse and poised in a stance of determination. Surrounding the statue, benches provided a place for locals and visitors alike to rest and soak in the vibrant atmosphere of the square.

As they continued their leisurely walk, Carmelo and Alex couldn't help but admire the charm and character of Plaza San Martin, a vibrant hub where the heartbeat of Malargüe could truly be felt.

Carmelo regarded Alex with a hint of suspicion, his brow furrowing slightly. "I didn't know your last name was Mendoza," he remarked, a note of curiosity in his voice.

Alex responded with a playful grin, his tone light and friendly. "You didn't ask," he quipped, a twinkle of mischief in his eyes.

Carmelo continued, a curious expression flickering across his features. "Alex Mendoza from the city of Mendoza in Mendoza Province. Is there some connection there?"

Alex met Carmelo's gaze with a steady, penetrating look, his deep green eyes seeming to hold a world of mystery. Carmelo tried to maintain his composure, resisting the urge to get lost in those mesmerizing pools of green. "There are many people with the name Mendoza," Alex replied, his smile disarming. "It's a very common name in Argentina, especially in Mendoza Province."

As Carmelo and Alex made their way back to the hotel, Carmelo's ears caught the sound of the concierge's voice calmly explaining to an irate couple that their suite had accidentally been double booked, and that the hotel was at capacity. The couple's frustration was palpable, but the concierge handled the situation with practiced ease, offering apologies and suggestions for alternative accommodations.

Noticing Carmelo and Alex walking by, the concierge flashed a nervous smile. Carmelo returned the gesture politely, though a hint of uncertainty flickered in his eyes. Was he somehow responsible for the conflict? And then, an unexpected thought crossed his mind: Had the concierge been flirting with him? The notion lingered as they continued on their way, adding a curious twist to the evening's events. They walked up to the reception desk and politely waited for the concierge to finish his conversation.

"I feel bad for what has happened," Carmelo whispered to Alex, discreetly gesturing toward the couple. "We could have found another hotel."

Alex calmly shook his head. "No, trust me. You want to stay in this hotel. They will not say a word to anyone about us if some of El Torre's men were to come around asking. We are safest here."

Carmelo gave Alex a look of fondness and gratitude. "I trust you, Alex."

As they stepped into the suite, they were greeted by the warm glow of soft lighting and the rich aroma of freshly cut flowers. The spacious room was elegantly furnished with luxurious fabrics and tasteful decor. Plush armchairs sat invitingly around a coffee table adorned with a vase of exotic blooms. To the left and right were rooms surrounding grand four-poster beds that dominated the center of each room, their crisp white linens inviting rest and relaxation. The walls were adorned with local artwork, adding a touch of charm to the sophisticated ambiance. Large windows framed stunning views of the surrounding mountains, allowing natural light to flood the room during the day. It was a sanctuary of comfort and tranquility, a haven from the chaos of the outside world.

Carmelo ran into one of the rooms and flopped down onto the bed sending a wave of air rippling through the goose-down duvet. As he collapsed onto the bed, the soft duvet enveloped him in a cocoon of comfort, its plushness inviting him to sink deeper into relaxation. He closed his eyes, savoring the sensation of the luxurious bedding beneath him, letting out a contented sigh. The events of the day melted away as he surrendered to the embrace of the sumptuous bed, allowing himself a moment of respite from the tumultuous journey they had endured.

"After today's escapades, this bed feels like a reward from the universe. Or maybe just the hotel concierge," Carmelo giggled. "I'm pretty sure I could sell tickets to this bed. It's the main attraction after all the chaos today."

Alex, noting Carmelo's evident comfort, offered to arrange for a vehicle for the next day, providing Carmelo with privacy to enjoy his shower.

When Alex returned from his errand, Carmelo was sitting on one of the armchairs in the lounging area with a towel twisted around his head, a thick white bathrobe enveloping his frame. "How was your shower?" Alex asked, his interest piqued by the sight of Carmelo wrapped in the luxurious robe.

"It was divine," Carmelo replied with a satisfied sigh. "The hot water felt like heaven after our adventurous day. I'm just not looking forward to putting my dirty clothes back on," he added with a look of disgust.

Alex perked up, a playful smile gracing his lips, "Well, it's funny that you said that because I went shopping while I was out, and I bought you something." He gave Carmelo a seductive grin.

Carmelo's eyebrows raised in surprise. "Oh? What did you get me?" He asked, unable to hide his curiosity. Like a kid on Christmas morning, Carmelo ripped the bag from Alex's hands and stuffed his hand inside. His smile gleamed from cheek to cheek. The first object he grabbed was a small bottle of some kind of thick liquid. He pulled it out of the bag. "Lotion?" His eyes squinting in confusion.

"Keep looking," Alex taunted.

Carmelo stuck his hand into the bag again. His hands wrapped around something long and cylindrical, shaft-like. He squeezed it firmly. "What kind of store did you go shopping at?" Carmelo asked with a slightly embarrassed look on his face.

"It's not what you think," Alex laughed, his own cheeks now blushing.

Carmelo pulled out a clear, plastic tube. "Socks?" He reached in again and felt the soft fabric of clothing in the bottom of the bag.

Alex chuckled, enjoying Carmelo's reaction. "Not just any socks," he teased, "they're thermal socks, perfect for keeping your feet warm in the chilly mountain air." Carmelo's expression shifted from confusion to amusement as he pulled out the clothing from the bag.

"The lotion is for your sunburn," Alex continued, still chuckling. "The back of your neck is almost as red as your face." He gestured at the clothing Carmelo had removed from the bag and was now inspecting. "I had to guess on the sizes but I hope they fit you," he added thoughtfully.

"Thank you, Alex! That was very thoughtful of you," Carmelo replied, getting up to give Alex a hug. "What do you say to us ordering room service and seeing how much damage we can do to the mini-bar? We can take a closer look at everything that is inside the package."

"That sounds like a great plan!" Alex gave a nod of approval, "It would probably be better than to be out in the public eye too much anyway."

As they sipped their second round of Argentine whiskey over ice, their food arrived. The aroma of sizzling meats and savory spices filled the air, whetting their appetites, a feast fit for kings.

The room service cart was adorned with succulent Argentine steaks, perfectly seared to medium-rare perfection, accompanied by a vibrant chimichurri sauce that danced on their taste buds. Alongside the steaks were golden-brown empanadas, their crispy shells giving way to a flavorful filling of seasoned ground beef, onions, and spices. A generous serving of fluffy white rice and charred vegetables completed the spread, offering a balance of textures and flavors that left them both eagerly anticipating the first bite.

Chapter Seven

After the meal was devoured, and as they still sat at the table in the hotel room, Carmelo reached into his messenger bag and pulled out the package.

"Well, here it is!" His eyes widened as he removed its contents and laid them on the table. He lifted the delicately folded document on top and slid the other items aside. Together they carefully unfolded the aged parchment, revealing an intricately drawn map. The map, weathered with time and yellowed with age, depicted rugged terrain, crude drawings, and cryptic symbols.

Alex traced his finger along the faded lines, his brow furrowed in concentration. "This map is a masterpiece of deception," he remarked, marveling at its maker's cunning. "Each symbol seems to hold a secret, a clue to unlocking the treasure's whereabouts."

Carmelo leaned in closer, his eyes scanning the map's intricate details with keen interest. "But what is the treasure, and what do these symbols represent?" He mused, his mind racing with possibilities. "Deciphering these cryptic messages won't be easy."

Alex, sensing Carmelo's intrigue, leaned forward. "What else was in the package?" He asked, his curiosity piqued.

"Lorenzo's journal," Carmelo said solemnly.   "He was my sister's husband who was murdered three months ago. Lorenzo was an archaeologist. One day his body washed up on the shore of the Rio de la Plata, nobody knows who was responsible."

"Maybe there are answers in there," Alex offered inquisitively.

"I hope so," Carmelo replied, his voice tinged with hope, "Otherwise, we're going to have to recruit someone who specializes in five-hundred-year-old obscure treasure map decryption." The binding of the journal creaked as he opened the cover. "It's all in Spanish. Lorenzo was known for his meticulousness. He might have left clues, but deciphering them won't be easy."

Alex nodded, understanding the gravity of the situation. "I will help you. We'll figure it out together," he assured Carmelo, placing a reassuring hand on his shoulder. He scooted his chair up next to Carmelo. Their thighs pressed against each other's. Carmelo could feel the muscular contour of Alex's leg as he leaned in close to examine the journal. He scanned the first few pages, "These first few pages seem to be transcribed excerpts from a document titled *El Primer Nueva Corónica y Buen Gobierno*, which means.."

"*The First New Chronicle and Good Government*?"

"I think that is correct," Alex admitted. "It doesn't make a whole lot of sense."

Carmelo interjected. "What does it say?"

As Alex read further, he remarked, "It seems to have been a handwritten manuscript to King Philip III of Spain. Its purpose was to give a historical account of the Andes from the earliest human beings to the Incas and the Spanish conquest; it was also meant as a call of attention to the deep problems caused by the Spanish government in Peru. In this transcription, it reads as if he is denouncing the ill-treatment of the natives of the Andes by the Spanish Empire after their conquest of Peru.

"Why would Lorenzo be interested in the history of Peru? Peru is a thousand miles north of Argentina and on the other side of the Andes mountains." He shook his head in confusion.

"I don't think Lorenzo was as interested in the history found in the text as he was in the man who wrote it." Alex flipped through the next few pages and scanned the text intensely. "Lorenzo's notes on these pages are talking about this man, Guaman Poma. His full name was Felipe Guamán Poma de Ayala, sometimes referred to as Huamán Poma or Waman Poma. It seems that he was a member of a noble family of the indigenous Huaman dynasty. He was a direct descendant of the eminent indigenous conqueror and ruler Huaman-Chava-Ayauca Yarovilca-Huanuco.

"Ok, so he was indigenous nobility," Carmelo deduced, trying to grasp a sense of the narrative.

"The journal says that Guaman Poma was born in 1535, shortly after the Spanish conquest of Peru, and he grew up in Huamanga, a central Peruvian district. It says that he was raised to speak several Quechua and Aru dialects, and also learned the Spanish language as a child or adolescent." Alex turned the page in the journal and heard a soft crackling sound. Stuck in between two pages was a thin piece of tracing paper folded in half.

Alex carefully pulled the sheet loose and unfolded it. It was a drawing that appeared to be traced from another source. "Look at this!" He exclaimed with a sense of wonder. "It says 'The Noble Jerónimo Luis de Cabrera in a dynamic and heroic pose as he founded the city of Córdoba.'"

In the foreground, Jerónimo Luis de Cabrera stood tall and resolute, with a determined expression on his face. He was depicted wearing the attire of a Spanish conquistador, complete with a gleaming breastplate and a feathered helmet, symbolizing his authority and leadership. His posture exuded confidence and purpose as if he were ready to conquer new frontiers and establish a lasting legacy.

Around Cabrera, the scene was filled with the rugged beauty of the landscape. Towering mountains loomed in the background, their peaks kissed by wisps of clouds, indicating the Andean region where Córdoba would eventually be founded. The rolling hills and valleys were lush with greenery, hinting at the fertile lands that would become the heart of the city.

In the sky above, a golden sun radiated warmth and light, casting a golden hue over the entire scene. This symbolic sun represented the dawn of a new era, marking Cabrera's pioneering efforts in establishing a Spanish presence in the region. Birds soared in the distance, adding a sense of freedom and exploration to the composition.

The attention to detail in the drawing was striking. Cabrera's features were meticulously rendered, from the rugged lines on his face to the determination in his eyes. His stance conveyed both strength and ambition, embodying the spirit of conquest and colonization that characterized the Spanish explorers of that time.

Overall, the drawing captured a moment frozen in time—a moment of courage, vision, and historical significance as Jerónimo Luis de Cabrera embarked on the monumental task of founding Córdoba.

"Córdoba, Argentina?" Carmelo's expression was one of piqued interest. "Now we're getting closer. What's the connection between Guaman Poma and Jerónimo Luis de Cabrera?"

Alex was silent for a moment as he read further into Lorenzo's journal. "Lorenzo wrote, 'Jerónimo Luis de Cabrera was born in Seville, Spain, in 1528. At the age of ten, he and his older brother Pedro migrated to the Viceroyalty of Peru.

As boys growing up in the vibrant Andean region of Peru, Jerónimo Luis de Cabrera and Guaman Poma shared a unique bond forged by their shared experiences and the diverse cultural tapestry of their surroundings. Cabrera, hailing from Spanish nobility, and Guaman Poma, from indigenous nobility, found common ground in their curiosity about the world beyond their immediate horizons.

Their paths often crossed in the bustling streets of Huamanga, where Cabrera's family had established connections, and where Guaman Poma was immersed in the rich traditions and teachings of his heritage. Guaman Poma, just a few years younger than Cabrera, was tasked with teaching Cabrera the Quechua language while Cabrera tutored Guaman in Spanish. Despite the societal divides of their time, their friendship blossomed, fueled by mutual respect and a shared thirst for knowledge.

Through their youthful adventures and conversations, they exchanged stories of distant lands, ancient legends, and dreams of exploration. Little did they know that their paths would diverge as they grew older, with Cabrera venturing into the realm of Spanish conquests and colonization, while Guaman Poma delved deeper into the preservation of indigenous histories and cultures.

Their childhood bond, however, remained a cherished memory for both, a testament to the enduring connections that transcended cultural barriers and shaped their respective journeys in profound ways.'"

"Interesting!" Carmelo exclaimed, "They were childhood friends."

"That seems to be what Lorenzo was saying," Alex confirmed as he kept reading. "So then they both grew into adults." Alex continued, "During that time, Guaman Poma went on to write his masterpiece, *Corónica, a* monumental work consisting of 1,189 pages primarily written in Spanish, interspersed with sections in the Quechua language, and some 398 full-page illustrations. It stands as the most extensive and sustained critique of Spanish colonial governance authored by an indigenous individual during the colonial era. The chronicle was addressed directly to King Philip III of Spain.

Within its pages, Guaman Poma meticulously detailed the injustices perpetrated under Spanish colonial rule, challenging the legitimacy of the Spanish presence in Peru by asserting that the land rightfully belonged to the indigenous peoples. He boldly proclaimed, "It is our country because God has given it to us," encapsulating his belief in the inherent rights of the indigenous population and their divine connection to the land.

Through his *Corónica*, Guaman Poma articulated a powerful narrative of resistance and advocacy for indigenous rights, highlighting the disparities and oppression faced under Spanish governance while advocating for a more just and equitable society. His work remains a testament to the resilience and courage of indigenous voices in confronting colonial injustices.

Guaman Poma advocated for a novel approach to governing Peru—a "good government" model that blended elements of Inca social and economic systems, European technology, and Christian theology, tailored to meet the practical needs of the Andean communities. He contrasted the treatment of subjects under indigenous governance with that under Spanish rule, arguing that indigenous rulers were more benevolent and just.

Despite his criticism of Spanish rule, Guaman Poma maintained a respectful stance towards King Philip, viewing monarchs as divinely appointed figures and holding a deep reverence for Catholicism. He urged the king to appoint indigenous individuals to positions of authority, believing that this would lead to better governance and fairness for the people.

In his writings, Guaman Poma not only proposed reforms but also highlighted perceived injustices, aiming to draw the king's attention to issues that needed redress. He saw the king as a representative of God and trusted that, if informed, the king would rectify these injustices, aligning with his vision of a just and equitable society under the auspices of the Spanish monarchy.

Unfortunately, before Guaman's manuscript ever arrived in Spain, it was intercepted by Spanish-Peruvian authorities and never reached the king.

Guaman Poma's lineage traced back to Inca royalty through three distinct family lines: Tarco Huaman Inca, son of Inca Mayta Cápac and cousin to Cápac Yupanqui, as well as grandson of Lloque Yupanqui; Huaman Achachi, brother of Tupac Inca Yupanqui; and Inca Huaman Taysi, the offspring of Inca Roca.

The Huaman family, affluent within the Inca Empire both pre and post-conquest, engaged in strategic matrimonial alliances among ruling families to consolidate political influence. Renowned as warriors and landholders across various Inca regions, they held reverence for the wild bird 'Waman', akin to a falcon, exclusive to highland areas above 4,000 meters altitude in the Andean region.

Legends circulating among the Spaniards suggested that direct descendants from the Inca Huaman lineage had amassed considerable wealth and harbored ambitions of reclaiming the Peruvian Empire's sovereignty, reinstating the Incan Huaman dynasty's supremacy. Fearing the potential upheaval of colonial governance, Hispanic occupiers initiated a merciless campaign of persecution against the Huaman family, systematically stripping them of lands, rights, and titles.

Consequently, much of the Huaman family's wealth in gold and ornaments was hidden away and remained concealed in a mountainous hideout. Most of the surviving family members fled to remote corners of Peru and beyond where many of them were eventually hunted down and executed. Among Andean folklore, tales prophesied the rise of the hawk symbolized by the phrase, "...Hawk will fly high, where the Sun surrenders..."

As this brutal campaign against the Huaman family raged through Peru, Jerónimo Luis de Cabrera, in his headquarters of Córdoba, was not immune to the pressure for participation. He was directed by his superiors to embark on an exploration of the Andean region southwest of Córdoba. In 1573, he organized an expedition of one hundred soldiers and forty supply wagons and set off to explore the region known today as Mendoza Province, Argentina.

Rumor has it that he stumbled upon a hidden stronghold nestled deep within the rugged terrain of the Andes Mountains. Inside, he uncovered a treasure hoard that whispered of ancient nobility and lost dynasties. This treasure belonged to the noble family of the indigenous Huaman dynasty, renowned for their wealth and power in the region.

The treasure hoard held not just material wealth but also tales of valor, lineage, and the intricate web of alliances and rivalries that shaped the Andean landscape.

Despite the riches and historical significance of his discovery, Jerónimo Luis de Cabrera chose to keep the location of the hidden stronghold and treasure hoard a closely guarded secret. His decision was not born out of greed or ambition but rather out of a deep sense of love and respect for his childhood friend, Guaman Poma.

Knowing the tumultuous history and exploitation that often followed such discoveries, Cabrera sought to protect the site and its treasures from falling into the wrong hands. He believed that preserving the legacy of the Huaman dynasty for their descendants was more important than personal gain or recognition.

Interestingly, when Cabrera returned to Córdoba, only a small fraction of his soldiers returned with him, and his expedition map, along with all documentation of the expedition were reported as having been lost during an attack by the Charrúa natives.

However, Cabrera's story seemed suspicious to many who suspected him of withholding information, which quickly led to accusations of insubordination, as his superiors questioned his motives and allegiance to Spanish interests in the region. Despite facing consequences for his actions, Cabrera stood by his conviction, guided by a sense of loyalty that transcended political pressures and ambitions.

In doing so, Cabrera's story became intertwined with the hidden history he sought to protect, a testament to the enduring bonds of friendship and the complexities of navigating colonial dynamics in pursuit of preservation and honor."

Alex turned the page and revealed another piece of folded tracing paper. "Here's another one."

As Carmelo carefully unfolded the new piece of tracing paper from Lorenzo's journal, a somber and poignant scene unfolded before his eyes. The drawing depicted Jerónimo Luis de Cabrera in his final moments, facing his execution in Lima, Peru.

Cabrera was portrayed with a solemn expression, his eyes reflecting a mixture of resignation and dignity in the face of impending death. He stood tall, despite the circumstances, embodying a sense of inner strength and resolve. His attire was simple yet dignified, a stark contrast to the grim reality of his fate.

The execution scene was captured with raw emotion and attention to detail. The executioner, clad in traditional attire, held a sharp executioner's axe poised to strike. The tension in the air was palpable, as onlookers gathered to witness the final act of a once-great conquistador.

In the background, the cityscape of Lima loomed, adding a sense of historical context to the scene. The architecture hinted at the colonial influence of the Spanish in the region, a stark reminder of the power dynamics and conflicts that defined the era.

The execution itself was depicted with a certain degree of restraint, focusing more on the emotional impact than graphic detail. Cabrera's posture and facial expression spoke volumes, conveying the gravity of the moment and the resilience of the human spirit even in the face of death.

As Carmelo studied the drawing, he couldn't help but feel a wave of solemnity wash over him. The artwork captured not just a historical event but also the deeper themes of sacrifice, loyalty, and the complexities of the colonial era. It was a testament to the enduring power of visual storytelling, bringing to life moments of triumph and tragedy from the annals of history.

Alex returned his attention to Lorenzo's journal, reading from the pages, "As Jerónimo Luis de Cabrera faced his impending execution in Lima, his old friend Guaman Poma stood among the onlookers, silently observing the somber proceedings. Despite the passage of time and the divergent paths their lives had taken, their bond from childhood remained unbroken.

In the quiet moments leading up to Cabrera's final days, Guaman Poma sought permission to speak with his old friend, longing to reconnect and share memories of their shared past. Allowed a brief meeting, they reminisced about their childhood adventures, the dreams they once held, and the paths that led them to opposite ends of the colonial world.

As they spoke, Guaman Poma, with his deep understanding of both Spanish and indigenous cultures, offered words of comfort and solace to Cabrera, recognizing the complexities and challenges they faced in their respective roles within the colonial system. Their conversation, steeped in nostalgia and mutual respect, served as a poignant reminder of the enduring bonds that transcended the trials of history.

In the moments before Cabrera's execution, Guaman Poma stood by, a silent witness to the passing of an old friend and a chapter in their shared journey through a tumultuous era in South American history."

"Wow, what a sad story," Carmelo said, wiping tears from his eyes. "If the story is true, that means Cabrera died protecting the legacy of his childhood friend. Even in his final moments, he didn't betray his friendship or his integrity."

"The last entry in the journal says that later in his life, Guaman Poma entered a series of legal battles, striving to reclaim ancestral lands and political status in the Chupas Valley, asserting his familial rights. However, these lawsuits proved disastrous; not only did he lose the legal battles, but by 1600, he was divested of all property and compelled into exile from the very towns where he once held noble sway."

"It's so tragic," Carmelo whispered sympathetically, his voice filled with a mix of sorrow and admiration. "I can't imagine what it must have been like living in those times, to have endured the kind of existential struggles that they faced in their everyday lives."

He paused, reflecting on the profound bond shared by the historical figures. "But the story of their enduring friendship despite societal pressures, and the sacrifices they made to remain true to their bond and their integrity is inspiring, and romantic even."

Carmelo's thoughts then turned to the map lying on the table in front of him. "So, if my logic tracks," he mused, "that means this map could possibly be the map of Jerónimo Luis de Cabrera's expedition. Is it possible that Lorenzo managed to track down this document after so many centuries?" His curiosity sparked a sense of wonder and intrigue, eager to unravel more mysteries hidden within Lorenzo's journal.

Alex gave Carmelo a grave look, his expression weighted with seriousness. "If it is," he began slowly, "this map leads to the lost treasure hoard of the great Incan Huaman dynasty."

Carmelo's eyes widened at the implication, his mind racing with the possibilities. The mention of a lost treasure hoard tied to such a legendary dynasty stirred a mix of excitement and apprehension within him. He could sense the weight of history and the potential for discovery looming before them. His hands trembled as he struggled to process the weight of the situation. "I need another drink," he murmured, his voice strained with emotion.

Carmelo returned from the bar with a fresh cocktail in hand, sinking deeply into one of the armchairs. "So what do we do now?" He asked, his voice heavy with uncertainty.

"I think it's pretty obvious. We should go find the treasure!" Alex exclaimed, his enthusiasm undiminished.

"But what about my sister?" Carmelo's concern was palpable. "Besides, didn't you say that you would take me to the nearest city and then you would go on your way?"

"Well, now I'm invested," Alex replied earnestly.

Carmelo raised an eyebrow, a sardonic smirk playing on his lips. "Oh, are you? Are you invested? Please explain to me how invested you are," Carmelo retorted, frustration evident in his tone. "The allure of ancient artifacts and adventures got you hooked, ey?"

"I care about you, Carmelo. I don't want to see you or your sister get hurt," Alex explained.

"Well, how do you suppose us going after the treasure ourselves is going to help Eloisa?" Carmelo's voice carried a solemn urgency as he spoke, his eyes fixed on the map before him. "No, this map is going to buy my sister's freedom and probably her life. I don't care where it leads. I only care about Eloisa."

"Listen to me, Carmelo. I know people like this man who has your sister. I have dealt with this kind of man before. Let me tell you, the kind of man who goes through all of this trouble to get this map is not going to just let you walk away. There's always going to be another question, another riddle, another clue, and he is not going to be satisfied until he has the treasure in his hands. Until then, you can potentially be useful to him. Once he has the treasure, you'll no longer be useful. You will just be a loose end. If we find the treasure before we give him the map, then we'll have the upper hand. When we go to face him, we will be holding all the cards."

"He said I had to come alone." Carmelo closed his eyes and sighed. "I don't know what to do now."

Alex reached out and gently took Carmelo's hand, pulling him close until their faces were just inches apart. Their eyes locked in a moment of shared intensity, the weight of their circumstances hanging heavy in the air. Alex's voice softened as he spoke, his words carrying a sense of determination and resolve. "Then we make a plan," he said firmly. "A plan to outsmart this man, to protect your sister, and to claim what is rightfully yours."

"Is it, though? Carmelo asked reflectively, "Is it rightfully mine?"

"The secrets of this map were lost 500 years ago," Alex explained, "Lorenzo found it. He did the research. He put together all of the pieces. Then, he put it all in an envelope and mailed it to you. It's yours. Those people outside Klaus' villa today, they're trying to kill you for it. I say we find it before they do!"

Their embrace was electric. Carmelo found himself lost in the cool green lagoons of Alex's eyes. In a moment of surrender, he threw his arms around Alex's neck, drawing him closer until their lips met in a tender kiss. Time seemed to stand still as they savored the warmth of each other's touch, their hearts beating in unison with the rhythm of their shared desire.

Carmelo's sudden recoil was palpable, his mind racing with a whirlwind of emotions. "I'm so sorry. Please don't be offended. I just..."

"It's okay, Carmelo," Alex reassured him, his voice soothing. "I didn't mind it." A playful smile danced on his lips as he leaned in to capture Carmelo's with another kiss, igniting a spark of longing between them, a spark that swiftly grew into a bonfire of lust and passion.

As they lay in each other's arms amongst the soft, disheveled linens, Carmelo felt a sense of peace wash over him. The warmth of Alex's embrace enveloped him like a comforting blanket. At that moment, he felt a deep connection to Alex, a connection that transcended words and barriers. With a contented sigh, he closed his eyes, allowing himself to bask in the intimacy of the moment, cherishing the closeness they shared.

"Tell me, what are your dreams for the future?" Carmelo asked softly. "I want to know everything about you. Tell me everything!"

"Well, I grew up in a bustling household in Mendoza, with one brother and two sisters, not to mention three nephews and four nieces. Family gatherings were always lively affairs," Carmelo reminisced, a hint of nostalgia in his voice. "My father passed away in 2015 from stomach cancer, and my mother lived a long, fulfilling life until 2020."

"I'm so sorry Alex." Carmelo caressed Alex's hand.

Turning more introspective, Alex continued, "When I turned eighteen, I ventured to the University of Buenos Aires to delve into the world of zoology." His expression briefly clouded with discomfort. "It was during those college years that I came to terms with my sexuality. It wasn't an easy journey, especially with a family like mine."

A shadow crossed Alex's features as he recalled the past. "I remember the day I told my father I was gay. He was furious, insisting I keep it hidden to maintain our family's reputation. It strained our relationship irreparably." He paused, the weight of the memories evident in his eyes. "Since then, I have mostly avoided returning to the place where I grew up."

Carmelo's heart went out to Alex as he listened to his story, feeling a pang of sympathy for the struggles he had faced. "I can't imagine how difficult that must have been for you," he murmured, his voice filled with empathy. "But you're incredibly brave for being true to yourself despite the challenges. Your strength inspires me, Alex." He reached out to gently brush a stray strand of hair from Alex's face, offering a silent gesture of comfort and solidarity.

"Amidst those challenges, I found solace in sailing," Alex's tone brightened, a spark of passion reigniting. "I learned the ropes at university and fell in love with the freedom it offered. Renting boats for weekend getaways on the Rio de la Plata became my escape."

"It sounds like sailing was a true passion of yours," Carmelo remarked, a soft smile playing at the corners of his lips. "There's something about being out on the water, feeling the wind in your sails, that's incredibly liberating. It must have been a wonderful escape from everything else." He gazed at Alex with admiration, marveling at the depth of his experiences and the resilience he displayed in pursuing his passions despite adversity.

"Ever since then, I haven't been able to stop thinking about it. You asked me what my dream is. My dream is to one day own my own sailboat, a symbol of independence and true freedom. I want to sail around the world. I guess you could say the open seas are calling to me."

"That's a beautiful dream, Alex," Carmelo said, his voice filled with genuine warmth. "To sail around the world, exploring new horizons and experiencing the freedom of the open sea—it's an adventure unlike any other. I believe you'll make that dream a reality one day, and when you do, I would love to be right there beside you, ready to set sail on the journey of a lifetime." He squeezed Alex's hand gently, offering silent reassurance and unwavering support.

Chapter Eight

As the morning sun gently filtered through the curtains of their hotel room, Carmelo stirred awake, the events of the previous day slowly returning to his consciousness. He turned his head to see Alex still asleep beside him, his features softened in the golden light. With a contented sigh, Carmelo stretched and sat up, taking a moment to appreciate the peacefulness of the moment before the day's adventures began anew.

As Carmelo approached the dining area, the sight of the map and Lorenzo's journal spread across the table reignited the questions that had plagued his thoughts throughout the night. Should they pursue the treasure, risking their safety and the safety of his sister for a glimmer of hope? What about Eloisa, trapped in the clutches of a dangerous man? Would she hold on? Would she survive the brutal conditions for just a few more days? Would she understand their decision and forgive him for not coming straight to Mendoza to rescue her? With a heavy heart, Carmelo knew that the answers would not come easily, but one thing was certain: they needed a plan.

As Alex entered the common room, he noticed the furrowed brow and distant gaze of Carmelo, indicating that he was already deep in contemplation.

"Good morning," Alex greeted, pulling out a chair and joining Carmelo at the table.

Carmelo looked up, a mixture of determination and uncertainty in his eyes. "Good morning," he replied, his voice tinged with apprehension.

"You woke up early," Alex observed, pouring himself a cup of coffee.

"Yeah, I couldn't sleep much," Carmelo admitted, running a hand through his hair. "I've been thinking about everything…the treasure, Eloisa, what we should do next."

Alex nodded, understanding the weight of the decisions they faced. "It's a lot to take in."

Carmelo sighed, his gaze returning to the map and journal on the table. "I just don't know if going after the treasure is the right move. What if it puts Eloisa in even more danger?"

Alex offered a reassuring smile, his voice steady as he addressed Carmelo's concerns. "Carmelo, I understand your hesitation. But think about it this way: no matter what we do, your sister's safety is already at risk. Showing up with just the map might not ensure her release. However, if we take the initiative and secure the treasure first, we'll have leverage. It's a risk, but it's a risk worth taking."

Carmelo pondered Alex's words, the weight of their predicament heavy on his mind. After a moment of silence, he met Alex's gaze with newfound determination. "Your perspective makes sense," he acknowledged, a newfound resolve settling within him. "Continuing passively isn't an option. We need to act, and pursuing the treasure might just give us the leverage we need. Somehow we need to turn the tables in our favor."

"Exactly," Alex affirmed, his expression unwavering. "Then, we'll be ready for whatever challenges come our way."

With a deep breath, Carmelo felt a surge of determination. "Alright then," he declared, his voice firm. "Let's make a plan."

Alex nodded, his mind already buzzing with ideas. "Alright, here's what I propose," he began, leaning in closer to Carmelo. "First, we need to gather as much information as possible about the treasure's location from the map.

"Right, we're going to need more coffee for that," he added with a playful smile, knowing that a caffeine boost would fuel their brainstorming session. Alex nodded in agreement, acknowledging the wisdom in Carmelo's words. "Oh yes! Coffee first, decoding treasure map second," he concurred, their shared grin indicating a sense of camaraderie as they embarked on their quest for answers.

As they sipped their coffee, and carefully scrutinized Jerónimo Luis de Cabrera's expedition map, the details leaped off the aged parchment, whispering tales of untold adventures and ancient mysteries. Carmelo's fingers traced the faded lines of the Conquistador's journey, each curve and mark a testament to the courage and resilience required to explore uncharted realms.

"This map seems to be incomplete," Alex announced.

"What do you mean?" Carmelo inquired. "Is there a piece missing?"

"No, what I mean is that it's not finished," Alex clarified. "For example, there's no compass rose here to provide us with bearings," Alex pointed out. "This map lacks a clear sense of orientation. The images and text are oriented in various directions, generally pointing inward from the edge of the map. I've seen other Spanish colonial maps drafted in this manner, but they always included a compass rose with north clearly distinguished. The absence of one here suggests to me that this map is incomplete."

"So we need some way of establishing the orientation," Carmelo suggested.

"Yes, then we will know where the features drawn on this map are located on land," Alex affirmed.

"Okay, well, we have one reference point here," Carmelo said, pointing to a familiar spot on the edge of the map. "Córdoba."

"Absolutely!" Alex agreed enthusiastically. "We know that the expedition started there, we just don't know exactly what course they took when they ventured westward, so we need at least one more point on the map that we can attribute to a real-world location, and then we will have our bearings."

"Ok, then there has to be something else on Cabrera's map that we can identify in a real-world sense," Carmelo added as his focus returned to the map laid out on the table.

"Indeed," Alex agreed, his eyes scanning the map intently. "Let's look for any distinctive landmarks or features that might provide us with a clue."

Together, they scanned the map meticulously, searching for any recognizable landmarks or features. Each symbol and illustration held the promise of a clue, a breadcrumb leading them closer to their goal. As they studied the map, their conversation ebbed and flowed, punctuated by moments of realization and speculation.

Carmelo's finger traced the outline of a symbol on the map, resembling a structure. "This looks like a settlement," he observed, his voice tinged with hope. "It says Charrúa. Is there a modern-day town that corresponds to this Charrúa settlement?"

"Probably not," Alex shook his head in response. "The Charrúa were nomadic. They migrated to different parts of the continent depending on the seasons. I highly doubt they would have established a permanent settlement that would have survived to the present day."

Carmelo's expression fell, disappointment flickering across his features, but he quickly refocused his attention on the map, determined to uncover more clues.

Carmelo traced a line on the map, squinting at the faded symbols. "These markings here, Alex, they seem to indicate a mountain range. Could this be the Andes?"

Alex leaned closer, studying the map intently. "It's possible. The Andes would fit the description." Alex's eyes widened with excitement. "If those are the Andes, then that means from this point," he placed a finger on Córdoba, "to this point," he indicated the depictions of mountains, "is roughly westward. That's a good start."

"But how do we narrow it down further?" Carmelo wondered aloud, his brow furrowed in concentration. "If our bearings are off by even a few degrees, we could end up being hundreds of miles off target."

"That is very true," Alex acknowledged, his tone filled with determination. "There's more to the puzzle, it seems."

Carmelo's finger trailed along a thin line on the map, tracing the contours of what appeared to be clusters of trees and a winding river. "I see clusters of trees here," he remarked, his voice tinged with frustration. "And what looks like a river, possibly. But which river?" He huffed in frustration, "Do you recognize the curvature of this river?"

Alex shook his head solemnly. "No," he admitted. "Judging by its orientation on the map, it could be the Rio Mendoza, but I can't be certain. Besides, rivers change their courses over time. This map is over five hundred years old. I doubt if we were able to lay this map over a present-day map, that the river drawn here would match up precisely with any of the rivers in Argentina today."

"Look here! There is a rainbow arching over the river. What do you think that suggests?" Alex asked.

"I don't know," Carmelo pondered, his brow furrowing in thought. "Could it possibly represent a waterfall? Maybe the rainbow symbolizes the spray of the waterfall creating rainbows," he added, his voice tinged with uncertainty.

"That's a possibility," Alex conceded, nodding thoughtfully. "Waterfalls are often landmarks in themselves, especially in mountainous regions like the Andes. If we can identify a significant waterfall along a river that coincides with the one here on the map, it could help us pinpoint a location. However, that will require some time to research, as I'm not so familiar with Argentina that I can identify which waterfall on which river this diagram represents if that's even what it is representing."

"That's true," Carmelo said with a deflated sigh, "There could be hundreds of waterfalls in Western Argentina alone. If only the map told us which one."

"Well, I believe it does," Alex said enthusiastically, "we just haven't found the key to figuring it out yet."

Amidst their exploration of the map, Carmelo and Alex unearthed personal notes—cryptic warnings of perils lurking in the wilderness.

"Look, there is something written here." Alex pointed to a section filled with annotations. "It says, 'Beware the guardian's watchful eye.' It sounds like there's more to this journey than just reaching the destination."

Carmelo nodded, a sense of determination in his voice. "It's like Jerónimo left clues for us, challenges to overcome before we uncover the treasure."

As they continued deciphering the map and unraveling its mysteries, Carmelo and Alex found themselves drawn deeper into the Conquistador's legacy, their excitement mounting with each revelation.

Alex delved into the map once more, his eyes scanning every detail in search of a clue. Frustration mounting, he flipped the parchment over, revealing its blank backside. Yet, amidst the emptiness, a block of elegantly scripted text caught his attention. "La Madre María nos protege y guía nuestros pasos," he read aloud, his voice steady despite the unexpected discovery. "Mother Mary protect us and guide our footsteps," he translated, the words resonating with a sense of significance.

Carmelo leaned in, his interest piqued. "Could this be significant?" He inquired, a hint of excitement in his voice.

"Perhaps," Alex sighed, his mind spinning with possibilities. "It seems to be a prayer of sorts to the Virgin Mary for guidance and protection written by Cabrera, possibly before the embarkation of their expedition. He was very Catholic, of course. It doesn't seem that unusual for an explorer of this era to write something like this. It could be just that, but it could also hold a clue about our next steps in this journey. I don't know."

Carmelo nodded thoughtfully. "It feels like we're getting closer to uncovering the truth."

Carmelo's enthusiasm was unmatched by Alex's demeanor. "I don't know, we still don't have a heading," he said, his voice tinged with uncertainty. Alex flipped the map back over and resumed his inspection of the map's features with forensic determination.

"I'm still not seeing anything," Alex declared, his eyes intently focusing on each unique feature drawn on the weathered parchment. "Here we have Córdoba," he added, softly gliding his fingers over the surface. He traced his fingers up one of the long edges of the document to the opposite corner and then inward slightly. "Here are the mountains. We think this direction is west, but where in the mountains exactly?" He sighed audibly, "The key has to be here."

A moment passed. Alex's eyes squinted as if he were in deep concentration. "Huh, that's interesting," he said, his voice suddenly taking a cautiously positive tone.

"What is it?" Carmelo asked, leaning in closer, his curiosity piqued.

Alex ran his fingers under the row of cone-shaped symbols that spread across the top right corner of the map. The row of symbols spanned approximately fifteen centimeters long, each symbol measuring about one and a half centimeters in height. Alex studied them intently, his eyes narrowing in concentration. "Take a look at these mountains," he remarked with a faint smile, his finger tracing the line of symbols. "Notice how they're fairly uniform in height, except for this one." He pointed to a symbol that stood out subtly, slightly taller than the rest, adorned with the sun setting behind it on the left side and a majestic bird soaring high on the right side.

"Yes, I see it," Carmelo concurred.

"This one is taller than the others. I think this is not just any mountain," his eyes widened with excitement, "I think this is a very specific mountain. If I am correct, this is Cerro Aconcagua."

"You've lost me," Carmelo said with a confused expression. "Cerro Aconcagua?"

"Aconcagua isn't just the tallest mountain in Argentina; it holds the title for the highest peak in the Americas, even surpassing all other mountains outside of Asia. It reigns supreme as the pinnacle of both the Western and Southern Hemispheres," Alex elaborated. "What better way to chart a course than to use the biggest geographical feature around? It's certainly something that would persist through the ages."

"That makes sense. And look! I just thought of something, too. Looking at this symbol, it reminds me of what Lorenzo wrote in his journal," Carmelo remarked with a smile. "See how the sun is behind the mountain on one side, and on the other, a bird soars high. It's like the legend he mentioned—the hawk flying high when the sun surrenders. The sun setting behind the mountain represents a symbolic surrender, while the soaring bird represents freedom and ascension."

"Carmelo, that's it! That has to be it! We have to go to Aconcagua, which means our next move is to head north, towards the city of Mendoza," Alex added, a hint of apprehension coloring his tone.

"Perfect!" Carmelo's voice was tinged with concern, "I'm coming for you, Eloisa."

With their next move slowly coming into focus, Alex and Carmelo swiftly collected their few possessions and exited the hotel, the weight of anticipation heavy in the air. Stepping onto the bustling street of Malargüe, they hustled to the address where Alex had arranged to rent a pickup truck for the journey ahead. As they embarked on this new chapter of their adventure, a sense of purpose propelled them forward, driving them closer to the elusive truth they sought.

As Alex and Carmelo embarked on their journey from Malargüe to Mendoza, the landscape unfolded before them in a breathtaking panorama of rugged beauty. The road stretched out like a ribbon, winding its way through the majestic Andes Mountains, their peaks towering against the vast expanse of the sky. The air was crisp and invigorating, carrying with it the scent of pine and earth.

As they drove, the scenery shifted seamlessly from barren desert to verdant valleys, each turn revealing a new marvel of nature. Sunlight danced upon the surface of rushing rivers, casting shimmering reflections upon the rocky terrain. Snow-capped peaks loomed in the distance, their icy summits glistening in the golden light of day.

Occasionally, they passed small villages nestled in the valleys, their quaint charm a stark contrast to the rugged wilderness that surrounded them. The sound of rushing waterfalls echoed in the distance, a symphony of nature's raw power and beauty.

Despite the challenges that lay ahead, there was a sense of excitement in the air, an anticipation of the unknown that fueled their determination to press onward. With each passing mile, they drew closer to their destination, their hearts filled with the promise of discovery and adventure.

As the wheels of their vehicle hummed against the pavement, Carmelo glanced over at Alex, the mountains passing by in a blur outside the window. "Hey, Alex," he began tentatively, "I've been meaning to ask you something. You mentioned earlier that you don't like going back home to Mendoza. Is there a reason for that? Isn't there anyone in your family that you still have a good relationship with?"

Alex's gaze drifted from the road ahead to meet Carmelo's earnest eyes. There was a flicker of hesitation before he responded, his voice tinged with a hint of sadness. "It's complicated," he admitted, his fingers tapping lightly on the steering wheel. "My family...well, let's just say we've had our fair share of struggles over the years. It's not easy going back to a place that holds so many memories, both good and bad."

Carmelo nodded in understanding, sensing the weight of Alex's words. "I'm sorry to hear that," he said softly, his empathy shining through. "Family can definitely be...complicated sometimes."

"Yeah," Alex agreed, a wistful smile playing at the corners of his lips. "Especially when your family is very religious and old-fashioned like mine is. When I finally gathered enough courage to tell my brother that I was gay, he punched a wall and broke his hand. For a moment I thought he was going to kill me. My oldest sister does not even talk to me anymore. When I told my parents, my mother cried and said that I had broken her heart, and my father wanted to send me to the conversion camps. My younger sister was the only person in my family who showed me support and kindness, but after she got married, I haven't heard much from her either. Her husband works for my brother now."

Carmelo listened with a heavy heart as Alex revealed the painful truth about his family's reaction to his coming out. The weight of Alex's words hung in the air, casting a shadow over their conversation.

"My parents have both passed now, leaving my brother in control of our father's business," Alex began, his voice tinged with a mix of resignation and resolve. "I attempted to reconcile with my brother by shouldering some of the family burdens, but our moral compasses couldn't be further apart. He's the type to engage in questionable deeds, only to seek solace in church, masking his actions with ostentatious displays of piety and generous donations. While I've forsaken the notions of religion and salvation, I still hold fast to the ideals of leading an authentic and morally upright existence. It became clear that assisting my brother compromised my integrity, so I made the difficult choice to distance myself. Yet, every return to Mendoza is met with his persistent attempts to ensnare me in his schemes, prompting me to keep my distance for many years."

"I'm so sorry, Alex," Carmelo murmured, his voice laced with empathy. "That sounds incredibly difficult. It seems like you've had to make some tough choices," Carmelo observed, his tone gentle yet understanding. "But staying true to yourself, to your principles—that takes real strength."

"Yeah," Alex replied, his expression a mix of sadness and resignation. "It's been a rough road, to say the least. But I've learned to find my own path, to be true to myself, no matter the cost."

Carmelo reached out a comforting hand, offering silent solidarity in the face of Alex's pain. "You're doing what's best for you," he affirmed. "And that's all anyone can ask for. I think you're incredibly brave, Alex," he said softly. "And you're not alone. You have people who care about you, who accept you for who you are."

A fleeting moment of understanding passed between them, a silent acknowledgment of the bond that had formed between them on their journey. As they continued on the road to Mendoza, Carmelo vowed to stand by Alex's side, offering support and friendship every step of the way.

"I'm grateful for the friends I've made along the way, like you, Carmelo. It makes the journey a little bit easier," Alex added with an appreciative smile. "What about you, Carmelo?" Alex inquired, his gaze fixed on the road ahead. "Tell me about your family."

Carmelo's eyes lit up with warmth as he began to speak about his family. "My family is everything to me," he said with a genuine smile. "My mother is the strongest woman I know. She's been through so much, but she always finds a way to keep us together. And Tia Paloma...she's like the glue that holds us all together. She's been there for us through thick and thin, always offering her love and support." He paused, a fondness evident in his expression. "Growing up, we didn't have much, but we had each other. And that's all that mattered."

"And then there's Eloisa," Carmelo added, a mixture of pride and concern in his voice. "She's the brightest star in our family. Smart, kind, and full of life. She's always had big dreams, and I've always done everything I could to support her."

Carmelo's voice softened, his gratitude evident. "They've always been there for me, especially when I came out. I'm incredibly thankful for each of them." His expression shifted, a hint of concern coloring his words. "But lately, I feel like they're worried about me like they think I'll end up old and alone." He sighed, a weight settling on his shoulders. "I just wish they could understand that I'm content with who I am, regardless of what the future holds."

"Your family sounds incredible, Carmelo," Alex said, his tone warm and reassuring. "And anyone would be lucky to have you in their life. You bring so much kindness and compassion to those around you. I do not doubt that your future is bright, no matter what path you choose."

Their conversation drifted into a comfortable silence, the hum of the engine filling the space between them. As they continued on their journey, Carmelo couldn't help but feel a deepening connection to Alex, their shared experiences weaving a bond that transcended the miles they traveled.

As they drove, Carmelo's eyes caught sight of a sign along the roadside, its urgent message demanding attention: '¡Despacio! ¡Prepárate para parar!' Alex reacted swiftly, his foot applying pressure to the brakes. Ahead, the road was obstructed by barricades, flanked by police vehicles on either side. The scene painted a picture of caution and control, with each vehicle permitted to pass through the checkpoint in a methodical procession.

"This is not good," Alex remarked, his tone laden with concern as they approached the barricade. He slowed the car to a stop, observing the situation ahead with growing apprehension.

"We need to find another route," Alex suggested urgently, scanning the surroundings for a potential detour.

As they searched for an alternative route, Carmelo spotted a narrow dirt road veering off to the right. "There!" He exclaimed, pointing excitedly. Alex nodded and quickly maneuvered the vehicle onto the unpaved path, hoping it would lead them away from the police blockade. They drove cautiously, unsure of where the road would take them but determined to evade any potential trouble.

The dirt road wound its way through rolling hills and lush greenery, leading them deeper into the countryside. Towering trees lined the path, their branches forming a canopy overhead that filtered the sunlight, casting dappled shadows on the ground. The air was fresh and crisp, filled with the earthy scent of foliage and the faint hint of wildflowers. Despite the uncertainty of their situation, the serene beauty of the surroundings provided a sense of calm as they continued their journey, hoping to find a safe path forward.

As Alex and Carmelo navigated the rugged country road, their truck rattled and bounced over the uneven terrain. Dust billowed up behind them, obscuring the trail they left in their wake. The landscape stretched out before them, a vast expanse of fertile agricultural land broken only by occasional clusters of hardy shrubs and towering trees.

Ahead, the road seemed to abruptly vanish into the wide expanse of a river, the rushing water shimmering in the afternoon sun. There was no bridge in sight, just the dirt road disappearing into the river's embrace before re-emerging on the opposite bank. Alex eased off the accelerator, his brows furrowing in concern as he surveyed the scene ahead.

"We're gonna have to cross that," he remarked, his voice tinged with uncertainty.

Carmelo leaned forward, squinting as he tried to make out the path of the road through the flowing water. "Looks like it's our only option," he replied, his tone resolute despite the hint of apprehension, "unless we turn around."

"I'd rather take my chances with the river than with those policemen blocking the highway," Alex admitted, his face revealing a heightened level of concern. "I can almost guarantee you that those officers are working for El Torre," he added, his tone edged with suspicion. "Besides, how bad could this be?"

In unison, they both turned their focus on the rippling water rushing over the road before them, their resolve strengthened by the urgency of the situation.

Carmelo seized a stick from the nearby brush, his movements quick and determined. He approached the edge of the flowing water with a mix of caution and determination, his eyes fixed on the rushing current. With a hint of humor, he theatrically plunged the stick into the water, stretching as far as he dared toward the center. Retrieving the stick, he inspected it closely, searching for any signs or clues hidden within the flowing stream.

"It's moving fast, but it doesn't seem too deep," he reported.

"Well, I think we are all out of options," Alex replied with a sigh of resignation. "I guess we're about to find out if this truck doubles as a boat."

"Aye aye, Captain," Carmelo replied with a playful grin. "I'll batten down the hatches."

With a deep breath, Alex steered the truck towards the riverbank, the sound of rushing water growing louder with each passing moment. As they drew closer to the water's edge, the truck's tires sank into the soft riverbed, the current tugging at them with unexpected force. With determination in their hearts, they pressed on, their eyes fixed on the distant shore, ready to face whatever challenges lay ahead.

The floorboards of the truck began to fill with water as the relentless current pounded against the driver's side door, pushing them steadily downstream. With a surge of adrenaline, Alex slammed his foot on the gas pedal. With a mighty roar, the truck lurched forward, its wheels gripping the riverbed as it propelled itself onto the dry bank ahead, escaping the grasp of the rushing waters.

As they put distance between themselves and the river behind them, the echoing roar of rushing water gradually faded into the background, replaced by the steady hum of tires on pavement—a familiar sound that signaled the presence of a nearby highway.

The auditory tapestry, woven from the rhythms of travel, filled the air with a sense of movement and journey, guiding them onward toward their destination. Like a steady heartbeat echoing through the landscape, the hum of passing vehicles resonated in the air, punctuated by the occasional rumble of larger trucks and the distant blare of car horns.

Alex's voice carried a mix of relief and determination as he spoke. "We've reached the eastern Route 40. This isn't the path I originally intended to take, but it'll lead us into Mendoza."

Carmelo nodded in agreement, a sense of anticipation mingling with the weariness in his expression. "At least we're back on track," he remarked, his eyes scanning the road ahead as their journey continued.

As they traveled north along Route 40, the imposing silhouette of Volcán Diamante loomed on the horizon. Its rugged slopes, etched with crevices and ridges, stood in stark contrast to the surrounding landscape. Wisps of clouds danced around its peak, adding to its aura of majesty and mystery. Despite the distance, the volcano's presence commanded attention, reminding travelers of the raw power and beauty of nature.

Chapter Nine

As they arrived at the Hotel Gran Mendoza, Carmelo and

Alex were greeted by the grandeur of its façade, towering above them with an air of sophistication. The entrance was adorned with gleaming glass doors framed by ornate pillars, while a valet stood ready to assist with any needs they might have upon arrival. The lobby exuded opulence, with marble floors, plush furnishings, and sparkling chandeliers casting a soft glow over the space.

As they stepped inside, the cool air-conditioned breeze enveloped them, offering respite from the warmth of the afternoon sun. The gentle murmur of conversation filled the air, mingling with the soft strains of classical music playing in the background. Carmelo couldn't help but marvel at the elegance of their surroundings, his eyes taking in the intricate details of the hotel's interior décor.

Alex guided Carmelo to the reception desk, where they were greeted by a friendly concierge who welcomed them with a warm smile. After a swift check-in process, they were handed their room keys and directed to the elevator, which whisked them up to their luxurious accommodations on one of the upper floors.

As they entered their room, Carmelo was struck by the breathtaking view of the city skyline stretching out before them, bathed in the golden hues of the setting sun. The room itself was tastefully appointed, with sumptuous furnishings, plush bedding, and all the amenities one could desire for a comfortable stay.

With a contented sigh, Carmelo sank into the soft embrace of the king-sized bed, feeling a sense of relaxation wash over him. As he glanced out the window at the twinkling lights of the city below, he couldn't help but feel a sense of gratitude for the opportunity to experience such luxury with someone as special as Alex by his side.

"Would you like to go out for dinner?" Alex asked Carmelo, a smile playing at the corners of his lips. "I know a little place close by where we can have a delicious dinner with a memorable atmosphere."

"Yes," Carmelo swooned as he sprawled out over the giant bed, "both of those things sound amazing!"

As Carmelo and Alex approached the upscale Argentine steakhouse, they were greeted by an elegant façade reminiscent of old-world Spanish colonial architecture. The building was adorned with intricately carved wooden doors and wrought-iron fixtures, exuding an air of timeless charm and sophistication. Large arched windows adorned with decorative grilles allowed soft light to filter into the interior, casting enchanting patterns on the cobblestone sidewalk below. A weathered sign above the entrance bore the name of the restaurant in graceful script, while potted plants and cascading vines added a touch of greenery to the warm terracotta walls. Patrons dressed in elegant attire came and went, their laughter mingling with the strains of live music, creating an atmosphere of romance and nostalgia.

As they entered, the enticing aroma of delicious cuisine mingled with the sounds of live music and the chatter of diners. The atmosphere was lively, with a live band playing on the stage and a dance floor inviting guests to join in the fun.

Almost as soon as they settled into their quaint little table next to the dance floor, food began to flow in, starting with a platter of golden empanadas and sizzling provoleta, followed by two perfectly grilled cuts of Argentine beef accompanied by roasted asparagus and potatoes, all adorned with the vibrant green hues of traditional chimichurri sauce. A bottle of Malbec, rich and robust, was swiftly uncorked, adding to the sensory delight of the evening. Finally, two large ramekins of decadent dulce de leche flan appeared, promising a sweet conclusion to their meal.

Amidst the laughter and the romantic strains of a tango, Alex leaned across the table with graceful elegance. "Carmelo, will you dance with me?"

Carmelo's eyes brightened with a mixture of surprise and delight as he glanced around the lively restaurant. With a charming smile, he extended his hand toward Alex. "Of course, Alex. I'd love to dance with you."

"Are you familiar with the tango?" Alex inquired.

"Not extensively, but I'm willing to give it a try," Carmelo replied with a hint of uncertainty.

As the music swirled around them, Alex and Carmelo took to the dance floor with a mix of anticipation and nervousness. Their movements were tentative at first, as they found their rhythm and synchronized their steps to the sultry beat of the tango. With each graceful turn and passionate embrace, their confidence grew, and soon they were lost in the intimate dance, their bodies moving in perfect harmony. Their eyes locked in a silent conversation, conveying emotions too deep for words as they surrendered to the passion and intensity of the moment.

"You know, the tango originated in Argentina, in the streets of Buenos Aires in the late 19th century," Alex said with a hint of wisdom in his expression.

Carmelo's eyes lit up with knowledge. "Actually, I did know that," he quipped. "So significant is this passionate Argentine dance that in 2009, the tango was added to the UNESCO Intangible Cultural Heritage List. I read that on Wikipedia before I flew down here."

With effortless grace and style, Alex glided across the dance floor as if the tango were ingrained in his very being. Each step was executed with precision and poise, his movements fluid and confident. With a commanding presence, he led Carmelo through the intricate choreography of the dance, guiding him with gentle yet firm hand placements and subtle cues. As they moved as one, their connection palpable, it was as if they were transported to another world, where only the music and the movement mattered.

"You're quite skilled!" Carmelo praised, his admiration evident.

Reflecting on his past, Alex responded with a nostalgic smile, "I began taking tango lessons around the age of fifteen. We'd gather in a small neighborhood garage, dancing together two or three times a week. The tango becomes a part of you, a need you can't quite explain," he mused. "There's an indescribable beauty in dancing the tango. It's like soaring through the air, when you catch that feeling. It feels like you're flying,"

The music ebbed and flowed as the two men surrendered to its seductive rhythm, their bodies moving in perfect harmony with each rise and fall of the melody. With each step, they embraced the passion and intensity of the tango, their movements a captivating display of connection and chemistry. As they danced, the world around them faded into obscurity, leaving only the pulsating energy between them and the intoxicating allure of the dance.

As the night wore on, they decided to take a leisurely stroll back to the Hotel Gran Mendoza. Along the way, they found themselves winding through a tranquil park, its pathways illuminated by the soft glow of streetlights and the gentle rustle of leaves overhead. The air was filled with the fragrance of blossoming flowers. Painted park benches lined the walkway, inviting passersby to pause and enjoy the tranquil surroundings. The cool evening breeze carried the distant hum of the city, a reminder of the vibrant life just beyond the park's borders.

There, as they walked amidst the peaceful serenity of the night, Alex reached for Carmelo's hand. "Being with you tonight, walking through this tranquil park under the soft glow of the moon, I feel a sense of clarity," Alex began, his voice gentle yet resolute. "Carmelo, you are more than just a friend to me. You've become someone incredibly special, someone I've come to deeply care for."

Carmelo's eyes widened with surprise, his heart quickened at the sincerity in Alex's words. "Alex, I...I don't know what to say," he stammered, overcome by the unexpected confession.

"There's no need for words," Alex reassured him, reaching out to gently touch Carmelo's hand. "Just know that I cherish every moment we spend together, and I hope to continue sharing these moments with you, exploring life's joys and challenges side by side."

Drawn together by the magnetic pull of their emotions, they embraced beneath the starlit sky, their passion igniting like a flame in the darkness. With each tender touch and whispered confession, they surrendered to the irresistible allure of their love, their hearts intertwining in a symphony of longing and belonging.

As they finally arrived back at the hotel room, the world outside faded away, leaving only the two of them enveloped in the warmth of their shared embrace. In the soft glow of the moonlight, they surrendered to the undeniable pull of desire, their souls entwined in a dance of passion and intimacy that knew no bounds.

"Carmelo!" Alex exclaimed with passionate fervor as he gently kissed Carmelo's neck. "Carmelo!" Alex gripped him tightly, swaying him from side to side with his muscular arms as if they were still in the midst of the tango, "Carmelo!" As Alex's passionate embrace and fervent whispers enveloped Carmelo, he felt a rush of emotions swirling within him. The sensation of being held close, the warmth of Alex's breath against his skin, it all felt so real, so intense. Alex grabbed Carmelo by the shoulders and shook him, "Carmelo!"

Suddenly Carmelo opened his eyes, his senses snapping back to reality. "I'm…I'm awake." He pealed his cheek off the side door panel. With a gasp, he blinked rapidly, trying to shake off the remnants of the dream that lingered in his mind.

"Carmelo! We're here. Welcome to my hometown, the City of Mendoza!" Alex's voice cut through the haze of Carmelo's thoughts, bringing him back to the present moment.

Mendoza, nestled in the foothills of the Andes Mountains, exuded a charming blend of old-world elegance and modern vibrancy. The cityscape was dominated by low-rise buildings with traditional Spanish colonial architecture, characterized by whitewashed facades adorned with ornate wrought-iron balconies and red-tiled roofs. Tree-lined avenues provided shade from the sun, while bustling plazas invited locals and visitors alike to gather and socialize.

Interwoven with the historic charm were contemporary touches, seen in sleek glass skyscrapers and stylish boutiques that dotted the city center. Amidst the urban landscape, verdant parks and tree-filled squares offered oases of tranquility, providing respite from the bustling streets.

Mendoza's architectural tapestry reflected its rich cultural heritage and the influence of European immigrants, creating a unique and captivating ambiance that enchanted the senses.

"Oh, okay," Carmelo replied, still feeling a bit dazed as he glanced around at their surroundings. "Are we checking into the Hotel Gran Mendoza?"

"No, of course not," Alex replied, his expression growing more alarmed. "The moment you check in there, you'll be announcing your presence in Mendoza. The man who has your sister chose that hotel for a reason. He has informants working there."

"So where should we go? We need to regroup and figure out what to do next," Carmelo asked.

"How about we find a spot that's a bit off the beaten path? Somewhere where we can gather our thoughts without drawing any unwanted attention," Alex suggested, his tone thoughtful yet urgent. "I know a place."

Alex drove to a secluded park tucked away from the main tourist traps of Mendoza, offering a serene refuge from the city's hustle and bustle, a hidden gem that only a local would know. As they stepped through the wrought iron gates of the park, the scent of blooming flowers enveloped them, mingling with the earthy aroma of freshly cut grass. Towering trees provided a canopy of shade, their leaves whispering secrets in the gentle breeze. Stone pathways wound through lush greenery, leading to secluded alcoves where benches beckoned weary souls to rest. In the distance, the soft gurgle of a fountain added a melodic backdrop to their surroundings, while birds chirped merrily overhead. Here, amidst the tranquility of nature, they found solace from the chaos of the world outside.

Carmelo unfolded the map onto a nearby picnic table, the warm rays of the afternoon sun casting a golden hue over its weathered surface. With each delicate movement, the intricate lines and symbols seemed to dance in the light, as if eager to reveal their secrets. Nearby, the gentle rustle of leaves and the distant chirping of birds created a serene backdrop to their quest for answers. As Carmelo and Alex leaned in, their faces bathed in sunlight, they resumed their journey through time and history, determined to uncover the remaining mysteries hidden within the ancient parchment.

Carmelo's keen eye caught sight of a deep diagonal crease in the top left corner of the map. With a gentle touch, he folded the corner over, revealing the short prayer to the Virgin Mary written on the backside.

Alex read the prayer aloud once more, the words echoing in the tranquil surroundings. "La Madre María nos protege y guía nuestros pasos," he read aloud, "protects us and guides our steps. What if it's not a prayer? What if instead of this passage being a plea for guidance and protection, it is literally saying Mother Mary guides the way?"

Carmelo's face brightened with a pensive expression as he delicately unfolded the flap of paper, revealing the upper corner of the map once more. "In my book, Midnight Rendezvous," he began, his voice tinged with excitement, "the monument statue marking the grave of Augustus Hopkins, a large plantation owner, pointed the way to the closest safe house for escaping slaves during the Underground Railroad. Could it be a statue of the Virgin Mary somewhere, pointing us in the right direction? Is there a well-known statue of Mary in Argentina?"

"Well, yes, of course, there are many statues of the Virgin Mary in Argentina, some of them are even famous," Alex admitted. "There's Nuestra Señora de Luján. The story of this famous statue began when two small statues of the Virgin were brought to Argentina from where they were crafted in Brazil. According to legend, a Portuguese landowner in Sumampa wanted to erect a chapel in honor of the Virgin Mary, in order to invigorate the practice of Christianity in his region. He asked a friend, a resident of Brazil, to send an image of the Immaculate Conception of Mary. For a better choice, his friend sent him two statues. When the statues of the Virgin arrived at the port of Buenos Aires they were placed in two boxes, and, along with other cargo, put on an oxen-pulled cart. After three days of travel, the cart halted overnight by the town of Zelaya, near the present city of Luján."

"But the next day the oxen were unable to move the cart. The oxen were changed and most of the wagon's contents were unloaded yet the replacement oxen still were unable to pull the wagon. Then, someone noticed that two small boxes had been left in the back of the wagon. Upon inspection, it was found that each of these boxes contained a different statue of the Virgin. One represented the Immaculate Conception, and the other was of the Virgin holding the baby Jesus.

First, the box with the statue of Mary and Jesus was removed, but the oxen were still unable to move the wagon. However, when the box containing the statue of the Immaculate was removed, the oxen proceeded easily. The assembled witnesses were astonished, and so they decided that the statue of Our Lady desired to stay there, and travel no further. The statue was later moved to its final sanctuary in Luján. Pope Pius XII gave the sanctuary the title of Basilica, and it was declared a National and Historical Monument in 1998. The second statue, depicting Mary holding the child Jesus, reached its destination, and is today worshiped there under the title of Our Lady of Consolation."

Alex's voice carried a tone of quiet reverence as he recounted the tale of Nuestra Señora de Luján, his words weaving a vivid tapestry of history and folklore. Carmelo listened intently, captivated by the rich narrative unfolding before him.

As Alex spoke, Carmelo's imagination painted images of the oxen-pulled cart halted in the moonlit town of Zelaya, the weight of divine presence bearing down upon the travelers. The miraculous intervention of the Virgin Mary, guiding the oxen with her unseen hand, filled Carmelo with a sense of wonder and awe.

When Alex concluded his story, Carmelo's gaze lingered on him, a newfound admiration shining in his eyes. "That's truly remarkable," he murmured, his voice filled with genuine appreciation.

"There's also La Virgen de la Rosa Mística," Alex announced with widened eyes, giving Carmelo a playful, almost eerie look.

Catching onto Alex's playful demeanor, Carmelo responded, "Ooh, the mystic rose! What's that?"

"It's a weeping statue of the Virgin Mary, except this one cries tears of blood!" Alex exclaimed with a mischievous glint in his eye, his voice dripping with playful spookiness. "It was a huge deal back in 2017. It was even on TV. Someone had filmed the statue weeping tears of blood. Apparently, it has happened on many occasions, and still does to this day. One woman claimed that the statue cured her cancer. That statue is in the town of Metan, in north-western Argentina. There are even more, but there's a problem with all of them, including the two I mentioned."

Carmelo gave Alex a puzzled look.

"None of them were around when Jerónimo Luis de Cabrera set off to explore the mountains of modern-day Mendoza Province. The closest Spanish settlements other than Córdoba were far to the east at Buenos Aires and Montevideo. There were no churches, no cemeteries, no statues. At least not any made by Europeans," Alex concluded, his tone laced with historical insight.

A glimmer of realization brightened Carmelo's gaze as he absorbed the flaw in his reasoning. "Right, of course," he admitted with a nod. "It's not a statue."

Alex paused, a moment of revelation washing over him. "It's not a statue," he exclaimed, his eyes widening with excitement. "But, it would have been here during Jerónimo Luis de Cabrera's time."

Carmelo leaned in, his curiosity piqued. "What are you thinking?" He asked eagerly.

Alex leaned over the map, scrutinizing it for the precise location. "It would be right around here," he remarked, pointing to an area west of Melargüe, deeper into the mountains. "Caverna de las Brujas," he declared.

"A cave of witches?" Carmelo peered at Alex as if he were not following the train of thought.

"Yes," he exclaimed with enthusiasm, his excitement palpable. "Well, no, not exactly. There are no actual witches. The cave was just named that...the name and the legends surrounding it are not important. What matters is what's actually inside the caves. In one of them, there's a large vaulted gallery known as Sala de la Virgen."

"The Virgin's room," Carmelo translated.

"Yes! It's a National Heritage Landmark in Argentina. In the center of this underground chamber, there's a large stalagmite that resembles the Virgin Mary, adorned in long flowing robes, standing in a slightly hunched position as if in prayer. Her hands are clasped in front of her. It's truly spectacular! The caves date back to the Jurassic period."

"Look at this," Carmelo exclaimed, pointing to the map. "The crease runs right through the spot that you indicated–the location of the Witch Caves."

Alex leaned in for a closer look. "And the other end of the crease aligns perfectly with that symbol we found earlier," he observed, tracing the rainbow with his finger.

Carmelo nodded, excitement building in his voice. "It's like a hidden pathway, connecting the caves to that symbol."

"Mother Mary protects us and guides our steps." Alex ran his fingers along the crease on the map, from the location of the Witch Caves to the rainbow symbol, "Could this be the clue we've been searching for?" Alex wondered aloud, his eyes sparkling with anticipation.

"What about these other creases," Carmelo pondered. "Look at this long one!" He pointed at a vertical crease that ran perpendicularly across the map. Carmelo's eyes widened as he followed the line of the crease, his finger tracing its path across the worn parchment. "This one runs all the way from Córdoba to Aconcagua! How did we not notice that before now?"

"We were focused on the symbols, not the creases," Alex explained, his voice brimming with excitement. "But now that we see it, look!" He placed his finger on the precise intersection point where the two lines met. It was an area deep within the mountains, slightly southwest of Aconcagua. "This is the spot."

Alex turned his attention to the unidentified symbol on the other end of the first crease. "That means, based on roughly where this symbol is located, it has to represent Puente del Inca, of course! The rainbow is not a waterfall, it is a bridge over a river!   Using a rainbow as a symbol for the Inca Empire makes sense. Rainbows were significant in Inca culture, representing the connection between the earthly and divine realms. The Incas revered nature and believed it held spiritual significance, with rainbows often associated with fertility, prosperity, and divine intervention. For the Incas, the rainbow was more than just a beautiful spectacle; it was seen as a gift from Inti, the sun god, and held deep symbolic significance."

"Prosperity?" Carmelo's eyebrow raised, intrigued by the sudden connection.

"Puente del Inca is a natural arch that forms a bridge over the Mendoza River, Alex continued, "It is said that the Incas would use the bridge to reach a place in the mountain where they would perform rituals."

"An Inca temple in the mountains? Perhaps a storehouse for Inca gold?" Carmelo's voice echoed with wonder as he exchanged a glance with Alex, their minds racing with possibilities. "Let's go find it!"

"Hold on a minute," Alex interjected, his tone cautious. "We can't go hiking out there this late in the day, especially with the wrong clothing and no supplies. It's fairly challenging terrain, and at night it's extremely dangerous to be out there. We will have to wait until the morning. I suggest we find a place to stay here in Mendoza for the night. We can get some hiking gear and supplies tonight, and then set out early in the morning."

Carmelo's expression was a blend of frustration and anticipation, tinged with excitement at the prospect of spending another night with Alex. "That sounds acceptable," a faint smile curled in the corner of his mouth.

After an exhausting two hours in a local sporting goods store, Carmelo and Alex arrived at the hotel that Alex had recommended. As they pulled up to the lobby entrance, Carmelo gave the place a thorough examination. He knew it was not the Hotel Gran Mendoza, but as long as Alex was with him, he knew everything would be perfect.

The hotel had a simple yet cozy vibe. Carmelo noticed the charming details that adorned the hotel's facade. Potted plants of vibrant blooms lined the windowsills, adding a pop of color to the otherwise unassuming exterior. Soft, warm lighting fixtures adorned the entrance, casting a gentle glow on the pathway leading up to the lobby. A wrought iron signboard displayed the hotel's name in elegant script, while wooden benches invited guests to pause and take in the tranquil surroundings. Overall, the hotel exuded a sense of understated elegance, promising a comfortable retreat from the bustling city beyond its doors.

"I hope this place isn't too shabby for you, Carmelo," Alex poked with a playful smile. "I know you've got refined American taste!"

Carmelo, sensing Alex's playful jab, retorted, "Of course not, Alex. I see you've chosen a hotel with a bit of character! It's got that 'charmingly outdated' vibe that makes you wonder if the elevator doubles as a time machine." Carmelo continued playfully, "Let's hope it doesn't take us back to the days of chamber pots and straw mattresses."

"It does have a certain rustic charm, doesn't it?" Alex added, his eyes sparkling with reflection from the overhead lights.

"It's perfect," Carmelo smiled appreciatively. "I wonder if we'll find any forgotten dirty socks left by the previous guests."

Alex's laughter echoed through the lobby, punctuating Carmelo's jest with an infectious joy that warmed the air.

As dusk settled over the city of Mendoza, casting long shadows across the streets, Carmelo and Alex found themselves seated at a cozy table in the hotel's courtyard. The soft glow of string lights overhead bathed the area in a warm, inviting ambiance, while a gentle breeze rustled the leaves of nearby trees. The evening air was filled with the tantalizing aroma of grilled meats and spices wafting from a nearby barbecue, mingling with the sound of laughter and conversation from other guests enjoying their meals.

Carmelo and Alex shared a bottle of wine and a quiet moment, savoring the tranquility of the evening and the promise of adventure that lay.

"Oh, Alex, I meant to ask you something." Carmelo's cheeks tinged with a hint of pink as he locked eyes with Alex.

"Okay," Alex replied, his curiosity piqued.

"You don't happen to know how to tango, do you?" Carmelo asked sheepishly.

Alex furrowed his brows, a faint smile tugging at the corners of his lips as he gave Carmelo a confused yet amused look.

Chapter Ten

By the time the phone rang to announce their wake-up call,

Alex and Carmelo were already wide awake and buzzing with excitement for their expedition. They quickly grabbed some breakfast pastries from the hotel lobby and washed them down with strong cups of coffee, fueling themselves for the day ahead.

In the early morning light, the city streets of Mendoza were bathed in a soft golden glow, casting long shadows that stretched across the pavement. The air was crisp and cool, carrying with it the faint aroma of freshly brewed coffee from the nearby cafes. As Carmelo and Alex made their way through the quiet streets, they passed by rows of charming colonial-style buildings adorned with colorful shutters and wrought-iron balconies. Occasionally, they encountered early risers going about their day, their footsteps echoing against the cobblestone sidewalks. Despite the stillness of the hour, there was a sense of bustling energy in the air, as if the city itself was just beginning to awaken from its slumber.

As dawn broke over the horizon, painting the eastern Andes with hues of gold and amber, Carmelo and Alex were eager to begin their quest. With each breath they took, the crisp morning air filled their lungs, energizing them for the adventure that lay ahead. Making their way to the outskirts of the city, they were met with the rugged terrain of the mountain range, looming in the distance like a silent sentinel.

The drive from Mendoza to Puente del Inca, at the base of Aconcagua, was a two-hour journey through breathtaking landscapes that showcased the natural beauty of the Andes Mountains. As they left the bustling city behind, Alex and Carmelo found themselves surrounded by vineyards and olive groves, the fertile plains gave way to the rugged terrain of the mountains.

The road wound its way through narrow valleys and towering peaks, offering panoramic views of snow-capped summits and deep ravines. Along the way, they passed quaint villages and remote settlements, where locals went about their daily lives amidst the stunning backdrop of the mountains.

As they ascended higher into the Andes, the air grew cooler and thinner, and the landscape became more dramatic. They navigated hairpin turns and steep gradients, the road clinging precariously to the mountainside. Finally, they reached the base of Aconcagua, where the towering peak dominated the skyline, a majestic symbol of the natural wonders that awaited them.

Puente del Inca emerged from the surrounding landscape with an air of ancient grandeur. Like a natural marvel, its rust-colored rock bridge mightily spanned the rushing waters of the Rio Mendoza. The mineral-rich hot springs surrounding the bridge cast a surreal glow, giving the entire scene an otherworldly ambiance.

Surrounded by the rugged beauty of the Andes, Carmelo and Alex felt a sense of awe and wonder at the natural wonders that lay before them. As they stepped out of the truck to explore, the crisp mountain air filled their lungs, invigorating them for the adventures that awaited in this enchanting landscape.

As they stood at the foot of the majestic bridge, Alex shared his knowledge of the area with Carmelo. "Puente del Inca is known for its historical significance," he explained, gesturing towards the ancient rock formation. "There have been discoveries of Incan and indigenous settlements in the surrounding region, but nothing as extensive as an Incan temple or fortification has been uncovered so far."

Carmelo listened intently, absorbing the information as he scanned the landscape for any clues that might lead them to their ultimate destination. The air was filled with a sense of anticipation, as they stood on the threshold of a potential archaeological discovery that could rewrite history.

As he continued, Alex elaborated, "Today, Puente del Inca is a bustling tourist destination. The allure of its natural hot springs attracts visitors from far and wide. Moreover, its strategic location between the two primary trailheads for ascending Aconcagua, the tallest peak in the western hemisphere, adds to its popularity."

He pointed towards an abandoned railway station, now transformed into the "Museo del Andinista," a museum dedicated to mountaineering. "The museum was founded by a group of passionate mountain climbers," Alex explained, "and it offers insights into the rich history of mountaineering in the region. That might be a good place to start."

As Alex suggested, they began their exploration by visiting the Museo del Andinista, hoping to gather more information about the history and geography of the region. Excitedly, Carmelo and Alex arrived at the museum just as it was opening for the day. They could hear the creak of the door as they pushed it open, stepping into the cool interior filled with relics of mountaineering history.

The Museo del Andinista welcomed visitors with a warm and rustic ambiance as they stepped through its entrance. Inside, the museum's interior was adorned with wooden beams and earthy tones, evoking a sense of adventure and exploration. Display cases lined the walls, showcasing an array of mountaineering gear, vintage photographs, and artifacts from past expeditions. Maps and charts detailing the surrounding mountain ranges hung on the walls, offering a glimpse into the region's rich history of exploration. The air was filled with the scent of aged wood and adventure, inviting visitors to immerse themselves in the storied past of mountain climbing in the Andes.

After spending some time in the museum, studying maps and exhibits related to the area, they decide to speak with the museum guide, Daniela, a seasoned mountaineer with a wealth of knowledge about the local area and its history.

Daniela was a woman in her mid-thirties, with a warm smile that lit up her face. Her dark hair cascaded in gentle waves around her shoulders, framing her features with a touch of elegance. Her expressive brown eyes sparkled with intelligence and kindness, reflecting her passion for the mountains and their history. Despite her slender build, there was a noticeable strength to her, evident in the defined muscles of her arms and the way she carried herself with confidence. Her athletic physique hinted at a life spent exploring the rugged terrain of the Andes, adding to her aura of capability and resilience. Overall, Daniela's appearance conveyed a sense of approachability and warmth, making her a welcoming presence in the museum.

"Hola, ¿hablas inglés?" Carmelo asked while approaching Daniela.

"Yes," she replied with a warm smile. "Good morning to you both! My name is Daniela. How can I help you?"

"Good morning, my name is Carmelo and this is my friend Alex," Carmelo smiled brightly. "If it's not too much trouble, could you tell us a little bit about some of the archaeological sites in the area?" Carmelo asked.

Daniela nodded, her eyes alight with enthusiasm for the topic. "Yes, of course, you have Puente del Inca itself. This natural rock formation and hot spring site have historical significance and may have been used by indigenous peoples long before the arrival of Europeans. While many specific sites may not be well-documented, the region around Puente del Inca contains traces of pre-Columbian settlements and activities, as evidenced by artifacts and archaeological surveys in the area. A little further to the west is the town of Las Cuevas. This nearby area is known for its caves, which may have served as shelters or ceremonial sites for indigenous peoples. There are many other, lesser explored pre-Columbian sites in the Aconcagua region to the north of our location. The Aconcagua Valley and surrounding mountains have been inhabited for thousands of years, and archaeological sites in this region include rock art, stone structures, and other remnants of ancient cultures."

Carmelo's excitement grew palpable as he absorbed Daniela's words. "Stone structures," he repeated with a spark of curiosity in his eyes. "Have any significant structures been discovered in that area?"

Daniela paused, considering Carmelo's question. "Nothing exceptional has been uncovered to my knowledge—mostly ruins of pre-Columbian settlements. But that doesn't discount the possibility of more significant structures waiting to be found," she explained. "There are vast, unexplored areas in the Aconcagua region alone, holding untold secrets and mysteries of the past."

Alex's inquiry drew Daniela's attention to the map on the wall behind her. He pointed to a long, narrow river valley east of Aconcagua, slightly northward, the approximate location where the two creases intersected on Carmelo's map. "Are there any known structural sites in this area?" He inquired, his finger tracing the valley's path.

"Yes, but that area up there has been much less explored than the Aconcagua Valley. That area is part of the Rio Vacas Canyon, a trail used to access the eastern ascent, but the main trail turns toward Aconcagua south of the location you're looking at. If you keep going north it wraps around the mountain leading to the northern approach. It's a much longer route than the other routes. The climb is not significantly more thrilling or challenging than the other routes, and it's much more remote if anything bad were to happen, so it's not a very popular route. Most bucket-list mountain climbers take one of the two well-known southern routes. I'm actually pretty familiar with that area. I've taken that trail almost all the way around to the north side of Aconcagua. It takes a couple of days on foot."

Carmelo reached into his messenger bag and retrieved Lorenzo's journal. "You mentioned rock art. Have you ever seen anything that looked like this out there?" Carmelo showed Daniela several of the pages from Lorenzo's journal filled with Incan symbols.

As Daniela scrutinized the drawing, her brow furrowed in concentration. At first, nothing seemed to stir a sense of recognition. Then, as she delved deeper into the details, her eyes widened in realization. Amidst the ornate designs and cryptic symbols, Daniela recognized one symbol she had encountered before.

"This symbol, here," she gestured with her finger, "I may have seen something similar to it. I can't be certain. I haven't been back there in several years," Daniela confirmed, her eyes narrowing in concentration as she examined the symbol. "It looks familiar. I could show you where it is, but unfortunately, for the next four days, I will be running the museum."

"I understand and, unfortunately, we don't have that much time. Do you know anyone else who is familiar with that area that we could possibly hire to guide us there today?"

"I could ask my girlfriend, Lucia," Daniela suggested, her expression thoughtful as she considered the logistics. "She's not working right now and could use the money. We used to go exploring out there together. She's as familiar with the area as I am. But, like I said, on foot, it will take two days to reach the place and then two days to come back.

If you're in a hurry, you're going to need a faster way of getting out there. I know a guy in Punta de Vacas that will rent you some quads. With those, you can get out there in one afternoon and have some time to look around before nightfall, then you'll have to stay the night at Pampa de Las Leñas camp. Tomorrow you'll have most of the morning to explore before you need to head back. It's the best you can do."

"Then we would greatly appreciate Lucia's help if she is available," Carmelo accepted graciously. "Thank you so much for your assistance and information, Daniela."

"My pleasure," she replied with a smile, "Give me twenty minutes to make a few phone calls and I'll let you know how it goes! Meanwhile, you might consider going down the road to the Last Stop Supply Shop and buying some provisions for your excursion. You're going to need plenty of water, a tent or two, depending on your comfort needs; perhaps some blankets. It is hot out there during the day, but at night the temperature drops to nearly freezing. Once you get to Pampa de Las Leñas camp, you can make a campfire and cook, so consider taking whatever you might need to prepare a meal."

Carmelo and Alex expressed their gratitude to Daniela before leaving the museum, their minds buzzing with anticipation for the adventure ahead. As they stepped out into the crisp mountain air, they exchanged hopeful glances, eager to hear back from Lucia about their potential guide. With Daniela's recommendations in mind, they made their way down the road to the Last Stop Supply Shop, ready to stock up on provisions for their excursion into the rugged wilderness.

At the Last Stop Supply Shop, Carmelo and Alex purchased plenty of water to stay hydrated during their journey, along with some non-perishable food items that they could easily prepare over a campfire at Pampa de Las Leñas camp.

With their supplies gathered, Carmelo and Alex felt an increased sense of readiness for their adventure. Carmelo glanced at Alex with a hint of uncertainty, seeking reassurance in their preparations. "That should be good, right?"

Alex nodded confidently, affirming their readiness. "I think so. It's just for two days and one night. We bought that extra tent and blankets in Mendoza. I still have my tent. We have some good boots, and some hats and gloves. I think we are set up."

"Now we just need a guide," Carmelo concurred.

"And some quads!" Alex added with enthusiasm, eager to explore the rugged terrain that awaited them.

With their provisions secured and excitement building, Carmelo and Alex made their way back to the Museo del Andinista to check in with Daniela. As they entered the museum, they spotted Daniela behind the front desk, her powerful, athletic physique giving her a commanding presence in the room. She greeted them with a warm smile as they approached.

"Any luck finding a guide?" Carmelo asked eagerly.

"Actually, yes," Daniela replied, her smile widening. "Lucia is available to take you out to the area you mentioned. She just needs to gather a few things and then she will meet you in Punta de Vacas. I also called Miguel at the Andes Adventures quad rental place there and I took the liberty of reserving you three quads for two days."

Carmelo and Alex exchanged excited glances before thanking Daniela profusely for her help. With gratitude in their hearts and anticipation in their steps, they headed outside to embark on their adventure into the mountains.

As the clock ticked past 10 a.m., they arrived in Punta de Vacas, greeted by the crisp mountain air and the warm glow of the morning sun. Lucia awaited them under the large roadway sign that read 'Andes Adventures Quad Rentals', her presence a welcome sight in the tranquil surroundings.

Lucia was a striking woman with sun-kissed skin and dark, flowing hair that cascaded down her back in loose waves. Her piercing brown eyes held a spark of adventure, reflecting her love for the outdoors. She had a strong, athletic physique, evident from the way she carried herself with confidence and grace. Dressed in outdoor gear suitable for the rugged terrain ahead, she exuded a sense of readiness for the adventure that lay ahead.

As they got out of the truck, Lucia approached them with a friendly smile, "Carmelo and Alex, I presume?"

"Yes!" Carmelo declared, "And you must be Lucia!"

"Nice to meet you, Lucia," Alex said warmly, extending his hand.

"Likewise," Lucia replied with a friendly smile, shaking Alex's hand firmly. "Daniela told me that you guys want to go up the Rio Vacas trail today. Ready for an adventure?"

"Absolutely," Carmelo chimed in. "We're eager to explore!"

"I'm excited to guide you," Lucia said, her eyes gleaming with enthusiasm. "Let's get you set up with the quads, and we'll be on our way. We have a lot of distance to cover."

"Good morning, Miguel!" Lucia called out cheerfully as they entered the quaint office of Andes Adventures.

"¡Buenos días, amigos!" Miguel replied with a wide grin. "Here for some adventure?"

"Yes, we're looking to rent some quads," Carmelo replied. "We've got a little expedition planned."

"Ah, exploring the mountains, are we?" Miguel's eyes sparkled with excitement. "You've come to the right place. Let me show you what we've got."

With Miguel's expertise, they selected the ideal quads for their adventure, eager to set off into the day under the bright Andean sun.

With their gear securely fastened to the quads, Carmelo, Alex, and Lucia revved the engines and set off on their journey. The rugged terrain stretched out before them, promising adventure and discovery with each passing mile. The sun cast long shadows across the landscape as they navigated their way through the winding mountain trails, upriver, the roar of the engines echoing off the rocky cliffs. As they ventured deeper into the wilderness, anticipation filled the air, fueling their excitement for the exploration that lay ahead.

As Carmelo rode through the rugged terrain on the quad, he felt a mixture of exhilaration and apprehension. The powerful engine roared beneath him as they traversed rocky paths and bumpy trails, jostling him with each bump and turn. The wind whipped through his hair, and the scent of pine and earth filled his nostrils.

Despite the occasional jolt and the unfamiliar sensation of riding a quad, Carmelo couldn't help but marvel at the breathtaking scenery around him. Towering mountains loomed in the distance, their peaks dusted with snow even in the warmth of the sun. Lush greenery lined the trails, interspersed with colorful wildflowers and the occasional glimpse of wildlife darting through the brush.

As they continued their journey, Carmelo couldn't shake the sense of adventure coursing through him. With each passing mile, he felt more alive, more connected to the rugged beauty of the landscape unfolding before him. Though the terrain was rough and unpredictable, there was a sense of freedom in riding through the hinterland, a feeling of being at one with the untamed wilderness of the Andes.

Three hours later, approaching fifteen kilometers approximately north by northwest of the tiny village of Punta de Vacas, the team reached the campsite known as Pampa de Las Leñas, unloaded their food supplies, and set up camp.

Pampa de Las Leñas camp was nestled in a picturesque valley surrounded by towering peaks of the Andes. The campsite, marked by a cluster of small stone structures, tents, and makeshift shelters, offered a rustic yet inviting refuge for weary travelers. The Rio Vacas meandered through the valley, its clear waters providing a soothing soundtrack to the serene surroundings.

Tall, swaying grasses carpeted the valley floor, interspersed with patches of wildflowers adding splashes of color to the landscape. The air was crisp and clean, tinged with the scent of pine and earth, while the distant call of birds echoed through the valley.

In the center of the camp was a large circular stone fire pit. Carmelo conjured images of a crackling campfire in the evening casting a warm glow, inviting weary travelers to gather around its flickering flames. He envisioned hikers and mountaineers from all over the world relaxing around the fire, exchanging stories and laughter, sharing the camaraderie that comes with a shared journey through the wilderness.

As Carmelo and Alex explored the rugged terrain near the camp, their eyes were drawn to the scattered remnants of a forgotten era. Amongst the rocky outcrops and winding trails, they stumbled upon ancient artifacts, each whispering tales of a bygone civilization. Pottery shards, weathered by centuries of exposure, bore intricate patterns and motifs reminiscent of pre-Columbian culture. Tiny strands of textiles, faded and frayed, yet still holding the essence of their craftsmanship, hinted at the skilled hands that once wove them. With each discovery, Carmelo and Alex felt the weight of history pressing upon them, urging them onward in their quest to unlock the secrets of the past.

"We still have a ways to go yet," Lucia said as she remounted her quad, "We will return here for the night. If you need to use the restroom, there is a flushing toilet in that building over there. There won't be any more where we are going." She gave Carmelo a mischievous grin.

Lucia's words echoed through Carmelo's mind as he glanced around the campsite, taking in the rustic beauty of their temporary home amidst the wilderness. The thought of venturing further into the unknown filled him with a mix of excitement and trepidation, but he trusted Lucia to lead them safely through the rugged terrain.

With a nod of understanding, Carmelo followed Lucia's lead, mounting his quad and revving the engine in anticipation of the journey ahead. As they set off once again, leaving the tranquil campsite behind, Carmelo couldn't help but marvel at the vastness of the wilderness stretching out before them, eager to discover what secrets lay hidden within its untamed beauty.

As they ventured deeper into the wilderness, the terrain became increasingly rugged, challenging Carmelo's newfound confidence on the quad. Lucia led the way with ease, navigating through rocky paths and dense vegetation with the skill of someone intimately familiar with the land.

Despite the bumps and jolts along the way, Carmelo found himself growing more accustomed to the rhythm of the quad, gradually gaining confidence in his ability to handle the rough terrain. With each passing mile, the breathtaking scenery of the Andean landscape unfolded before them, a symphony of towering peaks, lush greenery, and the winding river stretching as far as the eye could see.

As they continued their journey, Lucia pointed out various landmarks and natural wonders, sharing stories and insights about the rich history and culture of the region. Carmelo listened intently, soaking in every detail and feeling a deep sense of connection to the land and its storied past.

Despite the challenges of the journey, Carmelo felt a profound sense of exhilaration and freedom coursing through his veins, a feeling of liberation from the confines of everyday life. With each passing moment, he embraced the adventure wholeheartedly, eager to uncover the mysteries that awaited them in the heart of the wilderness.

As they reached a crossroads, Lucia slowed her quad to a halt, surveying their options with a thoughtful expression. Carmelo and Alex pulled up beside her, taking in the diverging paths that lay before them.

To the north, the massive Rio Vacas canyon stretched out before them, its depths shrouded in shadow as it wound its way through the heart of the mountains, slowly veering northwesterly toward the north face of Aconcagua. The sheer scale of the canyon was awe-inspiring, its towering walls loomed overhead like silent sentinels guarding the secrets of the wilderness.

To the west, a smaller tributary of the Rio Vacas meandered off into the distance, its waters disappearing into the rugged terrain of another connected canyon. The scenery was rugged and wild, with dense vegetation lining the banks of the stream, and the towering summit of Aconcagua looming overhead.

To the east, another, even smaller tributary stream flowed in from yet another connected canyon, its waters sparkling in the afternoon sunlight. Each path seemed inviting, promising new adventures and discoveries beyond each twist and turn.

With a knowing exchange of looks, Lucia directed their attention to the western trail. "That route leads to Plaza Argentina Base Camp, the common path for ascending Aconcagua from the east," she explained. "It has been heavily traveled, offering little in the way of new discoveries beyond the mountain ascent."

Turning to face the opposite direction, Lucia gestured toward the expansive canyon leading eastward. "This path leads to a vast area, relatively unexplored, stretching for many kilometers," she continued. "Daniela and I have only just started exploring this way. It is very intriguing; however, it's the straight path ahead that holds the greatest interest. That's where we'll find what you're seeking."

Forward, into the shadowy depths of the Rio Vacas Canyon, they continued for another hour, the rugged terrain challenging their every move as they pressed on towards their destination.

Finally, as they rounded a sudden bend in the canyon, they came to a stop. Lucia dismounted her quad as Carmelo and Alex circled theirs, killing the engines. "From here, we have to hike up that way," she pointed across the river and up towards a ledge jutting out of the cliff beyond.

After parking the quads and securing their gear, they followed Lucia's lead. The air was crisp, carrying on it the scent of pine and the roar of the rushing river in front of them. With each step, anticipation mounted, fueling their determination to uncover the secrets hidden within the ancient landscape.

Lucia guided them to a section of the riverbank where sturdy boulders protruded from the rushing waters. Carmelo noticed a rope securely anchored to a massive boulder on the river's edge, extending across to each boulder and onto the opposite bank. "The current is swift, and the riverbed is slippery," Lucia warned, her voice firm with authority. "Daniela and I set up this crossing on our last expedition." She gave Carmelo and Alex a cautionary glance as she handed each of them a harness.

"What you're going to do is put on these harnesses and clip onto the rope with your lanyards," Lucia explained. "Then you will slowly move across the current until you reach the first boulder. Once you're securely on the boulder, you will unclip your lanyard and move it to the other side of the anchor and continue the process until you reach the other side of the river."

Carmelo and Alex listened attentively to Lucia's instructions. "As you're wading across the river, keep both hands on the support rope and walk sideways facing upriver. Lean backward slightly so that your weight is angled against the current. If you lean into the current, it's more likely to sweep your feet out from under you. I will go first so that you can watch how I do it, then, Carmelo, you will go after me, and Alex, you will go last."

Lucia turned and headed out across the river, navigating the swift currents and rugged terrain with expert precision.

"Just when I thought I had mastered walking on solid ground, we leveled up to wading across rushing rivers,'" Carmelo quipped with a playful glint in his eyes. "I guess life decided to throw in a bit of white-water excitement to keep us on our toes!"

After securing his harness and receiving final instructions from Lucia, Carmelo cautiously stepped into the frigid waters of the Rio Vacas. Gripping the support rope tightly, he began his slow and steady journey across the swift current. The river tugged at his legs, its chilly embrace a constant reminder of the force he was contending with.

With each step, Carmelo felt the slippery rocks beneath his feet, his muscles straining against the pull of the water. Following Lucia's guidance, Carmelo leaned back against the current, his body angling to maintain stability. The sound of rushing water filled his ears, drowning out all other noise as he focused solely on his precarious crossing.

Step by step, he made progress, inching closer to the safety of the opposite bank. The boulders loomed ahead, promising solid ground and respite from the relentless current. As he reached each boulder, he carefully unclipped his lanyard, moving with deliberate precision to secure himself to the next length of rope.

Finally, after what felt like an eternity, Carmelo reached the far shore, his heart pounding with exhilaration and relief.

Alex approached the river with a blend of determination and caution, his rugged frame a stark contrast against the rushing waters. With each step, he balanced himself expertly on the uneven riverbed, muscles flexing under the strain. His eyes remained fixed on the opposite bank, unwavering in their focus as he navigated the swirling currents and jagged rocks.

With a final leap, he landed on solid ground, a victorious smile spreading across his face, embodying the triumph of overcoming nature's challenges.

Once Alex had safely crossed, they paused for a moment, catching their breath and reveling in the triumph of their river crossing. With Lucia's guidance, they continued their journey up the steep slope of the river bank, eager to uncover the secrets that awaited them in the depths of the canyon.

As they delved deeper into the canyon, the terrain became increasingly rugged, the rocky walls rising steeply on either side. Carmelo's gaze was drawn ahead to a large rock ledge protruding from the cliff wall, hovering about thirty-five feet above the canyon floor like a solitary sentinel.

The ledge beckoned to them, its sheer drop below hinting at the perilous journey that lay ahead. Yet, despite the daunting height, there was an air of excitement in the air, a sense of adventure that spurred them onward.

With each step, they ascended higher, the path growing steeper as they approached the looming precipice. The sound of their footsteps echoed off the canyon walls, mingling with the distant rush of the river below.

As they reached the base of the ledge, Carmelo could feel the adrenaline coursing through his veins, his heart pounding with anticipation. With a determined stride, he began the ascent, his eyes fixed on the rocky outcrop above, his mind filled with the promise of discovery that awaited them at the summit.

Once he had reached the top of the ledge, Carmelo's senses were heightened by the exhilarating rush of standing at such a lofty vantage point. As he surveyed the landscape spread out before him, a sense of awe washed over him.

The panoramic view stretched for miles in both directions, offering a breathtaking vista of the rugged canyon terrain. Below, the river wound its way through the rocky gorge, its waters glistening in the sunlight. To the west, the canyon walls rose majestically, their imposing presence casting long shadows across the valley floor where they had parked their quads, which now looked like little dots on the landscape.

From this elevated perch, Carmelo felt a profound connection to the untamed wilderness surrounding him. The sheer magnitude of the landscape filled him with a sense of wonder, reminding him of the boundless beauty and mystery of the natural world.

Carmelo felt a gentle tap on his shoulder. Lucia directed his attention away from the expansive view before him. Turning around, he was met with the imposing sight of the towering rock wall rising into the sky, its sheer size and smooth surface commanding his full attention.

Stretching hundreds of meters into the air, the rock face stood as a silent sentinel, its pristine surface gleaming in the sunlight with vibrant splashes of pink, gray, and blue. The polished appearance of the stone lent it an otherworldly quality as if it had been sculpted by the hands of some ancient deity.

As Carmelo gazed up at the colossal wall of rock, he couldn't help but feel a sense of awe and wonder wash over him. It was a reminder of the immense power and grandeur of the natural world, a testament to the forces that had shaped the landscape over countless millennia.

"Oh my goodness," Alex exclaimed, his eyes sparkling with wonder. "Look at that!"

"It's absolutely beautiful," Carmelo breathed, genuine amazement evident in his voice.

After giving them a moment to absorb the splendor of the site, Lucia urged them, "Check this out," gesturing further along the path.   "Here are some of the petroglyphs that you were wanting to see."

As Carmelo and Alex approached the spot indicated by Lucia, they were met with a breathtaking sight. Carved into the stone wall were intricate petroglyphs, their ancient lines etched deeply into the smooth surface. The glyphs depicted various symbols and figures, including geometric patterns, animals, and human-like figures adorned with elaborate headdresses. Each carving seems to tell a story, hinting at the rich history and cultural significance of the site.

Among the petroglyphs, they noticed a distinct central motif within the collection of images—a symbol resembling a stepped cross, consisting of three levels of steps on each arm that converged towards the center. The arms of the cross were equal in length, forming a square shape with a circular hole at the center where the arms intersected. The overall shape resembled a cross with a stepped pyramid-like structure. The symbol was surrounded by geometric patterns and swirling lines. Inside the central circle, there appeared to be a stylized eye.

The air was heavy with a sense of reverence as they stood in awe of this ancient artwork, marveling at the skill and creativity of the artisans who left their mark on the stone centuries ago.

"What is this place?" Carmelo scanned the skillfully carved stone, his eyes tracing the lines of the figures intricately chiseled out of the cliff wall. "Is this Incan?"

"I'm not sure," Alex answered. "It's definitely pre-colonial. This large symbol here in the center does look similar to the symbol that Daniela pointed out in Lorenzo's journal."

"Let's see," Carmelo gestured for Alex to turn around so that he could remove Lorenzo's journal from the backpack that Alex had been burdened with carrying. With a careful touch, he sifted through the pages until he found the page bearing the image of the symbol that Daniela had identified. "Look at this," he said, his excitement evident. "Daniela was right!

The symbol in the journal matches the one carved into the rock—this stepped cross symbol. This looks like it could be Incan!" Carmelo declared, his voice tinged with excitement and wonder.

Carmelo carefully examined the carved symbol, tracing its intricate lines with his finger as if trying to unlock its secrets. "What does the map say? 'Beware the guardian's watchful eye'. I wonder if that warning in some way pertains to this mysterious petroglyph?"

Alex leaned in closer, his eyes scanning the surrounding rock face for any other markings or clues that might shed light on the mysterious site. Lucia stood nearby, her expression a mix of anticipation and curiosity, waiting for their next move.

After studying the carved symbol and the surrounding area, Carmelo suggested exploring further along the ledge to see if there were any additional carvings or signs that could provide more insight into the site's significance. With Lucia's guidance, they continued their exploration, keeping their eyes peeled for any other clues that might help unravel the mystery of the Incan symbol and its connection to the hidden treasure.

As they advanced a few meters further down, the once expansive ledge began to narrow, gradually tapering until it seamlessly melded with the sheer face of the cliff. Their progress halted abruptly as they reached a dead end. Ahead of them, the ridge terminated abruptly, plunging precipitously into the depths below, a vertiginous drop spanning nearly forty feet.

Alex's words hung in the air, tinged with disappointment. "It looks like that's it," he remarked, his tone echoing the somber realization. "There's nothing past this point. It's a sheer drop-off."

Carmelo's voice carried a note of urgency as he approached the edge of the ridge, peering over in search of any sign of further passage. "That can't be it," he pleaded, a hint of determination in his tone. "Well, I guess we have to go back the other way."

The team made their way back along the ledge in the direction they had come up from. Along the way, Carmelo stopped to study the petroglyphs once more. "There has to be more than this. To me, this feels like a lookout point. Look at the vantage this location offers. You can see for almost a kilometer to the north and to the south. If the Inca did have something important stored near here, they would have been guarding it."

Alex nodded in agreement. "I agree, this canyon is like an ancient highway. The Inca would have built higher up, not down here in the canyon, but they would have had sentinels watching it."

"Absolutely," Lucia added, her voice carrying a tone of certainty. "This canyon served as a vital artery for communication and trade. The Inca were strategic in their placement of sentinels and lookout points along such routes to ensure the safety and security of their territories."

Carmelo paused, his gaze sweeping over the towering walls of the canyon, his mind racing with possibilities. "So, if we're looking for a way forward, perhaps we should think like the Inca and consider the landscape from their perspective," he suggested, his tone thoughtful.

"What do you mean?" Alex asked with an intrigued look.

"Well," Carmelo sighed softly as he delved into deep thought, "what do we know about the Incas? They primarily lived in the mountains, and they worshiped the sun, right?" Carmelo glanced at Alex, seeking confirmation.

Alex nodded, adding depth to the conversation. "Yes and no. Their main creator god was Viracocha, considered the most important deity in the Inca pantheon, and revered as the creator of all things. They also worshiped the sun as a god, Inti, the second most significant deity in their religion. They celebrated Inti Raymi, the Festival of the Sun, as a major religious event, which is still observed in Peru today. It's one of their most sacred days."

Carmelo's surprise at Alex's depth of knowledge was evident in his expression. "It's impressive how well-versed you are in South American history," he remarked, a hint of admiration in his voice.

Alex smiled coyly back at Carmelo, "I went to a great university! The one good thing my father did for me."

"That's right," Lucia chimed in, "I have been to Inti Raymi in Cusco twice. It's always in the third week of June —during the winter solstice which is also the Inca New Year. There was great music, amazing food, and so many vibrant colors."

"Ok, that's great! So, now I'm thinking about the significance of the winter solstice for the Inca," Carmelo replied thoughtfully. "They revered the sun as a deity, and the winter solstice marked a crucial celestial event for them. Perhaps there's a connection between the direction of the sunset on the winter solstice and the location we're searching for."

"That's an interesting idea," Alex said encouragingly. "So, you're suggesting that if the Inca built a settlement in this region, the site would likely have been chosen for its relationship to the position of the setting sun on the winter solstice."

"Possibly," Carmelo added with a pinch of uncertainty. "But in order for that to help us at all we would need to know where the sun would be located on the horizon during the winter solstice, and the other thing we need is a focal point —a third point that would be in alignment with the settlement and the position of the setting sun."

"A focal point," Lucia whispered knowingly as she looked upwards toward the western horizon, "like perhaps the tallest mountain in the western and southern hemispheres?"

Carmelo and Alex turned their attention to match Lucia's, their focus landing on the icy summit of the mighty Aconcagua. "Of course! That has to be it!" Carmelo's voice rang with excitement.

"So, if Aconcagua is the focal point, then we are on the right side of it," Lucia clarified. "Right now, the mountain is west of us—slightly southwest." She gestured towards the sun's current position. "During the summer solstice, the sun would be at its most southerly position on the horizon, close to where it is now." Lucia pointed with her left arm. "But during the winter solstice, the sun would be at its most northerly position, over there." She indicated with her right arm towards a more northerly direction.

"That means in order for Aconcagua to align with the setting sun on the winter solstice, we need to be southeast of the mountain," Alex concluded, connecting the dots.

"That's good for us because we have to go south to get back to the camp," Lucia observed, considering their options. "The sun will be setting soon, so that means we have about two hours until it is completely dark. I suggest we head back, and then in the morning we can search another area." Her practical suggestion resonated with Carmelo and Alex, who nodded in agreement.

As the sun dipped behind the steep canyon walls, painting the sky in vibrant hues of orange and pink, the river valley took on a magical quality, bathed in the soft glow of twilight. With the stars twinkling overhead and the promise of a new day on the horizon, the team made their way back to Pampa de Las Leñas camp, a tranquil haven amidst the rugged beauty of the Andes.

While the campfire was crackling with energy and warmth, Carmelo sat by the edge of the pit pouring over his thoughts, relieving the excitement of the day, and pondering other aspects of the next day's search. Alex handed him a bowl of hot stew that had been warmed over the flames.

"You're being awfully quiet," Alex noted with a tinge of concern. "Is everything alright, Carmelo?"

Carmelo gave Alex an appreciative smile. "Yes," he sighed, "I just keep thinking about Jerónimo Luis de Cabrera and his expedition. If we were correct in thinking that the creases on his map are intended to lead us here, that means somewhere nearby is likely where he discovered the site."

"Yes, most likely," Alex agreed, his tone reflecting a shared sense of solemnity. "Plus, there is Puente del Inca nearby which archeologists have already confirmed was used by the Incas."

"There's also Ranchillos," Lucia added.

"Ranchillos?" Carmelo asked, his interest piqued.

"Tambo de Ranchillos?" Lucia asked with a sparkle of recognition in her eyes. "I have been there. It is actually close by, but it is not in the Rio Vacas valley. It is near Los Penitentes, on the way back toward Puente del Inca."

Carmelo and Alex shared a brief silent gaze before turning their attention towards Lucia. "You've seen this site?" Carmelo asked, curiosity evident in his voice.

"Yes," Lucia confirmed. "It's a well-documented Inca site. It's about a 45-minute hike from the highway."

"So, it's an Inca settlement?" Alex asked Lucia, seeking clarification.

"Well, no," Lucia replied, "I wouldn't necessarily call it a settlement. It's more of an encampment. You see, the site is called Tambo de Ranchillos. In the Quechua language, the word Tambo means 'inn'. Tambos would contain housing and cooking facilities for travelers, they would sometimes have storehouses for supplies and weapons and would also often house military barracks.

"So it was basically a roadside outpost," Carmelo asked.

"Essentially, yes," Lucia confirmed. "If the Inca did have a more significant settlement nearby, it would have been further from the road, and it would have been higher in elevation. It would contain many more structures than are found at Tambo de Ranchillos. Tambo de Ranchillos primarily served as a stopover point for travelers, merchants, and military personnel."

"So, if there was an Incan highway nearby, and an inn for weary travelers and military personnel, it's logical that there could be an actual settlement or otherwise important site in this area."

"Yes," Lucia confirmed. "This is an ancient crossing through the mountains. There is evidence of use dating back almost one thousand years. I guess you could say that it is like a back door to the western side of the mountain range. It would make sense to have a permanent military presence guarding it, which would require a settlement and agricultural features."

"I can't wait to explore more," Carmelo confessed. "What is our plan for tomorrow?" Carmelo queried.

"My suggestion is that we go back to the crossroads and we take the trail heading east. It's a relatively unexplored area being that it is not on one of the main trails to climb Aconcagua and the river is uncrossable there," Lucia offered, "I've hiked a mile or so back in that area, but if memory serves me, the trail split off into several different directions, so there's no telling what secrets could be hidden out there. If we can find a route that heads roughly south, that would be where I would start looking first. It won't be an easy day physically, though. We will have to return to the location that we were at today and cross the river. Then, we will have to hike back to the crossroads from the other side of the river. Unfortunately, the river is too deep and swift to cross there."

Carmelo and Alex nodded their heads in agreement. Alex flashed his charming smile as if he had just remembered something funny. He reached into his backpack, "Well, now that is settled, would either of you like to help me finish off this bottle of whiskey?" Carmelo and Lucia both smiled widely and scooped up the paper cups that Alex was already filling.

As the crackling of the campfire softened and the glow of the embers dimmed, the rhythmic symphony of the night enveloped Carmelo, lulling him into a serene slumber under the vast expanse of the clear Andean sky.

CHAPTER ELEVEN

Carmelo, Alex, and Lucia woke up to the soft glow of the

rising sun casting a warm golden hue over the campsite. Stretching their limbs after a night's rest under the starry Andean sky, they began to prepare for the day ahead.

Lucia brewed a pot of rich Argentine coffee over the crackling campfire, filling the air with its enticing aroma. Meanwhile, Carmelo and Alex packed up their gear and double-checked their supplies for the day's exploration.

As they enjoyed their breakfast of fresh bread, cheese, and fruit, they discussed their plans for the day. With a sense of anticipation and determination, they set out on their journey, ready to uncover the secrets hidden within the ancient Andean landscape.

They followed the well-trodden path, retracing their steps from the previous day's journey. The landscape seemed familiar, yet with each step, they felt a renewed sense of anticipation. The air was crisp and invigorating, carrying with it the scent of pine and earth. The towering peaks of the Andes loomed in the distance, their snow-capped summits glistening in the light.

As the team reached the familiar river crossing, their journey took on a sense of familiarity mixed with anticipation. With practiced ease, they navigated the crossing, the glistening waters of the Rio Vacas flowing beneath them.

Once on the eastern bank, their path led them southward, back toward the area where the imposing cliffs of the canyon gave way to uncharted territory. Excitement pulsed through their veins as they approached the opening, ready to venture into new and unexplored passages that held the promise of ancient secrets waiting to be unearthed.

As they reached the familiar crossroads, they turned eastward. The canyon there was narrower, the walls rising steeply on either side, casting deep shadows that danced across the rugged terrain. The trail twisted and turned, leading them deeper into the heart of the mountains, where the sound of rushing water reverberated off the ancient stone walls, creating a symphony of nature that surrounded them.

The air grew cooler, tinged with the scent of damp earth and moss. Tall trees towered overhead, their branches reaching out like gnarled fingers against the clear blue sky. Occasional shafts of sunlight pierced through the dense canopy, illuminating patches of vibrant greenery that carpeted the forest floor.

With each twist and turn of the trail, the landscape seemed to change, revealing new wonders at every turn. Carmelo, Alex, and Lucia pressed onward, their senses alive with the sights and sounds of the wilderness that surrounded them, eager to uncover the secrets hidden within the heart of the canyon.

About a quarter of a kilometer along the narrow pathway, the trail branched off in several directions, each leading into another area of the labyrinthine canyon. The once-clear path now fragmented into a maze of options, each one beckoning them with its own allure.

Lucia halted their progress, her gaze scanning the diverging paths ahead. "This is where it gets a bit tricky," she remarked, her tone laced with uncertainty. "The canyon forks into several directions, and each path seems promising, but I think, if we want to pursue your theory from yesterday, we should probably take this route that looks to be heading more southward."

Carmelo and Alex exchanged a hesitant glance before nodding in agreement. They trusted Lucia's instincts, knowing she had a keen eye for navigating the rugged terrain of the Andes. With a sense of determination, they followed her lead, venturing deeper into the unknown expanse of the canyon.

After a few minutes along the southern path, the trail began to head upward fairly steeply, presenting a moderate challenge for the hikers. Carmelo, in particular, found himself struggling against the steep pitch, his breath coming in labored gasps as he fought to maintain his pace on the rocky incline. Every step forward felt like an uphill battle, but he pressed on, driven by a combination of determination and the tantalizing prospect of uncovering the secrets hidden within the canyon.

Carmelo chuckled as he remarked, "Hiking up this steep trail feels like we're auditioning for a mountain goat role in a wildlife documentary!"

The path slowly twisted from south to west and seemed to end abruptly on a leveled landing. Ahead of them, what seemed to be an impenetrable cliff face stood like an imposing barrier.

"It's a dead end?" Carmelo huffed with frustration.

"It looks like this is the end of the trail," Alex confirmed.

"This can't be it," Lucia said, scanning the rocks for any sign of a way forward. She paced from one side to the other, inspecting the surface of the wall. "Look here! You can't see it from head-on, but from this angle, you can see that there is a crack in the rock. I think it's wide enough to pass through. It's going to be tight though. Are you guys up for a little rock squeezing?"

Carmelo's frustration suddenly turned into curiosity. "Well, if we wanted an adventure, we certainly got it. It's a good thing I skipped dessert last night," Carmelo quipped, eyeing the narrow crack in the rock with a mix of amusement and determination. "Time to put these hiking boots to the test!"

Carmelo, Alex, and Lucia approached the narrow crevice with cautious fortitude. Alex led the way, his athletic build allowing him to navigate the narrow passage with relative ease, followed closely by Lucia, who expertly maneuvered through the rocky opening. Carmelo, always one for a witty remark, joked, "Right now I feel like a contortionist in a circus act," as he squeezed through the tight space.

Despite the challenging squeeze, their spirits remained high, fueled by the excitement of discovery and the thrill of overcoming obstacles together.

For approximately fifteen meters, they squirmed their way through the narrow pass until finally they were all through. On the other side of the giant rock formation, the pathway continued to rise in elevation, evolving from an earthen trail into a rocky, stair-like pathway, evidence of human intervention from a distant past. Each step revealed the careful craftsmanship of those who had traversed this route before, their labor evident in the precision with which the stones were laid and the way they seamlessly melded with the natural contours of the landscape. It was a testament to the ingenuity and resilience of those who had once called this rugged terrain home, a reminder of the enduring legacy they left behind for future generations to uncover.

"This doesn't look natural," Carmelo pointed out, "Is this an Incan road?"

From the cracks between the flat stones, tall weeds, and wildflowers sprouted, their vibrant hues adding a splash of color to the weathered pathway. Here and there, mature trees burst forth from the rocky ground, their gnarled roots intertwining with the ancient stones, occasionally obstructing the trail and displacing the pathway stones that had been meticulously laid long ago. Despite the encroachment of nature, the pathway retained an air of mystique, a silent witness to the passage of time and the ever-changing landscape it traversed.

"It could be," Alex admitted, "It looks to have been here a long time. "It's so overgrown in places, you could easily lose the path and go wandering off course without realizing, if you weren't careful."

As they ascended further along the Incan road, the landscape underwent a dramatic transformation. Rounding a bend, Carmelo, Alex, and Lucia were greeted by a breathtaking sight: the mountainside to their left had been meticulously carved into a series of agricultural terraces.

The terraces cascaded down the slope like giant steps, each level carefully constructed to retain soil and water, creating fertile platforms for cultivating crops in the rugged terrain. Lush vegetation had long ago overwhelmed the terraces, with areas so densely overgrown that the stepped features could barely be seen. On some terraces, the walls had begun to erode. Tree roots bursted through the rocks.

The stream that meandered through the canyon ran alongside the ancient Incan road, its waters essential for sustaining life in this rugged landscape. As Carmelo, Alex, and Lucia followed the terraced path, they noticed that the stream had been ingeniously harnessed to irrigate the agricultural terraces.

A network of carefully crafted irrigation channels had been skillfully constructed to divert a portion of the stream's flow, ensuring that each terrace received a steady supply of water. The channels snaked their way along the mountainside, following the contours of the land and distributing water evenly to the cultivated fields below.

The sight of the intricate irrigation system spoke volumes about the resourcefulness of the Inca people. By harnessing the natural flow of water and channeling it to where it was needed most, they had transformed the harsh mountain environment into productive farmland, enabling agriculture to flourish in even the most challenging terrain.

As they observed the ancient irrigation channels, Carmelo, Alex, and Lucia couldn't help but marvel at the engineering prowess of the Inca civilization. It was a testament to their deep understanding of the land and their ability to adapt to its unique characteristics, ensuring the sustainability of their agricultural practices for generations to come.

Carmelo looks out over the terraces, saying, "It's incredible to see how they transformed this rugged landscape into fertile farmland," he remarks, admiration evident in his voice.

Alex nods in agreement, his eyes scanning the terraces thoughtfully. "Absolutely," he responds. "Their ability to harness the natural resources and create sustainable agricultural systems is truly remarkable. It's a testament to their ingenuity and adaptability."

Lucia nods thoughtfully. "Yes, indeed," she remarks. "The Inca's mastery of agriculture allowed them to thrive in diverse environments and sustain their civilization for centuries. It's truly fascinating to witness their legacy still evident in these terraces."

Carmelo turns to Lucia with a curious expression. "Is this a known archaeological site, or could it be a new discovery?" He asks, his interest piqued by the sight before them.

Lucia furrows her brow in thought before responding. "It may be a new discovery," she says slowly, scanning the surroundings. "I haven't heard of the existence of Incan terraces in this region. But that doesn't mean it's not a known site. Given the extent of the overgrowth and dereliction, if it is a known site, it's perhaps one that hasn't been fully explored or documented."

"The Andean Mountains here in Mendoza province have seen varying levels of exploration," Lucia continued, "While some areas are extensively documented and studied by researchers and archaeologists, others remain relatively untouched. Factors like rugged terrain, dense vegetation, and limited resources contribute to this disparity in exploration efforts," Lucia elaborates.

Alex chimed in, "It seems like there haven't been any conservation efforts made to preserve this area. You would think there would be if the government were aware of this place," Alex added, his tone tinged with surprise.

Carmelo and Lucia nodded in agreement, "That makes sense. "Maybe we should document the site as best we can."

"Agreed," Lucia responded, her expression thoughtful. "Documenting the site could provide valuable insights into its history and significance."

What could we do?" Alex asked.

"Do either of you have a camera? We could document the site by taking photographs of the terraces, irrigation channels, and any other features of interest or artifacts that we find. We should also record our observations about the surrounding landscape and the condition of the site."

Carmelo reached into his pocket and pulled out his smartphone. "I'm glad I remembered to charge it at the hotel even though I don't get any service in Argentina," he exclaimed. "I can still take pictures."

After thoroughly examining the terraces and irrigation channels for a few minutes, Carmelo made sure to capture ample photo documentation of the area. Turning to Alex and Lucia, he inquired, "Shall we press on?"

"Yes," Alex exclaimed eagerly, "there must be more to discover beyond just these agricultural terraces."

"These terraces could have served to supply food for Tambo Inca de Ranchillos, or perhaps there's a larger settlement hidden nearby," Lucia suggested thoughtfully.

With eager anticipation fueling their steps, Carmelo, Alex, and Lucia pressed on, their curiosity driving them deeper into the heart of the ancient landscape. The rugged terrain whispered stories of ages past, beckoning them to unravel its secrets. Each stride carried them closer to the unknown, each moment filled with the promise of discovery. As they journeyed onward, their spirits soared, embracing the adventure that lay ahead.

Despite the centuries that had passed since its construction, the Incan road remained remarkably intact, a tangible link to the past. As they walked in the footsteps of ancient travelers, Carmelo, Alex, and Lucia couldn't help but feel a sense of awe and reverence for the civilization that had forged such a remarkable path through the mountains. Carved meticulously out of the mountainside, the road appeared almost seamlessly integrated into the rugged terrain.

Ahead of them, the road twisted and turned, winding its way around massive boulders and jagged cliffs with remarkable precision. At times, it ascended steep inclines, its stone steps hewn directly into the rock, providing footing for weary travelers. Other times, it descended into deep valleys, where the road followed the natural contours of the land, offering breathtaking views of the surrounding landscape. As they followed the road, they couldn't help but marvel at the craftsmanship of its builders. The stone walls flanking the road stood as silent sentinels, guiding their path and bearing witness to the passage of time.

As they journeyed deeper into the canyon, the path gradually narrowed until it led them to a sudden halt at the edge of a precipice. Before them stretched a yawning chasm, its depths obscured by swirling mists. At the brink of the abyss stood an ancient Incan rope bridge, its weathered fibers creaking softly in the breeze. Across the ravine, the road continued its winding journey, disappearing into another crevice in the rugged mountainside. A sense of trepidation mingled with excitement as they contemplated the daunting crossing ahead.

Carmelo nervously approached the edge, lightly tugging at one of the ropes interwoven into the bridge's construction.

"We have to cross that?" He asked, his voice tinged with apprehension. Alex and Lucia exchanged uncertain glances, silently debating the best course of action. "So, who should go first?"

Alex teasingly offered, "Well, I've read somewhere that the heaviest person should go first. It's about testing the strength of the bridge, you know?" His playful tone did little to ease the tension in the air.

Carmelo, acting comically outraged, objected, "But if the heaviest person goes first, whoever that may be, and that person collapses the bridge, then the rest of us will be stuck on this side with no way to get across!"

Lucia and Alex exchanged amused glances, acknowledging Carmelo's point.

Alex dug himself deeper, "Fair point. But if the two lightest people go first, what if the bridge still collapses under the third weight, or the second person even? Then one or two of us could potentially be stuck on that side of the ravine."

Carmelo and Lucia exchanged a concerned glance, realizing the gravity of the situation.

Alex continued, "So, no matter who goes first, we're each risking our lives crossing this bridge?" He gave Carmelo a caring smile, "If it makes you feel safer, I will cross the bridge first, especially since I have the backpack. That makes me the heaviest."

Lucia interjected, "I have an even better idea. I'm the lightest, I'm sure we can all agree," she smiled at both of them while pulling off her backpack. She set the bag on the ground and began to remove some of the gear she had been carrying.

She held up a coiled rope. "How about we anchor this rope to the rocks on this side, then I will take the rope across the bridge and anchor it on the other side. Then, both of you can put the harnesses back on and cross the bridge using this rope as a safety line."

Carmelo and Alex exchanged relieved glances, appreciating Lucia's innovative solution to the dilemma.

Alex playfully winked at Carmelo, "I would have gone first, you know." Carmelo looked deeply into Alex's eyes and then laughed, relieved that they had found a solution to their predicament.

Lucia swiftly delved into her backpack, extracting two camming devices, a pair of slings and a carabiner. With practiced hands, she secured the camming devices into crevices within the rocky outcrop, weaving the slings through them to create two sturdy anchor points. Once satisfied with the setup, she fastened the end of the rope to the carabiner and attached it to the ends of the two slings.

"There we go," Lucia announced, her voice confident. "That should hold. I'll take this rope across the bridge and anchor it on the other side. With this setup, we should be able to cross safely in both directions."

As Lucia stepped onto the weathered Incan rope bridge, it swayed gently beneath her weight, creaking agonizingly with each movement. The sound of the rushing stream below was muted, a distant murmur amidst the rustling of leaves and the occasional chirp of birds in the surrounding forest.

With each step, Lucia felt the unrelenting force of gravity pulling her downward, the ropes groaning as they bore her weight. The wooden planks beneath her feet were weathered and uneven, their surface worn smooth by centuries of use. As she ventured further across the ravine, the crevasse below widened, revealing jagged rocks and dense foliage far below.

From the midpoint of the bridge, Lucia gazed out at the breathtaking vista surrounding her. The towering cliffs of the canyon rose up on either side, their rugged faces softened by a veil of mist. In the distance, she could see the verdant expanse of the forest, stretching out as far as the eye could see.

Despite the precarious nature of her journey, Lucia had an expression of exhilaration on her face. With each step, she moved closer to the other side, her determination unwavering in the face of the challenge.

Carmelo and Alex watched with admiration as Lucia expertly maneuvered across the bridge, anchoring the rope securely on the opposite side. With the safety line in place, they donned their harnesses, ready to traverse the precarious crossing.

As Lucia finished testing the security of the safety line, she turned to face her companions, a triumphant smile gracing her lips. "All clear!" She called out, her voice echoing faintly against the canyon walls.

Carmelo, next in line, followed Lucia's lead, his movements cautious as he stepped onto the swaying bridge. With each careful stride, he focused on maintaining his balance, his hands gripping the rope tightly for support.

Meanwhile, Alex watched from the safety of the shore, his eyes fixed on his friends' progress. As Carmelo neared the halfway point, he couldn't help but feel a surge of anxiety knowing that Alex would have to cross after him, his concern for his companion outweighing his own eagerness to cross.

Finally, with a collective sigh of relief, Carmelo joined Lucia on the opposite side, his expression a mixture of exhilaration and relief. Together, they secured the rope, creating a lifeline for Alex as he prepared to make the crossing himself.

As Alex stepped onto the bridge, he focused solely on the task at hand. Gripping the rope firmly, he carefully moved forward, ensuring each step was steady and deliberate. The bridge swayed slightly under his weight, the ropes creaking softly with each movement.

The ambient sounds of nature surrounded him—the rustle of leaves in the breeze, the distant chirping of birds, and the gentle flow of water in the stream below. The bridge itself moaned beneath him, but Alex remained unfazed, maintaining his concentration on crossing safely.

As he reached the middle of the bridge, Alex paused briefly to glance down into the crevasse. The view was daunting, the depth of the ravine emphasized by the height of the bridge. He quickly refocused and continued forward, maintaining a steady pace until he reached the other side.

Upon reaching solid ground again, Alex breathed a sigh of relief, a sense of accomplishment washing over him. He turned to see Lucia and Carmelo waiting, their expressions calm and supportive.

They continued along the trail that led deeper into the mountain. The path became narrower and more rugged, winding through occasional tight crevices and rocky outcrops, each step becoming increasingly perilous.

Finally, they arrived at the end of a long, narrow pathway, where the mountain terrain transitioned into a high plateau, revealing a stunning vista beneath the expansive sky.

As they gazed out onto the high plateau, a breathtaking panorama unfolded before them. The vast expanse of the plateau stretched out under the broad sky, dotted with occasional clusters of shrubs and small trees. The plateau was ringed by the towering peaks of the Andes Mountain, Aconcagua looming high in the distance. Their rugged slopes were adorned with patches of snow and glaciers glistening in the sunlight.

Carmelo, Alex, and Lucia took a moment to catch their breath and absorb the stunning view around them. The air was crisp and clear, carrying with it a sense of tranquility and grandeur. They could feel the magnitude of the ancient landscape, filled with a history that whispered through the winds and echoed in the distant calls of birds soaring overhead.

"This is incredible," Alex murmured, his eyes scanning the horizon with wonder.

Lucia nodded in agreement, a smile of awe playing on her lips. "It's like stepping into a different world up here."

As Carmelo, Alex, and Lucia stepped out of the narrow pathway onto the high plateau, their eyes widened in awe at the sight that unfolded before them. Spread out across the vast expanse were the remnants of an ancient Incan city, each structure whispering stories of a bygone era.

Stone and adobe residential buildings stood in orderly rows, their walls weathered by time, yet still echoing the bustling life that once filled their interiors. Nearby, grand temples rose majestically, adorned with intricate carvings depicting Viracocha, the creator god, Pachamama, the goddess of the earth and fertility, Illapa, the god of thunder and storms, and Mama Killa, the goddess of the moon. Among them, the Temple of Inti, dedicated to the sun god, stood out with its golden hues catching the sunlight.

Further along, they could make out the imposing palaces, their multi-level designs hinting at the grandeur once enjoyed by Incan rulers and nobles. Surrounding these central structures were open plazas, their ancient stones having witnessed countless ceremonies, markets, and gatherings of the city's inhabitants.

As they walked through the city, they passed by administrative buildings, their well-defined rooms and corridors suggesting a place where governance and record-keeping were once meticulously carried out. Nearby, more terraced agricultural areas cascaded down the slopes, a testament to the Inca's mastery of engineering and agriculture, ensuring food security for their people.

Water management systems, intricately designed canals, and reservoirs crisscrossed the city, providing essential irrigation and drinking water. Stone-paved roadways led them from one part of the city to another, showcasing the connectivity and trade networks that once thrived here.

Amidst the structures, sections of sturdy walls and watchtowers hinted at the city's defensive prowess, a testament to its strategic importance in the region. Artisan workshops dotted the landscape, their remnants telling tales of skilled craftsmen who once created pottery, textiles, and metalwork, contributing to the city's vibrant artistic and economic life.

As they explored further, the city unveiled itself like a living museum of ancient civilization, offering glimpses into the daily lives, beliefs, and achievements of the Incan people who called this place home centuries ago.

Carmelo meticulously documented the scene with his cellphone camera, capturing every detail of the ancient structures. The site, with its intricate design and historical significance, was undeniably breathtaking and awe-inspiring. Despite their exhaustive search of the ruined city, they failed to stumble upon any artifacts that were particularly thrilling or remarkable. If anything valuable had been left behind by the city's ancient inhabitants, it seemed to have been removed long ago, perhaps centuries before their exploration. Yet, a lingering sense of curiosity gnawed at them, a feeling that there was still more to uncover in this enigmatic ancient city.

As Carmelo, Alex, and Lucia explored the perimeter of the plateau, their footsteps crunched softly on the grassy terrain, creating a rhythmic sound that echoed in the vastness around them. The plateau, surrounded by high cliff walls on about half of its perimeter, unfolded with a mix of dilapidated stone buildings peeking through the overgrown vegetation, remnants of ancient pathways meandering through the landscape, and faint traces of terraces hinting at the area's agricultural past. Dense foliage hugged the edges of the plateau, concealing potential secrets and adding to the air of mystery that enveloped the ancient site. Each step forward heightened their anticipation, fueling their curiosity about the hidden mysteries waiting to be unveiled beyond their current exploration.

As they ventured further, the towering cliff wall eventually gave way to a precipitous drop-off. Along the edge of this abrupt descent, a thick overgrowth of trees and wild brush formed a natural barrier, obscuring what lay beyond. Intrigued by the hidden potential, they pressed forward, and as they approached the cluster of vegetation, the landscape began to subtly reveal more of its secrets.

Amidst the tangled overgrowth and trees, they noticed a forgotten pathway winding its way through the vegetation, leading to a secluded area below. The pathway, once obscured by years of neglect, became clearer as they followed its meandering course. It soon transformed into a stone staircase, expertly cut into the side of the mountain, hinting at its ancient origins and leading them deeper into the heart of the mysterious site.

As they descended the curvilinear staircase, Carmelo, Alex, and Lucia were cautious, clinging to the wall of the mountain since there was no guardrail to prevent a misstep. The steep steps seemed to wind endlessly downward, leading them deeper into the heart of the ancient site.

During their descent, Carmelo's sharp eyes caught sight of mysterious symbols etched into the stone wall alongside the staircase. These symbols, weathered by time but still faintly visible, hinted at the rich history and cultural significance of the place they were exploring. Each symbol seemed to whisper a story of the past, urging them to unravel its secrets as they ventured further into the unknown. Finally, they reached a landing at the bottom of the staircase. The path then veered sharply to the right. Carmelo leaned forward, peeking around the corner, and his eyes widened in disbelief at what lay ahead.

"Oh my goodness!" Carmelo exclaimed with amazement.

As Alex and Lucia reached the landing, they, too, peeked around the corner and were awestruck by what they saw.

"Whoa!" Alex exhaled audibly. He put his hand on Carmelo's shoulder as they both stood there and stared at the sight with admiration.

"Beautiful!" Lucia commented excitedly.

Around the corner, at the end of the pathway, a cave opening beckoned. Surrounding the cave's entrance, a vast relief emerged from the stone wall, an immense and intricately carved depiction of a woman in a powerful and nurturing pose. Her figure was depicted with exaggerated features symbolizing fertility and abundance; her breasts were large, her belly full as if pregnant, alluding to the earth's capacity to give life and sustenance. A serpent coiled around her head, representing wisdom and protection, while a tortoise rested beside her thigh, a symbol of longevity and stability. In her right arm, she held a woven basket, a representation of the earth's bounty and the gifts it provides. Her left hand rested at her side, her flattened palm turned upward and protruding from the entrance of the cavern as if she were welcoming them to enter. The woman appeared serene and contemplative, seated with her legs crossed in front of her, embodying the essence of an earth goddess, perhaps

Pachamama herself, as revered in Incan mythology and culture.

"This is definitely something that has gone undiscovered until now," Lucia said with certainty.

"Indeed," Alex agreed, his eyes wide with awe. "It's remarkable to think that this has remained hidden for so long."

Carmelo looked around in wonder, his curiosity piqued. "What do you think this place is?" He asked, turning to Alex and Lucia.

Lucia pondered Carmelo's question, her eyes scanning the intricate carvings. "It looks like a temple dedicated to Pachamama, the goddess of the earth, fertility, good health, and good fortune," she remarked, her voice filled with awe and reverence.

Alex nodded in agreement, "Yes, and judging by how intricately carved it is, and how massive its scale is, I'd have to add that this was most likely a sacred place to the people who lived here. This isn't just a common shrine or temple."

"Where better to safeguard earthly treasures than within a sacred temple dedicated to the Earth goddess," Carmelo remarked, pondering the potential significance of their find.

"Well, we've come all this way, let's have a look!" Alex grinned enthusiastically. The trio prepared to delve deeper into the cave, their excitement palpable in the dimly lit chamber. Alex's enthusiasm was infectious as he distributed helmets and LED lights, ensuring they were equipped for the exploration ahead. Carmelo and Lucia followed suit, securing their protective gear and illuminating their path with the bright LED lights.

With their helmets on and lights in place, they were ready to uncover the mysteries hidden within the cave's depths. Each step echoed softly in the cavernous space, anticipation building as they ventured further into the unknown.

Inside the cave, the air was cool and carried a faint earthy scent. As their eyes adjusted to the dim light, they could make out intricate paintings adorning the walls. The paintings appeared to depict scenes from Incan mythology—the Incan creation story. One prominent image showed Viracocha, the creator deity, crafting the earth and all living beings, including Pachamama, the earth goddess. Pachamama's role was to watch over and protect the earth, ensuring its fertility and nourishment to sustain Viracocha's creation. In the paintings, Pachamama was surrounded by both earthly and mythical creatures, symbolizing the interconnectedness of life and nature in Incan cosmology. The walls were adorned with intertwining symbols and patterns, adding depth and complexity to the mythological narrative depicted in the cave.

Carmelo, Alex, and Lucia moved deeper into the cave, following the path illuminated by their helmet lights. They marveled at the ancient artwork, each painting telling a story of the Incan people's beliefs and traditions.

After some time exploring, they came upon a chamber that seemed to be the heart of the cave. In the center of the chamber stood a stone altar, adorned with offerings of colorful beads, shells, and small figurines. Above the altar, a natural skylight allowed a beam of sunlight to filter in, casting a golden glow over the sacred space.

Lucia whispered, "This must have been a place of worship, a sacred sanctuary where the Inca paid homage to Pachamama."

Carmelo nodded in agreement, his eyes scanning the chamber. He noticed another opening behind the altar that appeared to go even deeper into the cave. "Look, there's another passageway," he said, curiosity driving him toward the opening.

As Carmelo ventured deeper into the passageway, the darkness enveloped him, with only the limited reach of his helmet light illuminating a few feet of space around him. Beyond that boundary, pitch-black darkness loomed, creating an eerie atmosphere. The narrow passage twisted and turned, leading him further into the mountain's depths. After traversing several meters, the ground leveled off, and the space opened up into a vast, dark chamber.

Upon entering the chamber, Carmelo's light revealed a mesmerizing sight—a treasure hoard of the ancient Incas.

The walls of the cavern were adorned with faded but still discernible tapestries, depicting scenes of Incan life, ceremonies, and mythological tales. The colors, though slightly muted by time, still exhibited much of their former brilliance. On other parts of the walls, there were shelves filled with ceremonial pottery, golden plates, and cups.

As Carmelo's gaze swept across the chamber, he noticed stacks of precious stones—emeralds, turquoise, and sapphires—glinting in the soft light. Nearby, ancient textiles made from luxurious alpaca wool were neatly folded into piles, their intricate patterns and vibrant colors miraculously preserved, a testament to the Incan weaving tradition.

The center of the chamber held a raised platform where a golden throne stood, embellished with ornate carvings and jewels. Surrounding the platform, piles of golden artifacts caught Carmelo's eye. Intricately crafted figurines, ceremonial masks, and ornate jewelry adorned the space, shimmering faintly in the light. Among the treasures were ceremonial vessels, some adorned with feathered designs, showcasing the Incan artisans' skill and artistry.

In the corners of the massive chamber, there were large urns made of gold, statues of various Incan gods and goddesses dripping with intricately crafted jewelry adorned with precious stones. Stacks of golden coins, silver ingots, and precious artifacts were scattered around the room, glinting in the light of their headlamps. It was a breathtaking sight, a treasure trove preserved in the depths of the ancient cave.

The chamber exuded a sense of history and mystery, the strong scent of age lingering in the air. Carmelo couldn't help but feel a mixture of excitement and reverence, realizing the significance of this discovery—a treasure trove that not only held material wealth but also preserved the cultural heritage of an ancient civilization.

"Guys," Carmelo's heart was racing and he gasped for a breath of air, "You're going to want to see this. Come quickly!"

Alex's eyes widened in astonishment, his mouth slightly agape as he took in the sight of the treasure before him. Lucia's face lit up with amazement, her eyebrows raising in surprise as she scanned the chamber filled with priceless artifacts. Both of them were visibly captivated by the sheer magnitude and beauty of the treasure, their expressions a mix of wonder and excitement.

Carmelo's heart swelled with joy as his companions marveled at the treasure before them. "Carmelo, you found it! This is beyond amazing," Alex exclaimed, his eyes reflecting the flickering light of the treasure trove. "I'm in awe," he continued softly, his voice tinged with wonder.

"It's like a dream," Lucia whispered, her eyes sparkling as they wandered over the glittering artifacts. "To think that we've stumbled upon such a magnificent treasure together," she added, her voice filled with admiration for Carmelo's discovery. "It's like stepping into a mythological tale. I can't believe what I'm seeing," Lucia added, her expression reflecting awe and disbelief.

The emotions swirling between Alex and Carmelo surged like a tempest as they stood amidst the ancient treasures. Unable to contain the burgeoning affection in his heart any longer, Alex's gaze softened with tenderness as he closed the distance between them. In a moment charged with anticipation, he wrapped his arms around Carmelo, their lips meeting in a passionate kiss that spoke volumes of untold desires. Breaking the kiss, Alex's voice carried a depth of sincerity as he confessed, "Carmelo, this discovery is astounding, but it pales in comparison to what I feel for you. You've shown courage, determination, and a passion that's truly captivating. For me, finding you is the greatest treasure of all."

Overwhelmed with emotion, Carmelo reciprocated the affection, his voice trembling with longing as he whispered, "Alex, I've felt the same way, too afraid to voice it until now. Being here with you, in this moment, is everything."

After their heartfelt exchange and the passionate kiss, Alex and Carmelo remained locked in each other's embrace, their hearts beating in unison. The air around them seemed to shimmer with newfound understanding and affection, deepening the connection between them.

As they pulled back slightly, their eyes met, conveying volumes of unspoken words and shared emotions. Without needing further verbal confirmation, they both knew that this moment had changed everything between them. Their bond had evolved into something profound and beautiful, blossoming amidst the ancient wonders that surrounded them.

With a gentle smile, Alex caressed Carmelo's cheek, wordlessly promising to explore this newfound path together. In that sacred space, amidst the treasures of the past, they found a treasure of their own—a love that transcended time and history, igniting a bright and promising future.

As they stood in the cave, enveloped in the warmth of their newfound connection, a sense of peace and contentment settled over them. They knew that their journey had led them not only to a magnificent treasure but also to a deeper understanding of themselves and each other.

With renewed determination, they turned their attention back to the treasure hoard, ready to document and carefully examine each artifact and symbol. Alex and Carmelo worked side by side, their collaboration infused with a newfound closeness and trust.

Lucia, sensing the shift in dynamics, smiled knowingly at her friends. She continued to explore the cave, admiring the intricate details of the ancient artwork and marveling at the richness of Incan culture.

Realizing the significance of their discovery, Carmelo had an epiphany. "We can't take any of this treasure for ourselves. It must stay here, untouched," he stated firmly.

Lucia nodded in agreement. "We must reach out to authorities and archaeology experts immediately. Preserving this treasure in its original context is crucial."

Alex added, "These artifacts are priceless pieces of our history. They deserve to be studied and protected for future generations."

Their shared resolve echoed through the cavern as they made plans to safeguard the precious discovery.

"Furthermore, we cannot allow anyone to plunder this site, not Eloisa's kidnappers, and certainly not El Torre." Alex continued, looking deeply into Carmelo's eyes.

Carmelo protested, "Well, hold on just a minute. The only reason I came to Argentina in the first place was to rescue Eloisa! I don't want to see these treasures fall into the hands of criminals and smugglers either, but I will do whatever is necessary to save my sister's life, even if it means giving them whatever they want."

Alex comforted him gently, saying, "Of course, Carmelo. Give them what they want, the map, that's it."

Carmelo considered Alex's suggestion, "Right, they have not mentioned anything about Lorenzo's journal, or the treasure for that matter. It's possible that they are not yet aware that the journal accompanied the map, which means they are unaware of key information. I think it is a good idea for us to separate the two documents. I'll keep the map and you can hold onto the journal, for now."

"Good idea, babe!" Alex beamed, his white teeth gleaming in the sunlight. Carmelo looked up at him, blushing, a mixture of surprise and exhilaration swirling through him. "Too soon?" Alex laughed and playfully poked Carmelo.

Carmelo was stunned for a second until a subtle grin curled in the corner of his mouth. "I'll allow it," he said, diverting his gaze as a smile fully formed on his face. "What were we talking about?"

Chapter Twelve

The hours passed and daylight filtered through the cave entrance as they meticulously cataloged their findings, capturing the essence of the treasure and the history it represented. Each item told a story, and together, they pieced together the narrative of a civilization long gone but not forgotten.

As they made their way back through the cave and eventually out into the open air, Carmelo's mind buzzed with the implications of their discovery. He knew that this treasure hoard could shed new light on Incan history and culture, and he was eager to share their findings with the world while ensuring the artifacts were protected for future generations to appreciate.

When they finally emerged from the cave, the sunlight greeted them warmly, casting long shadows as it began its descent toward the horizon. The three friends stood at the mouth of the cave, their faces illuminated by a mixture of awe and determination. Carmelo was filled with a sense that their discovery was not just a stroke of luck but a responsibility to protect and preserve history. As they gazed out at the landscape before them, Carmelo, Alex, and Lucia shared a silent understanding of the journey that lay ahead, filled with challenges and new concerns, but also with the promise of revealing to the world their incredible discovery.

As they made their way back through the narrow passageway and up the stone staircase, a sense of accomplishment and wonder filled the air between them. They marveled at the beauty of the city around them, the intricate architecture, and the rich history that surrounded them.

As they walked through the deserted streets, the evening breeze carried whispers of the past, and Carmelo couldn't help but feel a profound connection to the people who once thrived in this remarkable place. The decision to preserve the treasure and share their discovery with the world weighed heavily on his mind, but he knew it was the right thing to do.

And so, under the fading light of the sun, Carmelo, Alex, and Lucia continued their journey, carrying with them the knowledge that they had played a part in rediscovering a piece of history that would leave a lasting impact on the world. With each step, they reaffirmed their commitment to protecting the heritage of the Incan civilization and ensuring that future generations could learn from and appreciate the wonders of their ancestors.

They passed by the familiar landmarks—the grand temple with its intricate carvings, the bustling plaza, and the quiet residential buildings that once echoed with the laughter of Incan inhabitants. The air was filled with a sense of reverence and awe, knowing that they had uncovered a piece of history hidden beneath the layers of time.

The sun cast long shadows across the ancient stone structures, painting the surroundings in a golden hue. Carmelo, Alex, and Lucia walked in silence, each lost in their thoughts. As they reached the rope bridge that spanned a deep ravine, a familiar sense of nervous anticipation returned. The wind had picked up considerably since their initial crossing, and now the bridge swayed dramatically with each gust and current of air ripping through the ravine. The team paused briefly to slip into their safety harnesses.

Carmelo took the lead, his eyes focused on the sturdy ropes and the wooden planks that formed the bridge. With cautious steps, he tested each plank before putting his full weight on it. The creaking of the old wood echoed in the canyon below, adding to the suspense of the crossing

At one point, a strong gust of wind lifted the bridge upward and caught Carmelo off guard, sending him slamming into the thin rope guardrails. The strain of the sudden weight on the ropes caused one of the weathered cords to snap loudly, almost sending Carmelo plummeting into the void below, if not for the harness and lanyard tethering him to Lucia's safety rope.

"Carmelo!" Alex gasped with mortal concern as the bridge bucked and twisted in the wind.

Carmelo screamed loudly, his arms flailing as he tried to find something to hold onto and regain his balance. The sound of ropes scraping against the sharp and jagged rocks across the ravine echoed off the cliffs. Despite the obvious age of the bridge and the turbulent wind currents, he managed to regain his footing and continue slowly. The bridge held firm as he continued across, each step a testament to his determination and resilience.

Alex followed closely behind, his hands gripping the ropes for stability. He marveled at the breathtaking view below, where the ravine stretched out like a yawning abyss, revealing layers of rock and vegetation. As the wind whipped up again, Alex bent his knees into a crouched position and gripped the safety rope tightly with one hand while white-knuckling the bridge guardrail rope with the other. The planks beneath his feet undulated and cracked, adding to the tense atmosphere.

He remained crouched until there came a short reprieve from the wind. Sensing his opportunity, he stood up slowly, his muscles tensed with each step across the swaying bridge. The sound of strained ropes and groaning wood filled his ears, but he focused on each step, determined to reach the other side safely.

Lucia brought up the rear, her steps measured and deliberate as she balanced herself on the narrow path. The bridge heaved and twisted beneath her like a bullwhip, but she expertly clung to it like a spider clinging to a web. Her fingers traced the weathered ropes, feeling for stability with each movement. The wind tugged at her clothes and hair, adding to the challenge of crossing the swaying bridge.

Once each of them had reached the security of terra firma once again, they exchanged relieved glances. "Just look at it this way." Alex joked to Carmelo, "this will be great fodder for your next novel!"

"Do you think there's a market for 'Incan Treasure Hunter' action figures? I could use the royalties to fund my therapy after all these near-death experiences," Carmelo quipped.

With their hearts still racing from the adrenaline-filled crossing, they turned all of their determination and excitement towards the hike again, hoping to reach their quads before nightfall. The sun dipped lower in the sky, casting long shadows over the rugged landscape as they pressed forward, eager to continue their adventure.

By the time they reached their quads, dusk had settled over the landscape, casting long shadows and painting the sky in hues of orange and purple. The air was filled with a sense of accomplishment and anticipation as they mounted their vehicles, their minds buzzing with thoughts of the day's discoveries and adventures.

"Such a beautiful sunset," Lucia remarked, her gaze fixed on the horizon where the sun dipped below the mountains.

Carmelo nodded, a sense of peace washing over him. "It's moments like these that remind us of the beauty and wonder of the world."

As the sky darkened and nightfall set in gradually, stars began to twinkle overhead. The distant calls of wildlife echoed through the valleys as they rode along the winding trails. Carmelo, Alex, and Lucia raced toward Pampa de las Leñas to collect their camping gear before returning to Puente de Vacas. Their journey back was filled with a mix of exhaustion and exhilaration. Carmelo mentally recounted their experiences, revisiting moments of awe and excitement from their exploration of the ancient Incan city.

On their approach to Puente de Vacas, the familiar sights of the town gradually came into view. The quaint buildings, the lively market square, and the welcoming atmosphere of the town felt like a warm embrace after their adventure-filled day. They planned to rest and regroup before deciding on their next steps in preserving and sharing their remarkable discovery.

As they neared Andes Adventures to return their quads, Alex's eyes widened as he caught sight of something ahead, causing him to slam on the brakes and cut the engine. Carmelo and Lucia, sensing his urgency, pulled up beside him, their expressions mirroring his concern.

"What's happening?" Carmelo inquired, his voice edged with worry.

Alex silently pointed across the highway to a nearby restaurant and bar, where four unmarked military vehicles were parked. "Those belong to El Torre's men," he explained grimly."

"Who exactly is this El Torre?" Lucia's brows furrowed in concern, her expression a blend of confusion and unease. "I feel like I've heard that name before."

Alex leaned in, his voice lowered. "El Jefe de la Policía Federal Argentina, the Chief of the Federal Police."

Lucia's eyes widened with understanding. "I've heard of him. Should we be worried about running into his men?"

"Absolutely," Alex replied grimly. "El Torre is notoriously corrupt. He doesn't hesitate to eliminate anyone who opposes him." He paused, his gaze intense. "We've been on his radar for days now, hunted like prey by him and his goons."

"So, he's after your map?" Lucia redirected her focus to Carmelo, seeking clarity amid the unfolding situation.

Carmelo nodded solemnly. "I believe he has already attempted to kidnap me to acquire it. I would probably be dead by now had Alex not come along to rescue me."

Lucia inquired, "Is this the same man who kidnapped your sister?"

"No, someone else has my sister. I don't know his name, but he wants me to bring the map to him in Mendoza to trade for my sister's life," Carmelo explained.

Lucia nodded, her concern deepening, "I see. I'm so sorry, Carmelo."

Carmelo's voice carried a weight of worry as he continued, "Somehow, this El Torre knows that I have the map and that I brought it with me to Argentina. He knew exactly when I flew into Córdoba and had a man waiting for me at the airport when I arrived. I don't know how he knows all of this, but if he gets his hands on the map, he will not only likely kill me, but he will prevent me from saving Eloisa."

Lucia's expression mirrored Carmelo's concern, her brows furrowing with unease. "So, what should we do? If we all drive up on quads, that will surely draw a lot of attention at this late hour," she voiced her apprehension.

Alex, who had been quietly considering a plan, chimed in, "First off, Lucia, they are not looking for you, and it's best if you stay off their radar altogether. What I suggest is that you two hang back, out of sight. I will drive closer and hopefully catch their attention. I will try to draw them out of town so that the two of you can return your quads and get to the automobiles. You can explain to Marco that I will return my quad later tonight once I've managed to shake them off my tail. Carmelo, you should forward copies of all your photos to Lucia. Lucia, you and Daniela can collect all of the documentation and photos to send to the property antiquities authorities, but don't contact them until Carmelo has a chance to rescue Eloisa, he will contact you when she is safe. Carmelo, you will take the rental vehicle back to Mendoza and check into the Hotel Gran Mendoza as instructed by Eloisa's kidnappers. I will find you after I shake off El Torre's men."

"You want me to leave you behind?" Carmelo protested.

"Consider the situation, Carmelo," Alex responded calmly. "Having all three of us visible and involved will only complicate things. I can handle myself and ensure they don't follow me back to you and Lucia. This way, we minimize the risk for everyone. Besides, I can't assist you in rescuing your sister directly. This plan will hopefully keep El Torre off your back until you can fulfill your mission."

Carmelo hesitated, grappling with the weight of Alex's words and the gravity of their situation. After a moment of contemplation, he nodded in reluctant agreement. "Okay, Alex. I understand," he finally conceded, though a trace of unease lingered in his eyes. "But, you had better come after me!"

Their intimate moment blossomed with a passionate kiss, a testament to the unspoken understanding that had flourished between them amidst the tumultuous events unfolding around them. It was a heartfelt gesture that solidified the bond they shared, affirming the depth of their connection amid uncertainty and danger.

As the warmth of their kiss lingered, time seemed to slow down around them. Carmelo felt a rush of emotions flood through him, a mixture of gratitude, excitement, and a newfound sense of belonging. He pulled back slightly, his gaze locked with Alex's, searching for the right words to express the whirlwind of feelings inside him.

"Alex," Carmelo began, his voice soft yet filled with sincerity, "I never expected any of this, when I set out on this journey. Meeting you, experiencing all of this together—it's been like a dream." His hand reached up to gently brush against Alex's cheek, his touch conveying a depth of emotion he struggled to put into words.

Alex's eyes sparkled with affection as he listened, his heart swelling with each word Carmelo spoke. "Carmelo," he whispered, his voice filled with tenderness, "These past few days have been the most exciting of my life. Thank you for crashing into my life, Carmelo," Alex expressed, his eyes reflecting genuine gratitude and affection.

"Quite literally," Carmelo quipped with a laugh, his heart warmed by Alex's words.

Alex's grin widened as he continued, "Having you in my life now, I can't bear the thought of losing you. Please be careful, Carmelo. I'll be right behind you, watching your back."

They stood there, caught in a timeless embrace, their hearts beating in unison as they savored the precious connection they had discovered amidst the challenges and dangers they faced together. The world faded away around them, leaving only the echo of their whispered confessions and the promise of a future yet to unfold.

"Here, take these," Alex said, pressing the rental truck keys into Carmelo's hand as he turned to gracefully mount the quad. His thighs bulged as he straddled the warm machine. "Lucia, good luck. I hope we will see each other again!" With a swift motion, he fired up the engine and took off across the street.

As Carmelo watched Alex drive away, he felt like a piece of his heart was speeding off with him, leaving behind a mixture of longing and determination in his chest. He clenched his fists, his mind racing with thoughts of the impending rescue mission and the dangers that lay ahead. He turned to Lucia, a solemn expression on his face, and said, "We need to move quickly and cautiously. Every moment counts now,"

Lucia nodded in agreement, her eyes reflecting the gravity of the situation. Together, they gathered their belongings and prepared to execute the plan Alex had outlined. The night air was filled with tension as they waited for Alex's diversion to take effect. Every passing minute felt like an eternity, each sound amplifying their anticipation and apprehension. They kept their eyes on the road, their minds racing with thoughts of what lay ahead and the risks they were about to face.

The sudden commotion across the street caught their attention as armed men rushed out of the bar toward the military vehicles. Police sirens blared, and flashing lights illuminated the chaotic scene as the vehicles sped away from the parking lot.

"It looks like they took the bait," Lucia remarked in a hushed tone.

"It seems so. I just hate that Alex is the bait. We should proceed cautiously toward Marco's place, return these quads, and get to our vehicles. However, we must remain vigilant; there could be more of them lurking around that we haven't spotted yet," Carmelo replied, scanning their surroundings for any signs of danger.

A sense of relief washed over them as they both confirmed that the coast was clear. With silent determination, they navigated through the shadows, using the quiet buildings as cover, until they reached the parking lot of Andes Adventures. The closed doors and darkened lights indicated that the business had shut down for the day. Carmelo noticed a sign on the front door instructing late returns to drop keys into a drop box. They followed suit, relinquishing their quad keys, and turned towards their respective vehicles.

"Thank you for everything, Lucia!" Carmelo expressed his gratitude, reaching out for a friendly hug. "Please convey my heartfelt thanks to Daniela for all her help as well. If you could share your email address, I'll send you all the photos I took."

"Of course," Lucia responded, pulling out her notebook and jotting down her email address on a page. "You be careful too, Carmelo. I hope you reunite with your sister safely! Please get in touch with us as soon as you can!"

"I will," Carmelo promised with a reassuring smile, appreciative of Lucia's support and well wishes.

With a heavy sigh, Carmelo climbed into the driver's seat of the truck and discreetly pulled out onto the highway heading east, towards the city of Mendoza. The road stretched out before him, a path fraught with uncertainty and danger, yet filled with determination to rescue his sister.

"I'm coming Eloisa," he whispered to himself, the words a vow echoing his resolve.

The drive from Puente De Vacas to Mendoza was a journey filled with a tumultuous mix of emotions and thoughts for Carmelo. The dark, empty road stretched ahead, illuminated only by the headlights of his vehicle, creating an eerie atmosphere that mirrored his inner turmoil.

As Carmelo drove alone, the silence of the night was deafening, broken only by the sound of his engine and the occasional rustle of wind and passing car. With each mile driven, he couldn't shake off the nagging worry about Alex. His friend's safety weighed heavily on his mind, and doubts crept in about whether they had made the right decision in parting ways.

The landscape outside his window seemed to fade into a blur of shadows and moonlit fields, reflecting the uncertainty and anxiety that gripped Carmelo's thoughts. Memories of their shared adventures, laughter, and camaraderie flashed through his mind, contrasting sharply with the current situation.

Every turn of the road felt like a step further into the unknown, amplifying Carmelo's sense of responsibility and determination to ensure not only Eloisa's but now also Alex's well-being. The isolation of the night heightened his senses, making him hyper-aware of every sound and movement around him.

Despite the doubts and fears clouding his mind, Carmelo's resolve remained firm. He repeated his vow silently, a mantra of determination and hope amidst the uncertainty. The road to Mendoza became a metaphorical journey of introspection and resilience, with Carmelo grappling with the consequences of their decisions and the uncharted path ahead.

As the drive continued, the lights on the horizon gradually came into focus, revealing the distant glow of Mendoza's city lights. The outskirts of the city started to take shape, their presence marked by the twinkling lights against the night sky.

The last few kilometers of Carmelo's journey through the night were guided by these distant lights, serving as a beacon of hope, and a reminder of his impending arrival in Mendoza. The contrast between the darkness of the surrounding countryside and the illuminated skyline ahead created a surreal yet comforting scene.

The city lights on the horizon grew brighter with each passing mile, casting a warm and inviting aura over the landscape. Despite the late hour, Mendoza seemed to welcome Carmelo with open arms, offering a sense of familiarity and safety in the midst of his journey.

As he drew ever closer, the city became more defined, outlining the buildings and streets that awaited him. Carmelo's destination was clear: the Hotel Gran Mendoza, a landmark that represented the last respite before his dreaded confrontation with Eloisa's kidnapper.

As Carmelo's vehicle approached the Hotel Gran Mendoza, the grandeur of the establishment became increasingly apparent. The hotel stood as a towering structure amidst the cityscape, its facade adorned with intricate architectural details that spoke of elegance and luxury.

The exterior of the Hotel Gran Mendoza boasted a blend of modern design elements and classic charm. A marbled entrance with tall columns welcomed guests, leading to a spacious lobby illuminated by crystal chandeliers that cast a warm, inviting glow.

Upon pulling up, Carmelo was greeted by the sight of uniformed valets ready to assist with parking. The hustle and bustle of guests coming and going added to the vibrant atmosphere of the hotel's entrance, creating a sense of activity and liveliness.

As Carmelo stepped out of his vehicle, he was met with the sound of soft music playing in the background, adding a touch of sophistication to the ambiance. The air carried a faint scent of flowers from the beautifully landscaped gardens that surrounded the hotel, enhancing the overall sensory experience.

The Hotel Gran Mendoza's reputation for impeccable service and attention to detail was evident from the moment Carmelo arrived. The front desk staff welcomed him with warm smiles, offering assistance with check-in and any other needs he might have.

The interior decor of the hotel was equally impressive, with plush furnishings, tasteful artwork adorning the walls, and expansive windows that offered panoramic views of the city and the nearby mountains. Carmelo couldn't help but feel a sense of relief and comfort as he entered the hotel, knowing that he had found a temporary haven amidst his tumultuous journey.

Carmelo approached the front desk of the Hotel Gran Mendoza, his footsteps echoing softly on the polished marble floor of the lobby. The warm ambiance enveloped him as he reached the elegant reception area, where friendly staff members awaited to assist him.

A courteous receptionist greeted Carmelo with a genuine smile, her demeanor exuding professionalism and hospitality. "Bienvenido al Hotel Gran Mendoza," she said warmly, prompting Carmelo to feel a sense of ease after his long and eventful journey.

Carmelo provided his information, and the receptionist efficiently processed his check-in, ensuring that his stay would be comfortable and hassle-free. She handed him a key card enclosed in a sleek envelope, along with a brochure highlighting the hotel's amenities and services.

As Carmelo made his way to his room, he couldn't help but admire the interior of the hotel. The corridors were adorned with tasteful artwork and soft lighting, creating an atmosphere of tranquility and refinement.

Upon entering his room, Carmelo was greeted by a spacious and elegantly appointed space. The decor featured a blend of modern comforts and classic elegance, with a plush bed, a cozy seating area, and a well-appointed bathroom with luxurious amenities.

The view from the window showcased the city lights glittering in the night, adding to the allure of his temporary sanctuary. Carmelo took a moment to relax and unwind, grateful for the comfort and hospitality offered by the Hotel Gran Mendoza after his eventful journey.

There was only one thing left to do. Carmelo's hand trembled slightly as he reached for the telephone. His fingers hovered over the familiar numbers, dialing them with a mix of anticipation and apprehension. His stomach twisted with nerves, and his heartbeat quickened in his chest. Each ring seemed to echo loudly in the quiet room, adding to his sense of tension.

After a few rings, a voice answered on the other end of the line. The sound of the voice, so familiar yet distant, sent a jolt of emotions through Carmelo. His throat felt tight as he struggled to find the right words, the weight of unspoken thoughts and feelings hanging in the air between them.

"Hola?" The voice on the other end cut through the silence with a calculated and cautious tone, devoid of any semblance of friendliness or warmth. Its detached coldness hinted at a personality steeped in callousness and criminality, sending an unmistakable chill down Carmelo's spine.

Carmelo took a deep breath, steeling himself for the conversation ahead. "This is Carmelo Quiñones De La Cruz," he finally said, his voice steady despite the racing of his heart. "I have arrived in Mendoza. I'm at the Hotel Gran Mendoza. I have the map. I'm here for my sister." The silence that followed was filled with unspoken questions, emotions, and the uncertainty of what the kidnapper's next words would be.

"It's about time, Mr. Quiñones. I was starting to think you had done something stupid and gotten yourself killed," the voice on the other end remarked with a hint of sarcasm.

"That almost happened," Carmelo admitted, his voice carrying a mix of relief and tension.

"Fortunately for your sister, that didn't happen. Rest for tonight, Mr. Quiñones. Tomorrow, at 7 p.m., I will send a car to pick you up outside of the hotel," the voice instructed, its tone leaving no room for argument or negotiation. Carmelo heard a click as the phone call abruptly ended, leaving him with a sense of unease and a flurry of thoughts swirling in his mind.

"Rest for tonight," Carmelo replayed the kidnapper's words in his mind. Rest. That sounded really good. After the tension and uncertainty of the past hours and the physically demanding day he had been through, the prospect of a peaceful night's rest felt like a rare luxury.

Chapter Thirteen

The next morning, Carmelo woke up early, feeling a mix of

anticipation and anxiety about the events to come. He decided to make the most of the day while waiting for the driver to pick him up at 7 p.m.

In the morning, Carmelo took a leisurely stroll around the hotel grounds, enjoying the fresh air and peaceful ambiance. He took time to appreciate the beauty of Mendoza, soaking in the sights and sounds of the city.

Mendoza, nestled in Argentina's wine country, held a charm that captured Carmelo's heart as he wandered through its streets. The backdrop of the Andes Mountains, their peaks bathed in the morning sun, painted a breathtaking scene against the clear blue sky.

Walking along the tree-lined streets, Carmelo was surrounded by lush greenery, parks, and gardens bursting with fragrant flowers. The Botanical Garden, with its colorful blooms and serene ponds, offered a peaceful retreat amidst the city's hustle and bustle.

The architecture of Mendoza was a blend of old-world charm and modern elegance. The ornate facades of historic buildings, each telling a story of the city's rich heritage, caught Carmelo's eye at every turn. Plaza Independencia, alive with activity, revealed the vibrant spirit of the city.

The sounds of Mendoza were equally captivating. The cheerful chatter of locals and the melodies of street musicians filled the air, creating a lively and welcoming atmosphere. Carmelo paused to listen to a guitarist playing traditional Argentine folk music, his soulful tunes adding to the city's charm.

Exploring Mendoza's culinary scene was a delight for Carmelo's senses. The aroma of freshly baked empanadas and grilled meats from local eateries tantalized his taste buds. Cafes buzzed with energy, offering a taste of the city's culinary culture.

Throughout the day, Carmelo's mind drifted back to the phone call from the kidnapper and the upcoming meeting. He tried to stay focused and composed, channeling his emotions into productive activities while keeping a watchful eye on his surroundings.

After a relaxing lunch of traditional Argentine cuisine, Carmelo gradually made his way back to the Hotel Gran Mendoza where he spent some time in his room, going over his plans and making sure he was prepared for the meeting later that evening. He checked his belongings, reviewed all of his important documents, and mentally rehearsed what he wanted to say. He spent some time relaxing in his room, taking deep breaths to calm his nerves, and steeling himself for whatever challenges may arise during the meeting with the kidnapper.

At three minutes past 7 p.m., the phone rang loudly, jolting Carmelo from his near-meditative state of existential introspection. He sat up quickly and answered the call, "Hello?"

As Carmelo answered the call, he heard the voice of the front desk clerk informing him that the car had arrived to pick him up. With a sense of readiness, Carmelo stood up, pulled his messenger bag over his shoulder, and made his way down to the lobby.

As Carmelo stepped outside, he spotted a sleek, fancy car waiting for him. The doorman opened the car door with a polite nod, and Carmelo slid into the luxurious interior. "Bueno noches, señor," greeted the driver warmly as he settled into the plush seat.

"Buenos noches," Carmelo replied, a sense of anticipation tingling in the air. He couldn't help but notice the opulence of the car's interior as the driver started the engine.

Before they set off, the driver leaned towards Carmelo and said, "Señor, por favor, ponte la funda de almohada sobre su cabeza."

Carmelo's eyebrows furrowed in surprise, but he complied, feeling a mix of curiosity and apprehension. With the pillowcase gently covering his eyes, the journey took on a mysterious and suspenseful tone as they made their way toward the inevitable confrontation with the man who held captive and threatened to murder his sister. The tension in the air was palpable, and Carmelo's thoughts raced with anticipation and determination as he braced himself for what lay ahead.

The drive took about twenty minutes, and Carmelo's keen observation noted the gradual fading of city sounds, signaling their transition from urban sprawl to a quieter, rural environment.

The car slowed down, and Carmelo could feel the gentle vibration as it came to a stop. The faint squeak of the brakes echoed in the stillness, signaling their arrival. Despite the pillowcase covering his head, Carmelo's senses were heightened, and he could sense the change in motion.

He heard the driver get out of the vehicle and close the car door. He waited in anticipation, listening intently for the sound of someone approaching the rear passenger side. The silence seemed to stretch, each moment filled with anticipation and uncertainty about what awaited him. Suddenly his car door opened and the driver removed the pillowcase from his head.

"¡Ándale!" The driver commanded abruptly, accompanied by a gesture signaling Carmelo to get out of the car. With a sense of urgency, Carmelo complied, stepping out into the unknown.

As Carmelo stepped out of the car, he found himself standing in front of a remote villa nestled amidst the sprawling countryside of Mendoza. The villa's location was carefully chosen for its seclusion, tucked away from prying eyes among the vineyards and rolling hills.

The exterior of the villa exuded a sense of quiet luxury, with traditional hacienda-style architecture featuring terracotta roofs, whitewashed walls adorned with climbing vines, and arched doorways leading into hidden courtyards. Tall cypress trees lined the perimeter, providing both privacy and a sense of mystique.

At first glance, the villa appeared peaceful and intoxicatingly alluring, but Carmelo knew better. Beneath the tranquil facade, the compound was a lair of villainy and criminal activity. Surveillance cameras discreetly positioned around the property kept a vigilant watch, ensuring that any approach was carefully monitored.

As Carmelo took in the sight, he couldn't shake off the feeling of being watched, of unseen eyes observing his every move. The remote villa seemed to hold its secrets close, hinting at the mysteries and dangers that awaited within its walls.

To his left, a winding path led further into the property, disappearing into the dense foliage. To his right, a gentle breeze carried the scent of wildflowers, adding a touch of tranquility to the scene. Despite the peaceful setting, Carmelo couldn't shake off the feeling of tension and uncertainty that hung in the air. Every detail of his surroundings seemed to amplify the anticipation of what awaited him.

As Carmelo reached the main entrance of the villa, he found himself surrounded by a team of security personnel. They quickly ushered him inside, where the atmosphere shifted from tranquil to tense. Inside the villa, Carmelo underwent a thorough scan and pat-down by the security team, ensuring he was not carrying any weapons. They also meticulously searched his messenger bag for any potential threats.

Once cleared by security, Carmelo was guided through the interior of the villa, passing through elegant halls and rooms adorned with luxurious decor. The air was filled with a sense of anticipation and apprehension as he followed the security team's lead.

Emerging from the villa's back entrance onto a vast Saltillo tiled patio, Carmelo's gaze was drawn to the expansive view of the surrounding countryside and the Mendoza River glistening in the distance. The security guard urged him to keep following, leading him down a long stone walkway that wound its way towards a grand Spanish-style pergola overlooking the river.

As Carmelo approached the pergola, he could see a man waiting at the end, his imposing figure framed against the scenic backdrop. He could feel the weight of anticipation and uncertainty hanging in the air, knowing that his encounter with this enigmatic crime boss awaited just a few meters down the pathway.

As Carmelo approached, the man stood up and turned towards him. "Ah, Mr. Quiñones, at last we meet. Please, have a seat," the man said with a polite yet authoritative tone.

Carmelo's concern for Eloisa overshadowed any formalities. "Who are you, and where is Eloisa?" He demanded, his voice edged with urgency and worry.

The man maintained his composure, offering reassurance. "Don't worry, Mr. Quiñones," he said calmly. "Your sister will be along shortly. You will find that no harm has come to her."

The tension in the air was palpable as Carmelo awaited more answers, hoping that the man's assurances were genuine and that Eloisa was indeed safe.

Carmelo's brows furrowed in skepticism. "I need to see her, to make sure she's unharmed," he insisted, his voice tinged with both urgency and determination.

The man nodded understandingly. "Of course, Mr. Quiñones. I will arrange for you to be reunited with your sister as soon as possible," he assured Carmelo, gesturing for him to take a seat at the pergola's table.

As Carmelo sat down, his mind raced with questions and concerns. He couldn't shake off the feeling of being in the lion's den, surrounded by unknown intentions and hidden dangers. Despite the picturesque setting of the pergola overlooking the Mendoza River, the underlying tension and uncertainty cast a shadow over the scene.

The man, sensing Carmelo's unease, attempted to ease the atmosphere. "Would you care for something to drink while we wait?" He offered, motioning to a nearby serving cart with refreshments. "Our vineyard produces some of the best wines in Argentina."

Carmelo hesitated for a moment, then nodded. "Yes, please," he replied curtly, his focus still on getting assurances about Eloisa.

The man stood up to pour Carmelo a glass of wine, introducing himself as Fernando Mendoza. "My family are the direct descendants of the famous conquistador and first governor-general of the Rio de la Plata, Pedro de Mendoza the namesake of the city and province of Mendoza—this river as well," he added, as if to establish his lineage and background. "Most people refer to me as Don Mendoza."

Carmelo, seemingly unimpressed by Don Mendoza's pedigree, surveyed the landscape around him. "This is a beautiful place you have here, Don Mendoza. How many people did you have to kidnap to pay for it?" He remarked with a hint of sarcasm.

Don Mendoza, unfazed by Carmelo's jab, chose not to react harshly. Instead, he maintained a composed demeanor and replied, "Beauty often comes at a cost, Mr. Quiñones." His response was measured, hinting at a deeper layer of secrecy and ambiguity surrounding his wealth and lifestyle.

As Carmelo took a sip of his wine, the distant sound of the Mendoza River reached his ears, accompanied by an unusual symphony of clicking and occasional chirping sounds.

"That's an interesting sound, are those birds?" Carmelo asked, curious about the unfamiliar noises.

Don Mendoza glanced towards the source of the sounds. "No, those are the sounds of the yacares," he explained. "It's almost feeding time for them. They make those sounds when they're hungry, anticipating their meal."

Carmelo's curiosity piqued further as he listened to the distinctive sounds of the yacares, adding another layer of intrigue to his surroundings.

"Don't you find it fascinating, Mr. Quiñones?" Don Mendoza interjected, his tone shifting to one of educational interest. "The yacare caiman were hunted almost to extinction in the 1980s for their valuable skin, sought after for leather production."

Carmelo raised an eyebrow, intrigued by the unexpected turn in conversation. "I had no idea," he admitted unenthusiastically.

"However," Don Mendoza continued, "trading restrictions placed since then have caused their population to rebound significantly. Now, it's estimated that they number in the tens of millions, a remarkable recovery." He spoke with a hint of admiration for nature's resilience despite human impact.

"They are amazing, intelligent creatures, with voracious appetites," Don Mendoza remarked, a flicker of fascination in his eyes. "I enjoy having them nearby. I find their nature relatable. You see, I too have a voracious appetite."

Carmelo's curiosity was piqued. "For what, Don Mendoza?" He inquired, sensing a deeper meaning behind the crime boss's words.

"That is why you are here, Mr. Quiñones," Don Mendoza replied cryptically. "You have something in your possession that I am very hungry for." His words hung in the air, laden with unspoken implications and veiled threats.

Carmelo's voice trembled with a mixture of fear and determination as he spoke. "Yes, I have the map. It's right here in my bag," he said, reaching into his messenger bag and pulling out the map. "You can have it, just give me back my sister!" His plea was heartfelt, driven by the desperation to ensure Eloisa's safety above all else.

Don Mendoza's eyes widened at the sight of the map Carmelo pulled out from his messenger bag. He gave Carmelo a skeptical glance, his expression hardening with caution.

"First things first," Don Mendoza began, his tone firm. "I must verify its authenticity. I hope that you are not trying to trick me with a forgery. That would be very unwise. I will know if it is fake." His words carried a weight of warning, emphasizing the serious consequences of attempting deception in their precarious situation.

Carmelo's stomach churned with nervous anticipation as Don Mendoza sprang from his chair, ready to conduct his examination of the map. The sudden movement and the gravity of the situation added to Carmelo's unease, highlighting the tension in the air as Don Mendoza delved into the process of verifying the map's authenticity.

"First, Mr. Quiñones, I will use this magnifying glass to closely examine the details of the map," Don Mendoza explained, holding up the magnifying glass to the map. "This will help me assess the quality of the paper, the ink used, and any signs of aging or wear that are typical of authentic historical documents." He scrutinized the map intensely for several minutes.

He then switched to a more serious tone, adding, "Next, I will use this ultraviolet light to detect any hidden features or alterations on the map. Modern inks or repairs would show up under UV light, which could indicate forgery." He clicked on the UV light and began sweeping it over the document.

Don Mendoza stood there silently for several minutes, his expression serious and determined. The weight of verifying the map's authenticity hung in the air. Suddenly, he reached into the pocket of his slacks and pulled out a handheld radio transceiver. With a calm and expressionless tone, he said, "Vente," signaling someone to come over. The atmosphere became tense as Carmelo waited, unsure of what would happen next.

A few minutes passed before Carmelo began to hear footsteps approaching from behind him. He stood up and turned around quickly, his heart pounding with anticipation. There, walking towards him, was Eloisa, flanked by two armed men. She was wearing a dirty black dress, her hair unkempt and unwashed, indicating days of captivity. Despite her disheveled appearance, there was a mixture of excitement and desperation in her eyes as she finally reunited with her brother.

Carmelo's heart clenched as he reached out to embrace his sister. Eloisa, overwhelmed by the emotions of the moment, burst into tears, her sobs echoing the relief and anguish of their reunion after days of uncertainty and captivity. The weight of their shared ordeal hung heavily in the air, but in that embrace, there was also a glimmer of hope and resilience.

Carmelo wrapped his arms around Eloisa, holding her close as she sobbed. "Eloisa, it's okay now. You're safe," he whispered soothingly.

"I thought I'd never see you again," Eloisa choked out between sobs, her voice trembling with emotion.

"We're together again, now. That's all that matters," Carmelo reassured her, his voice filled with a mix of relief and concern.

Carmelo and Eloisa turned to look at Don Mendoza again, who stood there silently and expressionless during the emotional moment. Don Mendoza's gaze shifted between the map on the table and Carmelo, his expression unreadable. "My driver will take you back to the hotel. You are both free to go," he said calmly, his tone neutral yet decisive. He then reached for the map, snatching it off the table and securing it in the breast pocket of his suit jacket.

Carmelo grabbed Eloisa's hand tightly, his instincts kicking in as he turned to lead her away from the pergola and up the stone pathway toward the villa. They had barely taken two steps, when suddenly a gunshot rang out, the sound echoing off the surrounding walls. A bullet ricocheted off the stone masonry nearby, sending fragments flying. Startled, Eloisa let out a piercing scream, her hand gripping Carmelo's tightly as they scurried for cover.

Don Mendoza spun around, his hand instinctively reaching for his pistol. He found himself face to face with the notorious El Torre, and six armed men brandishing assault rifles. At the same time, five members of Don Mendoza's security team came rushing down the pathway from behind Carmelo and

Eloisa, their expressions tense as they assessed the situation.

For a moment, the scene froze into a silent standoff, the tension palpable in the air as each side gauged the others' intentions. The night was filled with the sounds of heavy breathing and the faint rustle of leaves, punctuated only by the distant rush of the Mendoza River.

"¡Deténgase ahora mismo! ¡Suelte las armas!" El Torre yelled out above the commotion, repeating himself in English, "Stop where you are and put down your weapons!"

"We will not put down our weapons! Don't take another step onto my property, or my men will use you for target practice," Don Fernando Mendoza threatened, his tone carrying a cold edge of authority, his gaze unwavering as he addressed El Torre and his men. The standoff remained tense, each side calculating their next move amidst the threat of imminent violence.

El Torre responded defiantly, "I am Santiago Vargas, La Policía Federal!"

Don Fernando Mendoza lunged toward Carmelo, his grip firm as he grabbed him by the shirt and lifted him up. Carmelo could feel the cold metal of Don Mendoza's gun pressing against his back, the tension in the air palpable as Don Mendoza's anger flared. "You fool! I told you not to do anything stupid. You brought the Federales here! I should kill you right now!" His voice seethed with frustration and rage.

"No! Don't hurt him!" Eloisa pleaded, her voice filled with fear and desperation.

"Tell your men to stand down, or I will kill your little pig American informant!" Don Mendoza threatened El Torre, his voice dripping with menace. The standoff intensified as the threat hung in the air, each side poised for potential escalation or resolution.

Amid the intense confrontation, Carmelo was overcome with fear and anxiety. His emotions ran high as the situation teetered on the brink of violence. "I didn't go to the Feds or the police. I don't know who this man is! He has been trying to kill me since I arrived here in Argentina!" Carmelo's words were filled with desperation and a plea for understanding, as he tried to defend himself amidst the chaos.

"Señor Quiñones es verdad," El Torre said with no hesitation. "I would have killed him in Tejas if he had been at home." Carmelo's eyes widened in shock.

"It was you who ransacked my house in Austin!" The realization hit him like a ton of bricks, connecting El Torre's actions in Argentina to the events back in Texas.

"Si, señor. I should have gutted you and thrown your body in the river as I did with that archaeologist who tried to double-cross me," El Torre declared, his voice cold and unforgiving. "Go ahead, Don Mendoza, kill him. It makes no difference to me. I'm here for the map. I will take it now."

The tension in the air escalated as El Torre made his intentions clear, showing no remorse for his violent past and no hesitation in pursuing his goal of obtaining the map.

Don Mendoza, recognizing that Carmelo was not serving as a useful bargaining tool, released him abruptly, throwing him to the ground behind him. The sudden action added to the chaotic and unpredictable nature of the confrontation, leaving Carmelo vulnerable and uncertain of his next move.

"I never thought I'd say this, but I miss the simplicity of writer's block," Carmelo groaned under his breath as he scurried back toward Eloisa. "At least then, the only thing chasing me was a blinking cursor."

Don Mendoza turned his gun back towards El Torre, his voice filled with determination. "I will never give you the map. If you want it, you'll have to come through all of my men and take it off my dead body." His words carried a resolute defiance, indicating his unwavering resolve to protect his possession at any cost.

El Torre responded, "I was worried that you might be objectionable about handing it over, so I arranged for a little trade." He gestured to his men to bring their prisoner. Suddenly, two more of his men came up the steps from the river's edge, dragging a beaten and bloodied man at gunpoint.

When the man raised his head, Carmelo audibly gasped. It was Alex, and he had been severely beaten. Seeing his friend in such a state made Carmelo feel physically ill. He couldn't help feeling responsible for getting Alex mixed up in this horrible situation. The sight of his friend battered and in danger weighed heavily on Carmelo's conscience, adding to the emotional turmoil of the moment.

"Here is my final offer," El Torre said to Don Mendoza. "You give me the map, and I will give you your brother." His proposal created a tense and precarious situation, with Alex's fate hanging in the balance of a high-stakes exchange. "If you don't, I will shoot him in the face right in front of you."

"¿Qué es esto?" Don Mendoza studied his brother from a distance, a mix of disbelief and caution in his voice as he made sure that this wasn't some sort of trick. "Alejandro?" The use of Alex's full name hinted at the gravity of the situation and the deep-seated emotions surfacing in Don Mendoza's mind as he processed the unexpected revelation.

"Hola, hermano," Alex groaned, spitting blood out of his mouth before speaking. Alex's face bore the brutal marks of the beating inflicted by El Torre's men. His once handsome features were now marred by bruises, cuts, and swelling. Blood trickled from a split lip, and his eyes, once bright and lively, were now clouded with pain and exhaustion. Despite the grim condition of his face, there was a defiant glint in Alex's eyes as he greeted his brother, a testament to his resilience and determination amidst adversity.

At that moment, Carmelo's mind was a whirlwind of conflicting emotions. He felt a sense of shock and disbelief, realizing that he had been kept in the dark about Alex's true identity. The revelation stirred feelings of betrayal and confusion, as he grappled with the idea that someone he trusted had concealed such a crucial piece of information. On one hand, there was the relief of knowing Alex was alive, for now, but on the other, there was a deep sense of unease and mistrust, wondering what other secrets might be lurking beneath the surface.

The internal conflict weighed heavily on Carmelo. His thoughts raced with dozens of 'what if?' questions. What if Alex had been working for his brother the whole time? What if Alex had been manipulating him and toying with his emotions? What if Alex wanted the treasure for himself? These uncertainties left Carmelo questioning the authenticity of their past interactions and the trust he had placed in Alex. The revelation added a layer of doubt and suspicion to their relationship, making him wonder if anything Alex had said was the truth.

Carmelo studied Alex's face intently, searching for any hint of emotion or authenticity within his eyes. The intensity of the moment reflected Carmelo's inner turmoil and the need to discern the truth amidst the uncertainty surrounding Alex's motives and actions.

"Hermanito, where have you been?" Don Mendoza asked Alex with a mix of concern and relief. "I haven't seen you in months. Temía que estuvieras muerto."

"¡Trabajando para mí!" El Torre proclaimed proudly, indicating that Alex had been working for him during that time.

Don Mendoza's focus shifted between Alex and El Torre, a look of confusion on his face. "You're working for the Feds?" Don Mendoza asked Alex, his tone a mix of surprise and suspicion. The revelation added another layer of intrigue to the unfolding drama, as Don Mendoza tried to make sense of the unexpected turn of events involving his brother and the authorities.

"Fernando, let me explain," Alex pleaded, desperation evident in his voice as he tried to explain his situation to his brother amidst the chaotic and tense atmosphere,

"What is there to explain, Alejandro?" Don Mendoza's voice elevated as his anger began rising. "That you betrayed me—that you betrayed your whole family?" His words were laced with hurt and disappointment, reflecting the deep sense of betrayal he felt upon learning about Alex's involvement with El Torre and potentially with the authorities.

"It seems he betrayed all of us," El Torre added, casting a shameful glance at Alex. His words echoed the sentiment of betrayal and disappointment felt by both Don Mendoza and Carmelo, highlighting the complexity of Alex's actions and the consequences they had on multiple fronts.

In that heated moment, Alex looked directly into Carmelo's eyes, a mix of regret, apology, and a silent plea for understanding reflected in his gaze. Carmelo could feel a torrent of emotions surging within him as he met Alex's gaze. There was a sense of shock and disbelief at the unfolding revelations, mingled with anger and confusion. Beneath it all, there was a lingering hope for some explanation or resolution amidst the chaos and turmoil surrounding them.

"Well, what is your answer?" El Torre pressed for a response from Don Mendoza, his tone demanding and expectant, eager to hear Don Mendoza's decision in the midst of the tense standoff.

"My little brother is already dead to me," Don Mendoza replied, his voice firm and resolute. "If you want the map, you will have to kill me for it." His words carried a weight of finality, indicating his unwavering stance despite the volatile circumstances.

El Torre's response was swift and decisive. "Very well," he said as he took aim and fired a shot, hitting Don Mendoza in the chest. The impact knocked Don Mendoza off balance, sending him crashing onto his back. The pistol he was holding slipped from his grasp and landed a few feet away from where Carmelo and Eloisa were crouched, intensifying the already tense and dangerous situation.

In the chaos, El Torre's men and Don Fernando Mendoza's men unleashed a barrage of gunfire at each other. Alex, seizing a moment of distraction, broke free from his captors and sprinted towards the ledge overlooking the river. With determination, he leaped into the rushing water. However, just as he reached the peak of his dive, El Torre turned and fired another shot, striking Alex in the abdomen. The impact sent Alex tumbling into the rapid current of the Rio Mendoza, where he disappeared into the murky depths.

Carmelo's cry of horror echoed as he witnessed Alex getting shot. His distress consumed him to the point that he hadn't noticed Eloisa was no longer beside him. Panic surged through him when he realized she had taken Don Mendoza's gun and was advancing towards El Torre, who had momentarily turned away. With a heavy heart, Eloisa lifted the .45 caliber pistol, aimed it at El Torre, and pulled the trigger, delivering a fatal shot. "That's for Lorenzo," she declared through tears, dropping the gun and fleeing from the scene.

Carmelo raced after Eloisa, calling out to her in desperation. "Eloisa, slow down! This way!" He gestured towards the main villa, emphasizing the need to find a vehicle and leave the dangerous situation behind.

Together, they ran up the stone pathway until they reached the front entrance of the main villa. Carmelo was cautious not to run into one of Don Mendoza's security guards, but he suspected most of them had been called down to the pergola to assist in the ensuing firefight.

As they approached the driveway in front of Don Mendoza's house, Carmelo noticed that the car he had arrived in was still parked just outside the entrance, the driver was nowhere to be seen.

Carmelo cautiously approached the car and peeked into the driver's side window. The keys were still in the ignition.

"Eloisa," he waved at her, indicating the coast was clear. "Get in!"

With lightning speed, they both jumped into the car and locked the doors. Carmelo swiftly turned the key, and the engine roared to life. The tires squealed loudly as they peeled out of the driveway, leaving behind the chaos and danger of Don Mendoza's villa, heading towards freedom and safety.

CHAPTER FOURTEEN

As Carmelo raced away from Don Mendoza's villa, panic and adrenaline fueled his driving. The narrow rural road twisted and turned sharply, challenging his control over the vehicle. The moonlit night added an eerie glow to the surroundings, casting long shadows as the car sped along.

Carmelo's thoughts raced with fear and urgency, his focus solely on escaping the dangerous situation he had found himself in. The road ahead seemed endless, flanked by tall trees and occasional glimpses of vineyards passing by in a blur.

With each turn, the car's tires screeched against the pavement, and Carmelo's grip on the wheel tightened. The lack of streetlights made visibility limited, adding to the tension of the moment. The air was thick with suspense, punctuated by the sounds of the engine roaring and the rush of wind as they flew down the road.

Suddenly, as Carmelo took a sharp turn, the car's tires lost traction. The vehicle skidded uncontrollably, veering off the road and crashing through the underbrush. The momentum sent them tumbling into the yacare wetland habitat, the car lurching and rolling until it came to a jarring stop amidst the dense foliage and murky waters, surrounded by the hungry yacares.

Carmelo's world was a blur of disorientation as he regained consciousness. His head throbbed, and the acrid smell of mud and water filled his nostrils. It took a moment for his senses to sharpen, and when they did, he realized he was still in the car, now partially submerged in the yacare wetland habitat.

The impact had knocked him out briefly, but the urgency of the situation jolted him awake. The car was sinking slowly into the muck, and Carmelo's first instinct was to check on Eloisa. He reached out, finding her shoulder, and shook her gently, calling her name until she stirred.

Carmelo's heart raced with relief as Eloisa regained consciousness. He carefully inspected her forehead, relieved to find that the wound dripping blood down the side of her face was just a scratch. The murky surroundings of the yacare habitat added urgency as he called out to her until her eyes flickered open, inhaling deeply.

"Eloisa, are you okay?" Carmelo's voice was filled with concern as he helped her sit up. The car continued to sink slowly, the muck and water seeping in through the doors. The sounds of the habitat—gurgling water, the distant calls of wildlife—filled the air around them, adding to the surreal atmosphere.

Eloisa nodded groggily, blinking as she took in their precarious situation. "What happened?" She asked, her voice still groggy from the impact and brief loss of consciousness.

"We crashed," Carmelo explained quickly.

"Where are we? What is that smell?" Eloisa asked, her panic level rising as she took in her surroundings.

"I think we crashed into a yacare habitat," Carmelo replied, trying to keep his voice steady despite the rising tension. "That smell is the mixture of mud, water, and…yacare."

He scanned their surroundings, noting the murky water and the occasional ripple indicating the presence of the yacare caimans. The sounds of wildlife and the distant rush of the Mendoza River added to the surreal atmosphere.

"We need to find a way out of here," Carmelo continued, urgency creeping into his tone. "We can't stay here. Can you move?"

Eloisa tried to move and suddenly she screamed out as if in pain.

"Oh my gosh, what's wrong? Are you okay? Are you injured?" Carmelo asked in a panic as he inspected her for more wounds.

"My hair is stuck in the thing," she scrambled to get free, flailing her arms around in unnatural positions in an attempt to free her entangled hair.

""¡Ay bendito! You almost gave me a heart attack. I thought you had a broken leg or something." Carmelo looked behind her and saw that her hair had gotten sucked into the retractable seat belt mechanism. "Here, sit still, and let me see if I can pull it out."

Eloisa's frustration was evident as she snapped at him, "It hurts, Carmelo!"

Carmelo reached over and tugged on Eloisa's hair. She groaned in discontent, but he couldn't pull her hair free. "When I pull on your hair, pull down on the seatbelt at the same time," he instructed her. "One, two, three, pull!" They both pulled in unison.

Frustration grew palpable in Eloisa's voice as she exclaimed, "The seatbelt is locked, I can't pull it anymore!"

Searching for a solution, Carmelo spotted a shard of glass in the back seat. He carefully picked it up and told Eloisa, "I'm going to cut your hair loose." Eloisa closed her eyes and nodded, bracing herself for the improvised haircut.

After a few minutes of careful cutting, Carmelo managed to free his sister from her entanglement. "Let's get out of here," he said urgently, noticing the car sinking further into the swamp with each passing moment. "See if you can roll down your window. We need to climb out on your side because it's closer to the shore."

"What about the yacares?" Eloisa asked nervously, her heart racing as she rolled down her window, cautious of the looming cayman nearby. Its menacing hiss sent shivers down her spine, adding urgency to their escape.

"We have to get away from them. We have to take our chances," Carmelo said while pushing Eloisa toward the open window. "Climb out of the window and get onto the roof."

Eloisa groaned, expressing her doubt, "Are you sure about this? I don't think I can!"

Carmelo, feeling the urgency of the situation, replied with a hint of frustration, "Listen, this is the second car wreck I've been in since I've been here. We don't have a choice. We have to get away from these yacares! Trust me, it's safer up there. ¡Ándale!"

Eloisa carefully executed Carmelo's instructions. She eased herself out of the window, twisting onto her back to sit up on the window sill. With a determined effort, she pushed with her legs and successfully ascended onto the roof of the car.

Next, it was Carmelo's turn. He took a deep breath, steadying himself for the precarious maneuver. He slowly slid across the center console into the passenger's side seat, pulled himself up into the window, using the door frame for support, and cautiously made his way to join Eloisa on the car's roof.

"Now what are we going to do?" Eloisa asked nervously.

"Well, we're going to have to make it to shore. It's only about four meters away. I think we're going to have to swim."

"With the yacares?" Eloisa shrieked.

"Well, look, this is where we crashed into the habitat. I think the crash probably scared most of them off at least for a few minutes. I don't see any here in between us and the shore. Just count to three, jump out as far as you can, and then swim the rest of the way until you reach the shore. Don't stop. I'll be right behind you."

Eloisa closed her eyes for a moment, breathing heavily. Carmelo nodded reassuringly, trying to mask his own apprehension. "You can do this, Eloisa. Just jump and swim straight to the shore. I'll be right there with you." He scanned the water's surface, looking for any signs of danger. "Ready? One, two, three, jump!"

Eloisa leaped out over the murky waters in a diving pose. As she made contact with the water, her momentum propelled her through the floating algae and debris until she lifted her head and saw dry land within reach. She dug her fingers into the mud, pulling her legs underneath her body, and bounded up onto the shore. As promised, Carmelo was right behind her, sending a wave of water in her direction as he splashed down. Eloisa reached out to grab his hand and helped pull him onto dry land. They sat there for a moment, their hands clasping in a silent acknowledgment of their shared escape.

They climbed the rest of the way up the embankment, out of the yacares habitat, and back onto the road, this time their clothes drenched with smelly water and without transportation. They silently turned in the direction they were headed and began slowly walking.

Carmelo and Eloisa trudged along the road, their steps heavy and their clothes clinging uncomfortably. The smell of the murky water lingered around them, a constant reminder of their recent ordeal. Despite the exhaustion and discomfort, they pressed on in silence, each lost in their own thoughts as they walked toward an uncertain future.

Suddenly, from behind them came the sound of an approaching vehicle. Carmelo's heart raced as the sound of the approaching vehicle grew louder. Fear gripped him, wondering if it was someone coming to finish them off. They both turned to face the source of the noise, their expressions tense with anticipation.

The brakes of the car squealed as it rolled to a stop, its headlights blinding Carmelo and Eloisa momentarily. With apprehension, they watched as the driver's door swung open, revealing Alex slowly emerging from the driver's seat. His hand pressed against his abdomen, and his shirt was soaked with blood.

Alex walked directly toward Carmelo, his hand still covering the wound on his abdomen. "Are you both alright?" He asked, genuine concern evident in his voice.

Carmelo stood in silent shock, emotions swirling within him—anger, relief, and confusion. He watched Alex approach, his expression unreadable.

"Are either of you hurt?" Alex repeated, his concern deepening as he took in their soaked and disheveled appearance.

"No," Carmelo finally answered. "Well, not really. Just some scratches and bruises."

"Good, I need one of you guys to drive," Alex said abruptly. "Get in the car."

Carmelo's emotions were a whirlwind of concern, disbelief, and a touch of sarcasm. He questioned Alex's sudden appearance and the tangled web of events they had just escaped from.

"Wait, what?" Carmelo's voice carried a hint of outrage as Alex tried to usher him into the vehicle. "I was so worried that you were dead in the mountains somewhere, and nobody would ever find your body, like Lorenzo, may he rest in peace. Then, you show up at the bad guy's house, and it turns out you're his brother," Carmelo almost laughed at the ridiculousness of the situation. "Oh wait, and you were working for the man who tried to kill me! Why should we trust you?"

"Please, Carmelo!" Alex pleaded urgently. "We have to hurry or he's going to die!" He gestured towards the passenger seat, his eyes filled with desperation.

Eloisa, looking through the window, saw Don Mendoza in a critical state, bleeding profusely in the passenger seat. "Oh, hell no! I'm not getting in this car with that monster!" She cried out, her voice filled with fear and anger.

"We don't have time for this!" Alex pleaded urgently. "We're both in really bad condition. I would drive myself, but I've lost a lot of blood and I feel like I might faint. We need to get to the hospital right away!" His voice carried a sense of urgency and genuine concern for their well-being.

Carmelo looked at Eloisa, a silent understanding passing between them. "Alright, we'll drive you both to the hospital, but then we're taking the car and we're leaving Mendoza," he said firmly. Alex nodded with a sense of solemn resignation, realizing the gravity of the situation.

"Wait!" Eloisa exclaimed as Carmelo was heading towards the driver's side. "This time I will drive!" She gave Carmelo a determined look, leaving no room for debate. She climbed in behind the steering wheel and Carmelo climbed into the back seat with Alex.

The drive to the hospital was tense. Eloisa couldn't resist a cruel grin as she navigated the bumpy road, purposefully hitting every pothole along the way. Glancing over at Don Mendoza, she taunted, "Enjoying the scenic drive, Don Fernando? It's the least you deserve after all that you've put me through."

Don Mendoza winced with each bump, his discomfort evident. Eloisa continued, her voice laced with sarcasm, "I hope you're comfortable," she said as she slammed into another pothole. "You're not looking very well."

Don Mendoza clenched his jaw, unable to respond as Eloisa's merciless driving added to his misery.

As they sped towards the hospital, Carmelo sat in the back seat, determined to ignore Alex's pleading expressions.

"Stop looking at me like that," Carmelo snapped, his eyes fixed straight ahead.

"Carmelo, can I explain?" Alex's voice was strained with urgency.

"No!" Carmelo's tone was firm. "Don't even talk to me."

"Carmelo, I didn't tell you because I couldn't—"

"Eloisa, will you turn on the radio, please?" Carmelo interrupted, reaching out to touch his sister's shoulder. "Turn it up loud."

Despite Alex's persistent attempts to explain himself, Carmelo remained resolute in his silence, drowning out Alex's voice with the blaring radio.

Alex guided Eloisa to the nearest emergency hospital and instructed her to pull up close to the entrance and stop. He tried to get out of the car, but as he stood up, he immediately fell back into the seat.

"Alex!" Carmelo cried out in concern. He quickly exited the car and rushed to Alex's side. Wrapping his arms around him, Carmelo helped Alex to his feet, supporting his weight as they made their way into the hospital.

"We need help!" Carmelo shouted. "¡Necesitamos ayuda!" Spotting an unused wheelchair in the admittance room, Carmelo directed Alex towards it and carefully helped him into the chair. "¡Hay otra persona afuera, crítica!"

The emergency room nurses quickly responded, rushing outside to attend to Don Mendoza and bring him inside on a stretcher. Shortly thereafter, a few nurses returned to collect Alex and wheel him off into the depths of the critical care unit and out of sight.

Carmelo stood there briefly, his gaze fixed down the hallway where Alex had disappeared. A whirlwind of thoughts raced through his mind. Would he ever see Alex again? Had he made a mistake by not giving Alex the chance to explain? He chastised himself for being so stubborn and dismissive of

Alex's pleas, feeling a pang of regret and uncertainty about their strained relationship.

Carmelo's heart raced with panic and desperation as he approached the admittance counter. "Excuse me, señora. That man in the wheelchair—el hombre que acaban de tomar," he gestured down the hallway.

The nurse nodded with a smile, "¿Sí?"

"Can you give him something for me?" Carmelo quickly grabbed a piece of paper from the counter and tore off a small strip. He reached across, snatching a pen, and began scribbling frantically on the paper. "¿Puedes entregarle esto?"

The nurse nodded once more, her smile reassuring.

Carmelo expressed his gratitude with a "Muchas gracias," handing the nurse the piece of paper with Eloisa's Buenos Aires address written on it. "Estoy muy agradecido." With that, Carmelo turned and walked out of the emergency room entrance, climbing back into the car's back seat. "Let's get out of here," he said to Eloisa, shutting the car door firmly.

The drive from Mendoza to Buenos Aires at night was a mix of exhaustion and tension. The road stretched out endlessly, flanked by dark fields and occasional clusters of trees. Streetlights became scarce as they left the city behind, plunging them into stretches of pitch-black darkness broken only by the car's headlights.

Eloisa's grip on the steering wheel was tight, her eyes focused on the road ahead, navigating through occasional curves and bends. The hum of the engine and the rhythmic sound of tires on asphalt filled the otherwise silent interior of the car. Carmelo sat behind her, occasionally glancing out the rear window, his mind still reeling from the events at Don Mendoza's villa and the hospital.

Outside, the night seemed to press in, amplifying the weight of their situation. The stars above were obscured by clouds, adding to the sense of isolation on the deserted highway. Occasionally, they would pass by small towns or gas stations, their lights flickering like distant beacons in the night.

Despite the fatigue and unease, there was a shared sense of determination. Each mile brought them closer to safety, away from the danger and uncertainty of Mendoza. The road stretched ahead, a path towards a new beginning, albeit one tinged with apprehension and unanswered questions.

As they approached the outskirts of Buenos Aires, the first signs of dawn began to paint the sky with soft hues of pink and orange. The city's silhouette gradually emerged against the fading darkness, with skyscrapers and buildings etched against the growing light. The streets started to buzz with early morning activity, cars, and pedestrians gradually increasing in number as the city woke up.

The transition from rural roads to urban sprawl was marked by a change in scenery. Fields and open spaces gave way to densely packed neighborhoods, each with its own unique character. Trees lined the streets, their branches casting long shadows that shortened as the sun climbed higher.

The air carried a mix of scents—fresh morning dew, hints of coffee from nearby cafes, and the faint aroma of breakfast being prepared in homes and eateries. Birds chirped energetically, adding a lively soundtrack to the awakening city.

As they drove deeper into Buenos Aires, the skyline became more pronounced, with modern buildings and historic landmarks blending together in a harmonious yet eclectic tapestry. The streets became busier, reflecting the city's vibrant and dynamic atmosphere.

For Carmelo and Eloisa, the sight of Buenos Aires at dawn brought a sense of relief and anticipation. It was a new chapter, a chance to regroup and gather their thoughts after the tumultuous events they had experienced.

They made their way to Eloisa's home in the Puerto Madero neighborhood of Buenos Aires. Her home, though in the process of being packed up, still retained its stylish and modern charm. The living room featured chic and tasteful decor, with contemporary furniture arranged neatly. Large windows illuminated the space, offering a breathtaking view of the Rio de la Plata, the shimmering water reflecting the early morning light. Despite the moving boxes and a few pieces of furniture covered in sheets, the home maintained an air of sophistication and comfort, a testament to Eloisa's refined taste and appreciation for contemporary aesthetics.

"Carmelo, we made it," Eloisa said with relief. "Thank you for coming to rescue me. You saved my life." She wrapped her arms around him and squeezed softly.

"Eloisa, I love you," Carmelo replied softly. "I will always do whatever I can to protect you."

"I'm going to take a shower and then go to bed," Eloisa said wearily. "I haven't slept much in the past few days."

"That sounds like a great idea. I'll follow suit shortly. There's something I still need to take care of," Carmelo told her. "Can I use your telephone?"

Carmelo dialed the numbers and heard the phone ring a few times before Lucia's familiar voice answered, "¿Hola?"

"Lucia, I'm sorry to call you so early, but I've just arrived in Buenos Aires, and my sister is safely back home."

"Carmelo, that's wonderful news!" Lucia's voice carried genuine happiness. "I'm so relieved to hear that."

"There's something else. You need to report the site. It needs to be protected for future generations. Tell them it was discovered by you and Alejandro Mendoza thanks to the research contribution of the late archaeologist Lorenzo Varela. I want it to have been discovered by Argentinians. I don't want to take any credit. And Lucia, I want you to know that I am deeply grateful for everything you've done to make this happen. I hope one day we'll meet again."

"Of course, Carmelo," Lucia responded warmly. "It's been a pleasure knowing you. I wish you and your family all the best. Goodbye, Carmelo."

"Goodbye, Lucia. Give Daniela my thanks as well."

"I will," she replied before disconnecting.

By the time Carmelo got out of the shower, Eloisa was already asleep in her bed. Carmelo crawled into the bed next to her, softly kissing the back of her head. "Goodnight Eloisa," he said softly as he drifted off into slumber.

Chapter Fifteen

Carmelo and Eloisa sat at the kitchen table in Eloisa's

Buenos Aires home, ready for a video chat with their mom, Isabella, and Tia, Paloma. They sipped coffee in the middle of the afternoon as Carmelo, feeling embarrassed about wearing Lorenzo's clothes to bed, had risen early to launder the dirty, smelly clothing from the day before.

The call connected, and the two women appeared on the screen. "Mijitos!" Isabella cried out, tears of overwhelming relief and gratitude flowing at the sight of her two children together. "¡Gracias a Dios! My prayers have been answered!" She clasped her hands tightly in the air, a gesture of profound thanks and emotion.

Their Tia, Paloma, held Isabella as she sobbed, tears of joy and relief quietly streaming down her cheeks as well. "Mijos, thank goodness you are alive. We are so happy to see you. Are you ok? Eloisa, ¿hicieron daño?"

"No," Eloisa replied.

"¡Bendigo María!" She called out, "Carmelo, are you okay?" She asked with concern, noticing the darkening bruise on his forehead.

Carmelo lifted his hand to gently nurture the puffy shadow above his left eye, "Yeah, I think so. We had a little accident on our way back to Buenos Aires and I hit my head on something, but I think it's just a bruise. I feel fine otherwise."

"Mijo, when are you coming home?" Isabella asked, desperate to have her children safely returned from this horrific ordeal.

Carmelo looked at Eloisa and then back to his mother on the screen. "We're flying out tomorrow afternoon," he explained. "Eloisa and I are going to meet with her real estate agent tomorrow morning. They'll take care of everything here so Eloisa can come back home and be with her family, which is where she needs to be right now."

"Yes, we need you to come home safely and as quickly as possible, both of you." Tia Paloma added.

"Carmelo, you look like you've lost some weight, Mijo," Isabella said with concern. "Are you sure you're okay? You look sad."

"Oh, thanks, Mama," he replied. "I'm fine. I'm just tired and a little sore. I think we're going to get something to eat, and then we might binge-watch some documentaries on Prime Video until we fall asleep again."

"Okay, Mijo," Isabella replied. "Lock all of the doors and windows. Be very careful when you go out. Call me as soon as you land!"

"Bye, Carmelo! Bye, Eloisa! We love you both!" Tia Paloma blew kisses into the camera.

"We love you too!" Eloisa added her goodbyes just before Carmelo disconnected the video chat.

As they stepped out onto the bustling streets of Buenos Aires, Carmelo's senses were overwhelmed by the sights and sounds of the vibrant city. It was a new world for him, filled with unfamiliar landmarks and the rhythm of a culture he had only experienced through stories and pictures.

Eloisa guided him through the bustling streets, pointing out the iconic spots she had come to love during her time in Buenos Aires. They passed by historic buildings with intricate architecture, colorful street markets brimming with handmade crafts, and quaint cafes where locals gathered for lively conversations.

Arriving at Lucia's favorite restaurant, Carmelo marveled at the warm welcome they received. The aroma of Argentine spices wafted through the air, enticing him with promises of flavorful dishes he had yet to try. The menu, a fusion of traditional and modern cuisine, intrigued him, and Eloisa eagerly recommended her favorite dishes for him to try.

As they enjoyed their meal, Eloisa shared stories about the city, its rich history, and the unique blend of cultures that defined Buenos Aires. Carmelo listened intently, absorbing every detail and savoring the experience of discovering a new place through the eyes of someone who cherished it dearly.

As Eloisa spoke, Carmelo's attention was abruptly captured by a familiar figure standing outside on the sidewalk. The man had his back turned toward Carmelo, triggering a fleeting moment of confusion where he mistook the figure for Alex. His heart raced at the sight, almost causing him to jump out of his seat. However, as the man turned around, Carmelo quickly realized that it wasn't Alex. The brief illusion shattered, leaving Carmelo relieved yet unsettled by the resemblance.

"Carmelo, what happened? You seemed focused, and then you tensed up. Is something wrong?" Concern was etched in Eloisa's features as she turned to look at Carmelo.

The nervousness in Eloisa's voice brought Carmelo back to the present moment. He took a deep breath, trying to shake off the sudden rush of emotions. "Sorry, I thought I saw someone familiar outside," he replied, his tone still tinged with the remnants of surprise.

"It's just...I thought it was someone else for a moment," Carmelo continued, trying to downplay the significance of the incident. "But it was just a passing resemblance.

Everything's fine." He forced a smile, hoping to reassure Eloisa and himself at the same time.

Eloisa gave Carmelo a sympathetic nod, "You know, we still haven't talked about what happened yesterday, and how you know that man, Don Mendoza's brother."

Carmelo swallowed nervously, "I know."

"Is that who you thought you saw?" She pressed Carmelo for information, "There's something between the two of you, isn't there?"

Carmelo nodded, "Yes. Well, I thought there was." He diverted his eyes in embarrassment, "I don't know what to think now."

"How did you get involved with him?" Eloisa's tone was sympathetic and genuinely curious, wanting to understand her brother's feelings.

Carmelo took a deep breath, collecting his thoughts before beginning. "Well, I guess I need to start when I arrived in Córdoba," he said, recounting the series of events that were set into motion when he landed in Argentina. Eloisa sat there wide-eyed as Carmelo told her everything, leaving nothing out.

"Do you believe there might have been a valid justification for his secrecy regarding his identity and affiliations?"

After a moment of reflection, Carmelo replied, "It's possible. Maybe he had legitimate reasons for keeping things secret. But there are still so many unanswered questions. Like why he was working with El Torre, and what El Torre meant when he said that Alex had 'betrayed all of us." It's hard to trust him completely after everything that's happened."

"Do you think Alex betrayed you?" Eloisa delicately broached the subject.

Carmelo quietly considered the question before answering, "No, not really. I mean, I don't like that he withheld important information from me, but I understand why he might have felt trapped or unable to share everything," Carmelo continued. "The situation with his brother and El Torre, it's all so complicated. I think there's more to the story that I still don't know." He sighed deeply. "Maybe he was trying to protect me in his own misguided way. I mean, I don't think he was trying to take the map or the treasure for either himself, Don Mendoza, or El Torre. If that's all he was after, he had plenty of opportunities to make his move, but he didn't. He could have easily killed me and left me in the mountains. I probably would have just been added to the list of foreigners gone missing in the Andes."

"Maybe he was trying to prevent either Don Mendoza or El Torre from getting their hands on the treasure," Eloisa offered.

Carmelo nodded in agreement, "That's a possibility too. Alex always seemed conflicted about his family dynamics, what little he told me about them. He mentioned once that he wanted to preserve the cultural heritage of the treasure and ensure it wasn't exploited for personal gain. Maybe his actions were driven by that desire, even if they were misguided or secretive."

Eloisa leaned back, deep in thought. "It's hard to know for sure, especially with everything that's happened. But regardless, it's clear that Alex was caught in a web of conflicting loyalties and dangerous circumstances."

Carmelo sighed again, the weight of uncertainty heavy on his shoulders. "I just hope we can find some answers and closure soon. This whole situation has been overwhelming, to say the least."

"You might have to accept that we will never get answers or closure," Eloisa said gently, "but at least we are together, and safe!"

"That is true! I would have been devastated if you had gotten hurt." Carmelo admitted, reaching out to grasp his sister's hand. "We're both safe and we're going home tomorrow. I'm so thankful for that."

After they finished their dinner and conversation, they made their way back to Eloisa's home, Carmelo still buzzing with adrenaline from the misidentification of the stranger outside the restaurant. Locked safely inside, they settled into Eloisa's sofa, surrounded by the comfort of familiar snacks and the glow of the TV, creating a cozy retreat where they could relax and enjoy their final evening in Buenos Aires together.

As Carmelo lay sprawled out on the sofa, the room bathed in the soft glow of the television's light, he was jolted awake by an ominous knock at the door. His heart quickened with a mix of apprehension and curiosity as he glanced at the clock—2:33 a.m.. Who could be knocking at this hour?

With hesitant groans, Carmelo rose from the comfort of the plush sofa, the faint bluish light from the television casting elongated shadows across the floor. He paused for a moment, listening intently to the silence that followed the knock, half expecting it to be a figment of his imagination.

But then it came again, a persistent rap on the door that echoed through the quiet house. Carmelo padded softly across the room, his bare feet sinking into the plush carpet, and reached for the doorknob, his hand hesitating before making contact.

The television continued to murmur softly in the background, casting flickering shadows on Carmelo's face as he cracked the door open just enough to peer into the dimly lit hallway beyond. As he peeked through the crack, a voice cut through the silence, sending a chill down his spine.

"Carmelo, you need to come with me right now!" The voice sounded like Alex's, but something was off, distorted. The shadows in the hallway twisted Alex's features. His words cut through the silence of the night, sending a shiver down Carmelo's spine.

Carmelo hesitated, his instincts tingling with unease. Nevertheless, he opened the door to find a figure that resembled Alex standing in the hallway, bathed in dim light that obscured his features. "Alex? What's going on?" Carmelo's voice wavered with uncertainty.

"There's no time to explain," Alex insisted, his eyes darting nervously. "We have to go. Now. Where's Eloisa?"

Carmelo's mind raced with questions, but something in Alex's demeanor told him that this was urgent. Without another word, he stepped out into the hallway, the cool air of the corridor sending a chill down his spine.

Alex was leaning against the wall in the dimly lit hallway cradling the gunshot wound in his abdomen, blood seeping through his fingers.

"Alex, you're still bleeding!" Carmelo exclaimed with concern in his voice. "I thought the hospital would at least stitch you up."

"They did, and they removed the bullet," he assured Carmelo, "but I was supposed to stay in bed for several days. Instead, I snuck out of the hospital and came to save you."

"To save me?" Carmelo asked with a confused expression. "Save me from who?"

"El Torre, he's still alive and he's coming for revenge!" Alex's words expressed the urgency of the moment. "He wants to kill you and Eloisa. We must leave now!"

"Wait!" Carmelo protested, "Eloisa is still asleep! I have to go wake her up. I can't leave her behind."

"Of course not," Alex agreed. "We just need to hurry. We don't have a lot of time."

Without a word, Alex turned and started down the hallway. Carmelo followed, the corridor stretching endlessly, the walls closing in with each step. As they walked, Carmelo noticed something unsettling—a faint trail of blood, leading deeper into the darkness.

"Alex, wait!" Carmelo called out, his voice echoing in the empty corridor. The figure ahead seemed to fade in and out of focus, its form shifting and distorting with each passing moment.

Finally, they reached a dead end, where a mirror hung ominously on the wall. The figure gestured for Carmelo to look into the mirror. As he did, the reflection morphed, revealing not Alex, but the menacing visage of El Torre with a chunk of his skull dangling off the side of his head by a thick, hairy patch of scalp.

"Your escape is futile, Mr. Quiñones," El Torre's voice reverberated through the void. "Leaving this country alive was never an option. You've underestimated the extent of my ruthlessness!"

Suddenly, Eloisa and Alex appeared behind him. "Carmelo, get back!" Eloisa cried out.

El Torre laughed maniacally. "You thought Alejandro Mendoza would save you? Your hombre has been working for me this whole time."

"Don't listen to him, Carmelo!" Alex pleaded urgently. "Come on, this way! Hurry!" He darted away, and Carmelo struggled to keep pace, his heart pounding with a mix of fear and determination.

"Alex, stop running!" Carmelo cried out, his voice filled with desperation.

"Carmelo, wait!" Eloisa called after them, her voice tinged with urgency. Then, she let out a blood-curdling scream that pierced the air.

Hearing Eloisa in distress, Carmelo halted in his tracks and swiftly turned back toward his sister. As she came back into view, he was horrified to see a man's arm wrapped around her throat, choking her. At first glance, it appeared to be Alex, but as the man's features came into focus, Carmelo realized with dread that it was Don Mendoza. The glint of a machete against Eloisa's throat added to the chilling scene unfolding before him.

Don Mendoza's cold, lifeless eyes bore into Carmelo, sending a shiver down his spine. Blood seeped from his chest wound as he spoke with a chilling calmness. "How ironic, Mr. Quiñones. You thought you could outsmart me, but all the while, my little brother was seducing you and manipulating you." He erupted into hysterical laughter. "Now, I'll chop you and your sister into pieces and feed you to the yacares. They're famished!" With a savage motion, Don Mendoza lunged toward Carmelo, the sharp blade of his machete slashing through the air toward him.

Carmelo recoiled, a surge of realization and fear coursing through him. Suddenly, the dream shattered, and he jolted awake, drenched in sweat, his heart racing.

Eloisa stirred beside him, concern etched on her face. "Carmelo, are you okay? You were thrashing in your sleep."

Carmelo took a deep breath, the remnants of the dream still haunting his thoughts. "I...I think so. I was just having a bad dream," he muttered, but deep down, he knew it was more than that. It was a reminder of the tangled web of deceit he was ensnared in.

Later that morning Carmelo and Eloisa had breakfast together at a nearby cafe and coffee shop, Café Tortoni, where they met with Eloisa's Real Estate Agent, Matteo.

As Eloisa and Carmelo entered Café Tortoni, they were greeted by the rich aroma of freshly brewed coffee and the inviting atmosphere of the historic establishment. The morning sunlight filtered through the café's vintage windows, casting a warm glow over the antique furnishings and ornate decor.

As they stepped further into the cafe, Matteo stood up, waving them toward a cozy table near the window, allowing them to enjoy views of the bustling Buenos Aires streets outside while immersing themselves in the café's old-world charm. The table was adorned with a crisp white tablecloth and a small vase of fresh flowers, adding a touch of elegance to their breakfast setting.

A waiter in a classic uniform approached their table with a friendly smile, presenting them with menus that showcased Café Tortoni's renowned coffee specialties, including cortados, café con leche, and medialunas, a staple Argentine pastry. Eloisa ordered a cortado, while Carmelo opted for a traditional mate tea, wanting to experience a local favorite.

As they savored their beverages, their conversation flowed effortlessly, surrounded by the café's rich cultural heritage and the gentle murmur of other patrons engaged in lively discussions. The ambiance was a perfect blend of relaxation and stimulation, with the aroma of freshly brewed coffee adding to the cozy atmosphere.

Amidst the elegant setting of Café Tortoni, they delved into the details of selling Eloisa's home and their upcoming return to Texas. Matteo, adding his expertise to the discussion, offered valuable insights into the local market dynamics.

Matteo exuded an air of sophistication and professionalism that instantly put both Carmelo and Eloisa at ease. His tailored suit and confident demeanor spoke of experience and competence in the real estate industry. His dark hair was neatly styled, complementing his sharp features and expressive eyes that conveyed attentiveness and understanding.

By the end of their short meeting, Eloisa handed Matteo the keys to her house with a genuine smile, as if that singular gesture marked the end of her old life and the unceremonious beginning of a brand new one. The exchange felt symbolic, a tangible step towards a fresh chapter filled with possibilities and opportunities. Matteo, with a reassuring nod, accepted the keys, understanding the significance of this moment for Eloisa.

After their meeting with Matteo, Carmelo and Eloisa decided to take a leisurely walk through a nearby park before heading to the airport. The park was a tranquil oasis amidst the bustling city, with lush greenery, winding paths, and benches inviting visitors to pause and enjoy the surroundings.

As they strolled along the pathways, they admired the vibrant flowers, tall trees providing shade, and the serene atmosphere that contrasted with the urban hustle outside the park. They passed by families picnicking, joggers enjoying their morning run, and couples taking romantic strolls, all contributing to the park's lively yet peaceful ambiance.

For Carmelo and Eloisa, the walk in the park was a moment of respite, a chance to soak in the beauty of Buenos Aires one last time before embarking on their journey back to Texas. It was a time to reflect on their experiences, discuss their plans for the future, and appreciate the natural beauty that the city had to offer.

Inside the park, nestled among the trees and overlooking a serene pond, was a secluded spot that held a special significance for Eloisa and Lorenzo. It was their favorite place to visit in the city, a hidden gem that offered a perfect blend of tranquility and natural beauty.

The spot featured a wooden bench positioned strategically to capture the best view of the pond and the surrounding greenery. It was a peaceful oasis away from the bustling city, where Eloisa and Lorenzo often spent quiet moments together, sharing stories, dreams, and laughter.

As Carmelo and Eloisa approached this cherished spot, memories flooded back. Eloisa recalled the times Lorenzo made her laugh uncontrollably with his witty remarks, or the moments they sat in comfortable silence, simply enjoying each other's presence amidst the serene ambiance of the park.

Sitting on the familiar bench, Eloisa took a moment to reminisce about Lorenzo and the beautiful memories they shared in this tranquil setting. It was a bittersweet moment, filled with nostalgia and gratitude for the precious moments they had experienced together.

The drive to the Buenos Aires airport was a journey through bustling city streets, characterized by a mix of modern architecture and historic landmarks. As Carmelo and Eloisa made their way, they passed by lively neighborhoods with colorful buildings, busy markets, and people going about their daily routines. The traffic was a blend of cars, buses, and motorcycles, creating a vibrant yet chaotic atmosphere.

Along the route, they caught glimpses of iconic sights like the Obelisco de Buenos Aires, a towering monument in the heart of the city, and the wide avenues lined with trees and cafes. The sounds of tango music drifted through the air, adding to the city's lively spirit.

Despite the traffic, the drive was smooth and efficient. As they approached the airport, the scenery transitioned to a more industrial landscape, with signs pointing towards terminals and parking areas. The anticipation of their journey back to Texas filled the air, blending with the excitement and nostalgia of leaving Buenos Aires and Argentina behind.

Carmelo and Eloisa entered the sprawling airport terminal and embarked on their journey back to Texas, leaving behind the tumultuous events and emotional rollercoaster they had experienced in Argentina. As they boarded the plane, there was a sense of closure and a newfound determination to move forward.

During the flight, Carmelo reflected on the lessons learned, the bonds strengthened, and the resilience they had discovered within themselves. He gazed out of the airplane window, watching the landscape change from the bustling cityscape of Buenos Aires to the vast expanses below.

Eloisa sat beside him, her gaze filled with a mix of nostalgia for her home in Buenos Aires and anticipation for the new chapter awaiting them in Texas. She leaned over and whispered, "We made it through, Carmelo. We're stronger now."

Carmelo nodded, a faint smile forming on his lips. "Yeah, we did," he replied, his voice filled with determination. "And we'll keep moving forward, together."

After a grueling fourteen hours in flight, the plane descended towards their destination. Carmelo and Eloisa exchanged glances, a silent understanding passing between them. They had faced challenges, and experienced loss, but also found courage, love, and hope amidst the chaos.

As they stepped off the plane, they were greeted by the familiar sights and sounds of Texas. They embraced the next chapter of their lives with renewed strength and a deep appreciation for the journey that had brought them to this moment.

Chapter Sixteen

Carmelo's meeting with Gale was a mix of excitement and

apprehension. As he entered Gale's office, he couldn't help but notice the celebratory mood, with balloons and a congratulatory banner hanging on the wall. Gale greeted him with a warm smile, congratulating him on making it to the New York Times Bestselling LGBTQ+ Authors list.

"Thank you, Gale. It's surreal, but I'm thrilled," Carmelo replied, a hint of excitement in his voice.

The meeting started with Gale sharing the good news and discussing the details of Carmelo's upcoming book tour. They went over the cities, venues, and promotional strategies, outlining a plan to make the tour a success. Carmelo felt a surge of pride and anticipation as he imagined connecting with readers across different cities.

"I can't wait to engage with readers and share my journey," Carmelo said, his enthusiasm evident.

However, amidst the buzz of success, Gale's question about Alex brought Carmelo back to a place of uncertainty. "Have you heard anything from Alex?" Gale asked, concern evident in her voice.

Carmelo's expression faltered for a moment before he replied, "No, nothing yet. I spoke with Lucia and Daniela the day the article came out about the discovery. They said that they have tried contacting him, but have not received any response." He tried to sound casual, but the worry crept into his words.

Gale nodded understandingly, offering words of encouragement. "Don't worry, Carmelo. Sometimes things take time. Focus on your book tour and let's make it a huge success. Alex will reach out when he's ready."

Carmelo appreciated Gale's reassurance, but the unease lingered in the back of his mind. As they delved into discussions about the news article regarding the treasure discovery and Carmelo's book progress, Carmelo couldn't shake off the nagging question about Alex's silence.

As Carmelo settled back into his life in Austin, he couldn't shake the cloud of unease that followed him. Days turned into weeks, each passing moment tinged with a growing sense of frustration and concern.

Carmelo tried to push Alex's absence to the back of his mind, attempting to convince himself that everything was as it should be. Yet, like a persistent echo, thoughts of Alex continued to reverberate through his mind, refusing to be ignored.

Every time his phone lit up with a notification, his heart skipped a beat, hoping it was a message from Alex. Each time it turned out to be something else—a mundane email, a social media update—the disappointment felt like a heavy weight settling in his chest.

He immersed himself in his daily routines, focusing on work and spending time with friends and family, trying to distract himself from the gnawing uncertainty. Yet, in quiet moments, when the noise of the world faded away, the silence felt deafening.

At times, he caught himself replaying memories of their shared adventures, wondering where Alex was, what he was doing, and if he was healing from his wounds. The unanswered questions danced on the edge of his consciousness, elusive yet ever-present.

Despite his attempts to rationalize and move forward, there was a lingering sense of incompleteness, a missing piece that only Alex's presence could fill. It was a struggle between acceptance and longing, between letting go and holding on to hope, as Carmelo navigated the tumultuous waters of uncertainty and unanswered questions.

One evening, the weight of uncertainty pressed heavily on Carmelo's shoulders as he sat in his room, surrounded by the quiet of the night. The glow of his phone screen illuminated the dimly lit space, a beacon of hope amidst the darkness of his unanswered questions. With hesitant fingers, he pulled out the scrap of paper that had Don Mendoza's phone number scribbled on it. He decided to give the phone number a try. He didn't know what to expect, or who might answer the call, if anyone. For all Carmelo knew, Don Mendoza could be dead. He figured that he had nothing to lose, so he dialed the number.

The phone rang, each tone resonating with anticipation and apprehension. But as the ringing persisted, it became a stark reminder of the unanswered connection, echoing in the silence of his room. There was no response, no familiar voice on the other end to dispel his worries.

Undeterred, Carmelo tried again later, the act of dialing becoming a ritual of hope and desperation intertwined. He left a voicemail, his words a mix of urgency and longing. "Alex, it's Carmelo," he spoke into the phone, his voice carrying the weight of unspoken concerns. "I don't know if you will get this message or not. I need to talk to you. Please, just call me back. I need to know that you're okay."

The room seemed to hold its breath as Carmelo ended the call, the silence once again enveloping him. He sat there for a while, staring at the silent device, his thoughts a whirlwind of unanswered questions and unspoken fears. The struggle with the lack of communication from Alex felt like a constant shadow, a presence that refused to dissipate despite his efforts to reach out.

During a dinner conversation with Eloisa, Carmelo brought up his concerns about Alex. "Eloisa, I don't know what to do about Alex," he admits, his voice tinged with worry. "It's been weeks since we returned, and I haven't heard a word from him. Do you think I should keep trying to contact him?"

Eloisa placed a comforting hand on Carmelo's arm. "I understand your concern, but maybe give it a bit more time," she suggested gently. "I'm sure Alex will reach out when he's ready. You've done what you could, Carmelo."

"Well, next week the book tour starts. I have to fly to New York for the 'kick-off' event." Carmelo explained. "I won't be back here for a couple of weeks. I guess I should stop dwelling on it and just get on with my life. Things are going well right now, honestly."

"I think that is a great decision," Eloisa said with a warm smile. "You should go enjoy your trip. Enjoy your success, Carmelo. You've earned it!"

Carmelo leaned back on the couch, the soft glow of the lamp casting a warm ambiance in the room. Across from him, Eloisa sat with a cup of tea in hand, her eyes reflecting a mixture of excitement and concern.

"Can you believe it's finally happening?" Carmelo's voice held a hint of disbelief, tinged with excitement. "The book tour, New York City, all of it."

Eloisa nodded, a smile playing at the corners of her lips. "It's incredible, Carmelo. You've worked so hard for this, and now you get to share your story with the world."

"I just wish..." Carmelo's voice trailed off, his thoughts drifting to the absence that lingered in his mind. "I wish Alex could be here to see it too."

Eloisa reached out and placed a comforting hand on Carmelo's arm. "I know, Carmelo. It's hard not hearing from him, but maybe he's just processing everything in his own way."

Carmelo nodded, a mix of emotions flickering across his face. "You're right. I'll keep hoping he reaches out soon."

Their conversation continued late into the night, filled with anticipation for the upcoming tour and the underlying hope of reconnecting with Alex amidst the whirlwind of success.

The bustling energy of Times Square pulsated through the air, a symphony of neon lights and excited chatter that seemed to welcome Carmelo as he arrived at "Pride and Prose Books." The bookstore, nestled in the heart of Times Square, was adorned with rainbow flags and banners celebrating LGBTQ+ literature and authors.

As Carmelo stepped inside, he was greeted by the warm glow of fairy lights and the aroma of freshly brewed coffee. The bookstore's interior was adorned with shelves filled with diverse books, colorful posters promoting LGBTQ+ events, and a stage adorned with a banner proclaiming Carmelo's achievement as a New York Times bestselling LGBTQ+ author.

The atmosphere was electric, filled with anticipation and pride. Attendees, a mix of fans, fellow authors, journalists, and LGBTQ+ advocates, mingled around, sipping on rainbow-themed cocktails and engaging in lively discussions about literature and queer representation in media.

On the stage, a podium awaited Carmelo, flanked by bookshelves showcasing his bestselling book and glossy copies of all his previously published works. A spotlight illuminated the stage, casting a warm glow on the podium and creating an ambiance of reverence and celebration.

As the ceremony commenced, Carmelo took his place at the podium, greeted by applause and cheers from the audience. A representative from The New York Times presented Carmelo with a framed copy of the New York Times Bestselling Author certificate commemorating his achievement, recognizing him as a bestselling LGBTQ+ author.

Carmelo stood at the podium, feeling a mixture of excitement, gratitude, and humility. The representative from The New York Times praised Carmelo's work, highlighting the impact of his book on LGBTQ+ representation in literature and the cultural significance of his achievement.

As Carmelo accepted the certificate, a wave of emotions washed over him. He thought about the journey that led him to this moment, from the challenges of self-doubt and creative struggles to the joy of connecting with readers and sharing his story.

Addressing the audience, Carmelo expressed his heartfelt gratitude, thanking his family, friends, readers, and everyone who supported him along the way. He spoke passionately about the importance of diverse voices in literature and the power of storytelling to inspire change and foster understanding.

The audience listened intently, captivated by Carmelo's words and the sincerity in his voice. They applauded, cheering him on as he shared snippets from his book and anecdotes from his writing process.

Before Carmelo left the stage, he made sure to express his gratitude once again. "Thank you all for being here today and for your unwavering support. None of this would be possible without you," he said, his voice filled with sincerity.

As he stepped down from the stage, Carmelo couldn't help but feel a surge of excitement and nervousness for the upcoming tour. The energy of the event, the cheers of the crowd, and the knowledge that he was now a New York Times bestselling author fueled his determination to make the tour a success.

After the formalities, Carmelo mingled with attendees, signing copies of his book and engaging in conversations with fans and fellow authors. The bookstore buzzed with excitement and camaraderie, a celebration of creativity, inclusivity, and the LGBTQ+ community.

Carmelo smiled warmly at each person he met, exchanging words of gratitude and connection. He listened intently to their stories, their experiences with his book, and how it had impacted their lives. Some shared personal journeys of self-discovery and empowerment, while others simply expressed admiration for his work and creativity.

"It's an honor to meet you all," Carmelo said, his voice filled with sincerity and appreciation. "Your support means everything to me, and I'm so grateful for each and every one of you."

He signed each book with care and personalized messages, taking the time to engage with each fan. The bookstore buzzed with energy as Carmelo connected with his readers, forging bonds that went beyond the pages of his book.

As he finished signing the last book, he looked out at the crowd with a sense of fulfillment and pride. This moment, surrounded by his supporters in the heart of New York City, was a testament to his journey as a writer and the impact of his words on others.

Carmelo sat there smiling, basking in the adoration and appreciation of his community. The room buzzed with excitement and congratulations, but amidst it all, there was a sudden hush as a familiar voice cut through the chatter.

"I don't mean to impose," the voice said, "but would you be willing to sign one more? I wanted to wait for everyone else to go first."

Carmelo's heart skipped a beat as he turned to see Alex stepping out from behind a row of bookshelves. "Alex? You're here!" His eyes widened with a mix of surprise and relief. "Are you okay?" Carmelo's voice was filled with genuine concern. "I've been so worried about you. Not hearing anything from you in weeks has been unbearable."

Alex nodded, a small smile playing on his lips. "I'm sorry for the silence, Carmelo. Things have been...complicated." He glanced around, taking in the atmosphere of the book signing event. "Can we talk? Somewhere private?"

Carmelo nodded eagerly, gesturing towards a quieter corner of the bookstore. "Of course, Alex. Let's catch up." The mix of emotions in his voice reflected the tumultuous journey of their recent past, now converging in a moment of unexpected reunion.

As they settled into a pair of cozy armchairs in a secluded nook of the bookstore, Carmelo gently took the copy of his book out of Alex's hand. He flipped it open, the pages crisp and inviting, and began to sign it with a flourish. His pen moved smoothly, leaving behind a heartfelt message inside.

After finishing, Carmelo set the book down on the table in front of him, his cheeks tinted with a slight blush. The note inside conveyed more than just gratitude for Alex's presence—it held a silent plea for understanding, a desire to bridge the gaps that had formed during their time apart.

As he looked up, Carmelo met Alex's gaze, a mix of emotions swirling in his eyes. "I've missed you, Alex," he admitted softly, the weight of their unspoken conversations lingering in the air between them.

Alex leaned forward, his eyes earnest as he continued, "I want you to know that I had absolutely nothing to do with that. As you probably can recall, Fernando admitted that he had not seen or heard from me in months before that night."

Carmelo nodded, recalling the uncertainty and fear he had felt during those chaotic moments. "Yes, I remember that," he admitted, his voice carrying a weight of memories.

"Remember how I mentioned our family falling out? It's because I couldn't stand by their actions and refused to partake in their illegal schemes," Alex revealed, a flicker of unease crossing his face as he repositioned himself to look Carmelo in the eyes.

"Alex, you seem to be in pain," Carmelo said, reaching out with sympathy. "How is your wound? Is it healing properly?"

Alex nodded slightly. "It's getting better, but I'm still sore," he admitted. "The doctor removed the stitches, and there are no signs of infection, but it's taking time to heal completely."

Carmelo's concern deepened as he listened. "I'm glad to hear it's improving, but please take care of yourself," he said softly.

"Carmelo, what El Torre said was true," Alex stated, his hypnotic green eyes commanding Carmelo's attention. "I was working for him."

Carmelo's brows furrowed in confusion as he shook his head. "I don't understand," he groaned, his eyes searching Alex's for some semblance of an explanation.

Alex's words echoed in the quiet bookstore, his voice tinged with regret and resolve. "You see, I didn't know what kind of a man El Torre was until after I had been working for him for two years," he began, his gaze fixed on Carmelo. "I was recruited by him a couple of years ago after my last visit to Mendoza, when I told my brother that I no longer wanted to be associated with the family business. El Torre offered me a substantial amount of money to help him bring down Fernando, to bring my brother to justice, and permanently dismantle the criminal legacy that my father built. These were things I wanted to see happen, and with the money, I would finally have the means to buy a boat and leave this place forever. So, I began to collect incriminating evidence against my brother and many of his business associates."

"That explains why El Torre said you betrayed Don Mendoza, but he also mentioned betrayal toward him. What did he mean by that?" Carmelo inquired, seeking clarity on El Torre's accusations.

"While I was up in the mountains documenting my brother's employees trapping endangered animals and smuggling them to Chile for collectors, whispers about El Torre's involvement in Lorenzo's murder began circulating. Back then, I had no clue about Lorenzo, the map, the journal, or your sister's abduction. My focus was on exposing my brother and his criminal cohorts. All I knew about El Torre at the time was his involvement in funding exploration and research for a missing archaeologist from Buenos Aires. The whispers suggested that Lorenzo was on the verge of a groundbreaking discovery with immense global significance. However, El Torre's motive seemed to be silencing Lorenzo to preserve the secrecy of this discovery for himself, leading to Lorenzo's murder."

Carmelo's eyes widened as Alex spoke, his voice laced with shock and disbelief. "What did you do when you put the pieces together?" His words trembled slightly, betraying the mixture of emotions swirling within him—curiosity, concern, and a hint of apprehension.

"I took what information I had gathered. I got on my motorcycle, and I left. I was headed back to Buenos Aires when our paths crossed." Alex gestured toward Carmelo, indicating that he was referring to the two of them. "When you told me what had happened to you on your way to

Mendoza, I knew El Torre was involved. Then, to make matters even more complicated, once I was made aware of your sister's abduction, I knew that my brother was also involved. It was exactly something he would do."

Carmelo grimaced, a visible sign of his displeasure at being reminded of that situation.

"By then, I was convinced that if both of them were entangled in this mess, there had to be truth to the rumors about Lorenzo's discovery. I realized I had to do everything possible to thwart their plans, but my priority was also to ensure your safety and help you rescue your sister," Alex explained earnestly.

"So, when El Torre said that I betrayed all of you, he was wrong about that. I never betrayed you, Carmelo," Alex emphasized.

Carmelo nodded, a mixture of relief and gratitude washing over him. "I know that," he affirmed, his voice carrying the weight of understanding tinged with apprehension. "You just kept important information from me, secrets," he added, his tone soft yet tinged with a hint of disappointment.

"Indeed," Alex admitted with a sense of true regret. "I did do that, and I'm sorry. I was worried that if I revealed who I was and how I was interconnected with the people trying to cause harm to you and your sister, you would never trust me, and you would likely have ended up dead because of it. The only way I could protect you was for me to stay close to you, which meant that I had to keep certain details secret for a while."

"Thank you for explaining," Carmelo replied, his tone a mixture of understanding and lingering concern. "I can see how complicated and dangerous the situation was. It's just hard to process all of this."

Alex nodded solemnly, his expression reflecting genuine remorse. "I understand. I wish I could have been more upfront with you, but I had to make some difficult decisions in the heat of the moment."

Carmelo sighed, the weight of everything settling on his shoulders. "I appreciate your honesty now, Alex. It's a lot to take in, but I'm glad we're having this conversation."

"Carmelo, I want you to know that I never lied to you. I need you to understand that I've always been honest with you. When I told you about my feelings for you, it was genuine, and those feelings haven't changed," Alex emphasized, his tone earnest and sincere, a hint of vulnerability in his eyes. "I just wanted to make sure you understood that, despite everything else."

Carmelo offered a small smile. "I do. Thank you for clarifying that."

"Also, I'm sorry it took me so long to get here to tell you this," Alex reached out and cupped Carmelo's hand in his.

Carmelo's gaze softened, a flicker of understanding crossing his features. "I know you've been through a lot too. I've been worried, wondering where you were, what you were doing, and how you were healing."

"I had to lay low for a while," Alex admitted, his gaze meeting Carmelo's with sincerity. "After Fernando was released from the hospital, he was transferred to prison. I wasn't sure if any of his associates would try to come after me. For the past few weeks, I've been cleaning up my family's business, cutting all ties with any of his agents involved in illegal activities and nefarious dealings. I sold my family's property in Mendoza—the Villa, orchards, the winery. I am going to take all the money and create a foundation dedicated to helping people who were victims of organized crime in the province of Mendoza. There's still so much more to do to make amends for the pain my family has caused, but I couldn't stay away, knowing what you must be thinking about me and how much pain that must be causing you."

Carmelo listened intently, his expression reflecting a mix of understanding and empathy.

"There's more," Alex said, his eyes widening with anticipation as he leaned in. "I also came to deliver some important news. The Argentine government has issued a financial reward as well as recognition to those involved in discovering and safeguarding the treasure site. Lucia, Daniela, and I claimed credit for the find, ensuring Lorenzo's role was acknowledged as per your request. But here's the important part: we unanimously decided that you and Eloisa deserve your rightful share of the reward."

"Wow, Alex, that's...incredible!" Carmelo replied, his surprise evident in his tone. "I didn't expect that at all. Thank you for considering us like that. It means a lot, especially after everything that's happened. How much money did we each get?"

"Well, we agreed that we would each keep two hundred and fifty thousand dollars, and the rest should go to you and Eloisa," Alex explained, his voice tinged with sincerity.

"Oh, my word! Two hundred and fifty thousand dollars! That's amazing!" Carmelo cheered excitedly.

"No, Carmelo." Alex's tone turned serious. "That still leaves one million, two hundred and fifty thousand dollars for you and Eloisa."

"Wait, Alex, you're telling me there's one million, two hundred and fifty thousand dollars waiting for us?" Carmelo's eyes widened in disbelief, his voice tinged with astonishment. "How is that possible? I don't understand."

"Carmelo, when we claimed the reward, we made sure to set aside a significant portion for you and Eloisa," Alex explained patiently. "It's in a bank account at the BCRA, the Central Bank of Argentina, waiting for you both to claim it."

"Alex, this is just...I can't believe it!" Carmelo exclaimed, his eyes shining with tears of joy. He sprang from his chair and enveloped Alex in a tight hug. "This is the best day of my life!"

Alex returned the embrace, his smile reflecting Carmelo's happiness. "I'm glad we could make this happen, Carmelo," he said warmly.

"So, where does that leave us?" Carmelo asked, his arms still clinging to Alex's shoulders. "Where do we go from here? You're not going to disappear on me again, are you?"

"Unfortunately, I can't stay for the rest of your book tour because I have some business to attend to in Buenos Aires," Alex explained. "But since you'll be busy for the next few weeks, it'll give me time to read your book!"

Carmelo's eyes brightened with curiosity. "Where can I find you after the book tour ends? How can I contact you?" He inquired eagerly.

Alex reached into his pocket and retrieved a sleek business card, handing it to Carmelo with a warm smile. "Here, take this. It has my contact details and where I'll be in Buenos Aires," he said, pointing to the card. "You can call me anytime, every day if you want. Carmelo, I want to be with you more than anything. Please, come find me after your tour ends. I have something very special to show you."

Carmelo nodded, his voice filled with sincerity. "I will, Alex. I promise," he said, feeling a surge of warmth and excitement. He hugged Alex tightly, expressing his longing to be with him.

"Oh, there's one more detail that I forgot to mention," Alex said with a playful smile. "My flight doesn't leave until 9 a.m., tomorrow morning, and I haven't booked a hotel room yet. Can I crash at your place?"

Carmelo laughed out loud, "I think we can make that work."

Alex's playful smile widened as Carmelo laughed. "Great! I promise I won't take up too much space," Alex joked, his eyes sparkling with anticipation.

"Of course, but I must warn you, I can be a little bit possessive. I might not let you leave so easily in the morning," Carmelo quipped with a grin, his smile reflecting the genuine happiness he felt. They exchanged a knowing look, both excited about the prospect of spending more time together.

CHAPTER SEVENTEEN

Carmelo completed his book tour with a mixture of relief and excitement. The journey had been challenging, but it had also been incredibly rewarding. As he boarded the plane back to Buenos Aires, he couldn't help but feel a sense of anticipation for what awaited him.

Upon his return to Buenos Aires, Carmelo wasted no time. He headed straight to the Central Bank of Argentina to retrieve the reward money, a significant sum that would undoubtedly shape his and Eloisa's future endeavors. With the transaction completed, Carmelo's thoughts turned to Alex.

He had been looking forward to their reunion ever since they parted ways in New York. The address Alex had given him led Carmelo to a marina, a serene and picturesque setting that seemed to promise new beginnings.

The marina was a tranquil haven nestled along the shimmering waters of the Rio de la Plata. As Carmelo walked along the marina's wooden boardwalk, he couldn't help but be captivated by the scene unfolding around him.

The marina was a bustling hub of activity, yet it exuded a sense of tranquility that was rare to find in such a vibrant city. Sailboats and yachts of various sizes bobbed gently in the water, their sails catching the breeze and their hulls gleaming in the sunlight.

The marina was lined with charming shops and cafes, their facades painted in cheerful colors that added to the nautical theme of the area. Wooden benches were strategically placed along the boardwalk, inviting visitors to pause and take in the scenic views.

As Carmelo strolled further along the marina, he noticed clusters of palm trees swaying gracefully in the breeze, their fronds rustling softly. The trees provided a welcome shade and added a tropical touch to the already idyllic setting.

The water in the marina was a mesmerizing shade of azure, reflecting the clear blue sky above. Fishermen could be seen casting their lines from the docks, their hopeful expressions mirrored in the crystalline waters below.

Seagulls soared overhead, their cries mingling with the sound of lapping waves and distant boat engines. The salty tang of the sea air filled Carmelo's lungs, invigorating him as he continued his exploration of the marina.

Everywhere he looked, Carmelo saw evidence of a vibrant maritime community. Sailors in crisp white uniforms worked diligently on their vessels, preparing them for upcoming voyages. Families and tourists wandered the marina, taking in the sights and sounds with a sense of wonder.

The marina's architecture was a blend of modern design and classic nautical elements. Dockside buildings boasted sleek lines and large windows that offered glimpses of luxurious interiors. Weathered wooden docks stretched out into the water, providing moorings for the elegant boats that called the marina home.

At the heart of the marina, a central plaza beckoned with its lively atmosphere. Here, musicians played cheerful tunes, and artists showcased their maritime-themed creations. The scent of freshly baked pastries wafted from a nearby cafe, tempting Carmelo with its irresistible aroma.

As the sun began to dip lower in the sky, casting a golden hue over the marina, Carmelo couldn't help but feel a sense of awe at the beauty that surrounded him. The marina, with its blend of natural beauty, maritime activity, and charming ambiance, was a fitting backdrop for the reunion that awaited him with Alex.

Walking along the marina, Carmelo felt a surge of emotions. He was eager to see Alex again, to hear his voice, to feel his touch. As he approached the designated yacht slip, Carmelo spotted Alex on the deck, moving about with purpose. The sight of Alex, framed against the backdrop of the shimmering water and the setting sun, took Carmelo's breath away.

"Nice boat!" Carmelo called out, unable to contain his admiration.

Alex turned towards Carmelo, a smile spreading across his face. "Thanks! It's been waiting for this moment."

Alex's sailboat was a breathtaking sight, a vessel that embodied elegance, functionality, and the spirit of adventure. As Carmelo approached the sailboat, he couldn't help but be captivated by its beauty and craftsmanship.

The vessel, named "Garcia Eterna," was a classic sloop-rigged yacht, boasting timeless design elements with modern amenities. Its hull was painted in a deep navy blue, contrasting beautifully with the white sails that billowed gracefully in the wind. The name "Garcia Eterna" was elegantly scripted in gold lettering on the transom, adding a touch of personalized charm.

The deck of the sailboat was expansive, providing ample space for relaxation and enjoyment of the open sea. Teak wood deck planks, meticulously maintained and polished, added warmth and sophistication to the exterior. Stainless steel fittings and railings gleamed in the sunlight, enhancing the overall aesthetic appeal.

At the stern of the sailboat, a spacious cockpit area welcomed guests with comfortable seating arrangements. Cushions upholstered in marine-grade fabric offered both style and durability, ensuring a comfortable experience while underway or at anchor. A folding cockpit table provided a perfect spot for al fresco dining while taking in the panoramic views.

The mast of "Garcia Eterna" rose majestically towards the sky, supporting a single main sail and a foresail, both expertly rigged for optimal performance. The rigging was meticulously maintained, with each line and cable inspected and adjusted to ensure smooth sailing in varying wind conditions.

With Alex's help, Carmelo stepped onto the yacht. The deck was bathed in soft light, creating a magical atmosphere. As they stood face to face, the air between them seemed charged with anticipation.

"I've missed you," Carmelo confessed, his eyes locking with Alex's.

"I've missed you too," Alex replied, his voice filled with sincerity.

The magnetism between them was palpable, a silent acknowledgment of everything they had been through and everything that lay ahead.

As the sun dipped lower on the horizon, painting the sky with vibrant shades of pink and orange, Carmelo and Alex found themselves drawn together by an irresistible pull. They moved closer, their breaths mingling in the warm evening air.

"I want to show you something," Alex said softly, taking Carmelo's hand in his. "It's down below."

Curiosity sparked in Carmelo's eyes as he followed Alex below deck. The interior of the yacht was elegantly appointed, with soft lighting and luxurious furnishings that exuded comfort and warmth.

Alex led Carmelo to the rear of the yacht, where a small table was set up with two glasses and a bottle of champagne. The sight brought a smile to Carmelo's face.

"This is beautiful," Carmelo remarked, taking in the romantic setup.

"It's just the beginning," Alex replied, pouring them each a glass of champagne. "To new adventures and new beginnings."

They clinked their glasses together, the sound echoing in the quiet evening. As they sipped their champagne, conversation flowed easily between them. They talked about their experiences since they last saw each other, sharing stories and laughter.

As the evening wore on, the sky painted a breathtaking backdrop for their reunion. The stars began to appear, dotting the sky like glittering jewels.

Carmelo couldn't shake the feeling of gratitude and happiness that filled his heart. Being with Alex, in this moment, felt like coming home.

"Let's go back up on deck," Alex suggested, rising from his seat and extending his hand to Carmelo.

They climbed the stairs to the deck, where they were greeted by a panoramic view of the night sky. The stars shone brightly overhead, casting a soft glow over the water.

Carmelo and Alex stood side by side, their fingers intertwined. They gazed out at the vast expanse of the sea, lost in the tranquility of the moment.

"I have something for you," Alex said suddenly, reaching into his pocket.

He pulled out a small box and handed it to Carmelo. With trembling hands, Carmelo opened the box to reveal a delicate silver bracelet, adorned with a single star-shaped charm.

"It's beautiful," Carmelo whispered, his eyes shining with emotion.

"It's a symbol of our journey together," Alex explained, taking the bracelet from the box and fastening it around Carmelo's wrist. "A reminder that no matter where life takes us, we'll always be connected."

Tears pricked at the corners of Carmelo's eyes as he looked at Alex. At that moment, surrounded by the beauty of the night and the warmth of Alex's love, Carmelo felt a sense of completeness he had never known before.

"Thank you," Carmelo said, his voice choked with emotion.

Alex pulled Carmelo into a tender embrace, holding him close under the starlit sky. They stayed like that for a long time, savoring the quiet intimacy of the moment.

As the night wore on, they watched the stars twinkle above them, each one a silent witness to their love story. The world seemed to fade away, leaving only Carmelo and Alex in their own little universe.

Finally, as the first light of dawn began to paint the sky in hues of blue and gold, Carmelo turned to Alex with a smile.

"Let's sail off into the sunrise," Carmelo suggested, his eyes shining with excitement.

Alex's smile mirrored Carmelo's as he nodded in agreement. Hand in hand, they stood at the bow of the yacht, ready to embark on their new adventure together.

As the 'Gracia Eterna' set sail, leaving the marina behind, Carmelo and Alex looked ahead to the horizon, where the sun was just beginning to rise. At that moment, with the wind in their hair and the sea at their feet, they knew that their love was a journey worth taking, full of promise and endless possibilities.

About the Author

Lancer Gareth's passion for storytelling ignited during his childhood, filling countless spiral notebooks with imaginative short stories, plays, and poetry. His talent quickly garnered recognition during his teenage years, earning him numerous awards for his creative prowess. At just 17, Lancer Gareth achieved a significant milestone by becoming a published author after clinching a college writing competition while still in high school.

Since then, Lancer Gareth has embarked on a multifaceted journey, expanding his creative horizons. Building on his literary achievements as a teenager, he has evolved into a record-producing musician, a self-published novelist, content creator, and business owner. Based in Texas, USA, Lancer Gareth continues to captivate audiences with his diverse talents and entrepreneurial spirit.